WHAT READERS ARE SAYING

"Well, this was riveting! Truthfully, I couldn't put it down. I love books with this kind of pace."

–CAROLE H.

"Great book and congrats. I'm sure many more will enjoy it as well. I loved it . . . stayed up late to finish it!"

–SHARON D.

"Our book club has been together for ten years. After staying up late to finish reading your book, I sent them an excerpt. It'll be our book of the month in May, and we want you to join us so we can ask you questions about it. I loved it!"

–KAREN B.

"Please tell me there will be a sequel to this book!"

–JESSICA M.

"I won't spoil it for others, but *why* did you do that? You know what I'm talking about! I couldn't believe it. A must-read!"

–LISA T.

A KNOCK
ON THE
DOOR

www.mascotbooks.com

A Knock on the Door

©2022 Roberta K. Fernandez. All Rights Reserved. No part of this publication may be reproduced, stored in a retrieval system or transmitted in any form by any means electronic, mechanical, or photocopying, recording or otherwise without the permission of the author.

This is a work of fiction. Names, characters, businesses, places, events, and incidents are either the products of the author's imagination or used in a fictitious manner. Any resemblance to actual persons, living or dead, or actual events is purely coincidental.

For more information, please contact:
Subplot, an imprint of Amplify Publishing Group
620 Herndon Parkway, Suite 320
Herndon, VA 20170
info@mascotbooks.com

Library of Congress Control Number: 2021921521

CPSIA Code: PRV0422A

ISBN-13: 978-1-63755-473-9

Printed in the United States

This book is dedicated to my daughter, her husband, and all of my friends and colleagues who encouraged me to take the leap and supported me throughout the process. This book is one among millions, but in me, you see only the one. My heartfelt love goes out to each of you.

Life's a
journey — Enjoy
the read!

Robertson

A KNOCK ON THE DOOR

ROBERTA K. FERNANDEZ

 SUBPLOT™

PROLOGUE

HIS INSTANT REACTION to the sound of gunfire was to duck his head and slam on the brakes. The car spun wildly across three lanes. Jack tried frantically to gain control as he realized that what he had heard was the sound of his tire blowing out. As he headed for the guardrail, he murmured a quiet "I love you" to Lori. He never felt the cold, dark water of the river.

CHAPTER

1

RITA JOHNSON SANK into the worn leather of the executive chair. She closed her eyes and took a deep breath. It still smelled like Jack. She could hear his thunderous laughter as he told her about surprising Lori on her birthday with an old-fashioned singing telegram. A faint smile crossed her lips. Jack would find a reason to laugh as often as possible.

She scanned the room. Pictures of Lori and Jack covered the wall he had faced every day. Jamaica, Venice, the Grand Canyon. Jack plunging toward Earth on his first bungee jump. Lori's face distorted from the g-force of the roller coaster. A toast at their last anniversary party. Silver. They had been married for twenty-five years. Jack never replaced photos; he just kept finding space to add more. Happiness filled that vast wall. It was a montage of their life together. Rita supposed it was a stark contrast to what she imagined Lori would be feeling today.

Rita thought she had cried all of her tears at his funeral last week, but now they resumed their flow down her cheeks.

Eighteen years of wonderful memories as Jack's assistant drifted through her mind as she returned to the task at hand. Quietly tapping the keys of his computer, the files flashed on the screen in front of her. But her eyes were only vaguely aware of what they were supposed to be focused on. She wiped at her cheeks, pausing to give herself yet another moment to reminisce.

Rita hadn't worked with Jack for two years now, but this office still felt familiar. The room still had the same blue plush carpet, worn a bit in places from frequent footsteps, and the inexpensive silver vase with the slightly faded artificial flowers. She remembered helping Jack choose the furniture and color scheme for his office about five years ago. She smiled at the memory of Jack's frustration when he said, "I can't possibly redecorate this place, Rita. You choose." Rita remembered the unfathomable look on his face when she told him he'd better look at her house before he asked for her decorating help. She had no knack for it at all. She laughed when he said, "What? I thought all women were good at this stuff!"

Over the past two years, she had adapted to working for Mark Mason, the vice president of SpringWare. But she had yet to experience the feeling of partnership that she'd had working with Jack. Working for Mason allowed very few opportunities to see Jack now that she was in a different wing of the building. Periodically, they'd run into each other in the cafeteria or coffee shop downstairs and have a chance to catch up. She hadn't talked to Lori since a few months before she started working with Mason.

Her eyes shifted back to the wall of photographs. Jack and Lori had physically changed over the years, but you could tell their relationship was strong. There were no forced smiles, no distance between their hugs. Lori was still beautiful in her maturity. Her eyes were alive and vibrant. The love they had for each other was palpable, even in their pictures.

Rita tucked her arms in against her stomach and let the tears come once more as she recalled the funeral. Lori's eyes had held nothing but sorrow, and there was a vacancy she was only beginning to experience. *I'm such a coward.* Rita chastised herself for not finding the courage to tell Lori how sorry she was and how much Jack had meant to her. She had snuck out a side door right after the service ended. Even the humidity and the hot September sunshine couldn't burn away the overwhelming sadness. Feeling as if she had lost her own son, Rita couldn't soothe herself, much less find the words that would comfort Lori.

A week later, the pain was still too much to bear. Now that she'd never be able to reconnect over coffee or the occasional lunch, she didn't know how she would cope. *Time heals all wounds.* But it hadn't healed her relationship with her daughter, and she didn't believe it would be true with Jack's death either. *They don't know what they're talking about. Whoever the hell* they *are.* Rita wished she'd made a better effort to stay connected to Jack and Lori. *Too many regrets.*

She made a mental note to get her own personal business in order. She cringed as she remembered how it took her months to find everything she needed to settle her mother's estate, and to sort through eighty-seven years of accumulated possessions. It was 2015, and she had now entered the last third of her life. She didn't want her own death to be as physically and emotionally challenging for her daughter as it had been for her when her mother died.

Rita flexed her hands in an effort to refocus her attention on the task at hand. Jack's assistant had left town to tend to a family emergency, so Mason sent her here to get everything she needed to finish a project that Jack had been working on. The deadline for delivery was near, and Mason needed files that pertained to the job so he could wrap it up himself and get it to the client on time.

Rita shook her head to clear the mental cobwebs and wiped her cheeks dry with her sweater. *Okay. Focus.* Deftly maneuvering the mouse, she scrolled through the many folders within the project file. She jotted down items on her yellow legal pad and copied items to a CD to take back to her office. Rita smiled. It pleased her to know that Jack had continued to use the systems they had perfected together years ago. She was an expert organizer and could pull any needed bit of information from a filing cabinet at a moment's notice, so it was easy for Jack to translate those same procedures to his computer's desktop.

She was just about to close a folder when a file in it caught her attention. It was named with a code word the two of them had used for highly sensitive projects. She tried to open it, but the file was encrypted. *That's odd.* Mason hadn't mentioned that this project was confidential.

"How's it coming, Rita?"

Rita's hand flew to her chest as Mason's deep voice shocked her. She looked up to see his intimidating presence filling the doorway. He took no notice that he had frightened her. Quickly regaining her composure, she casually slid her other hand to softly touch the F function key, clearing the screen, though she didn't think Mason could have seen it from his vantage point.

"Just fine, Mr. Mason. I have a clear understanding of what needs to be done. I only saw one folder with the project name on it. Jack would have made a great assistant. He was always so well organized." Rita managed a laugh. She popped the CD out of the tray, slid it into a jewel case, and handed it to him.

"Here are the files you need."

"Good. I need you in my office right away."

"I'll be right there; I just need to log off and gather my papers." She watched Mason turn and walk out. *A man of few words.*

Rita pressed a few additional keys and took her own copy of the files out of the CD drive. She carefully hid the disk between her papers and hurried back to her office, puzzled and deeply concerned about what she had seen.

CHAPTER

2

RITA SPENT HER lunch hour at the library downtown. Getting the CD out of the building required some quick thinking, but it was easier than she thought it would be. It was common knowledge that communications and logins were monitored, but not what specific activities were tracked.

Taking a seat at the computer that was the farthest away from the other patrons, she pushed in the CD tray and entered the old password she and Jack had used. The file sprang open.

A listing of dated emails appeared on the screen. *What is this?* With a furrowed brow, she clicked on the first one.

> **Mr. Mason, I'm detecting a problem with the software. I'm afraid it might cause issues with database entry. I may need a few more days to figure this out. I'll keep you up to date. Jack**

Rubbing her chin, Rita clicked on the next email.

> **I'm concerned that this program has been altered somehow. I need to run more diagnostics before we can release it. Please inform the client that we will not make the deadline. Jack**

> **Jack, I have reviewed your file and ran some tests of my own. I disagree with your findings. Please get the product ready to ship. Mason**

Rita clicked through the entries. It was like watching volleys in a tennis match, Jack finding problems, and Mason dismissing them. Jack's concerns were growing, and the problems he was finding became more glaring. Mason found explanations for all of them, however weak they seemed.

> **Mr. Mason, I don't know how, but I am certain that this project has been compromised. I believe there is great risk associated with the distribution of this program for SpringWare and the NSA. Jack**

> **Jack, I expect the product ready for delivery as promised. I do not share your conclusions. Move forward or I will ask George to finish this up. Mason**

NSA. *The NSA is the client?*

There was another file in the folder. None of the passwords she shared with Jack would open it. Her gut told her it was important. Rita's entire body shivered with dread over the tone of those emails, especially now that she knew the client's identity.

Her fingers played at the buttons on her coat, her eyes

unfocused on the computer in front of her. *What does this mean?* After all her years of working with Jack, she knew that if he was concerned about something, then there was something to be concerned about. He would never say anything that he didn't believe to be true. He was meticulous in his work and had the highest degree of integrity. Rita would never doubt his ethics.

Mason was a different story. In the two years she'd worked for him, she had observed only ego and ambition. Though she had never witnessed him doing anything unethical, she had seen nothing to make her think that he was beyond it. Mason had accomplished much in a short time at SpringWare. Because of him, the company was on the cusp of becoming a major player in a highly competitive software gaming industry.

We create gaming software. That's what was bothering Rita. *Why is the NSA a client?* Though Rita knew Jack had worked on a few non-gaming projects, that was the biggest change Mason had made at SpringWare. Their sole focus now was the gaming industry. *So why the NSA?*

Rita exited the library into another humid and hot September afternoon, contemplating what she had seen on the CD she had stuffed back in her purse. Somehow, she hoped that if she couldn't see it, it wouldn't be real. But she knew that ship had sailed. She would have to explore every port it stopped at to ease the seasickness she was feeling inside.

CHAPTER

3

MOONLIKE ORBS CAST a soft glow around the restaurant, creating sparkling effects from the polished silver and crystal glasses. Lori Crawford sat silently at a corner table near the back. It was their favorite place to sit in Café Amore, as it gave the vantage point of seeing all the other tables in the room. She noticed reserved placards placed carefully on nearly all of the crisply ironed tablecloths. It wouldn't be long before the dining room would be filled with people in the holiday spirit. She inhaled deeply. The smells of garlic, onion, and basil were a sensorial preview of the comfort food that would soon be placed in front of her.

Lori knew that when that party of ten sat down at the long table across from hers, the solitude would be shattered for the rest of the evening. That was fine with her. The loneliness she was feeling might be broken by eavesdropping on the conversations of others. Usually she and Jack would be reviewing the holiday gift list, making sure they hadn't forgotten anyone. This year, she hadn't found the energy to shop. She knew that friends and family would understand. There was just no way she could fake a holiday spirit so soon after the funeral.

The ornaments on the tree rattled when the door opened. The gentle breeze she had felt when she entered a half hour ago appeared to have gathered momentum. She was sure it had become colder as the winter sun had disappeared. The little boy entered, rushing right to the small reindeer hanging eye level in front of him. Strong hands quickly followed, hanging it back on the branch, as Dad pushed in ahead of those who were to be her companions for the rest of the meal. Lori could tell eavesdropping wouldn't need perfect hearing with this lively group. This family was very merry tonight, and from their grand entrance, it was clear they would be sharing their conversations with all the patrons.

Lori managed a melancholic grin, remembering how good Jack was at playing their game. They'd take turns guessing what celebrity they looked like, their occupation, or how they were related to each other. Tears welled up in her eyes as she realized she would have to enjoy this activity alone tonight.

The parents were obvious: Dad, rushing after the little boy as he headed for the kitchen, and Mom, carrying the baby bundled in wool and fur. The portable carrier went on the floor next to her chair at the end of the table. The gray-haired couple bringing brightly wrapped packages were surely the proud grandparents, and at even a quick glance, the resemblance would unmistakably make them the parents of the eager boy's father. The next two couples were certainly siblings and their spouses. A brother and sister to the mother of their nephew, as the likeness to their sister was also striking. The lone middle-aged woman trailing behind was not as easily identified. *A friend?* With much commotion, they all eventually found their seats and secured the boy in his booster chair. The servers quickly offered to take their coats to the rack they had obviously missed in the entryway.

This was her first Christmas alone. Watching this family interact and enjoy each other's company brought back memories. Even though she felt sad, a smile still tugged at her mouth as she attempted to focus on happier times. She had been alone now for three months—ninety-eight days, to be exact.

Jack had been the one person she had ever loved. The only one she had shared a home with since she left her parent's house. He was the only one she could ever imagine sleeping next to her. And yet, that had all changed . . .

Shouting jolted her from her mind's wanderings. The boy had overturned his glass on his aunt, who was sitting next to him. Dad was up in a flash, grabbing napkins from all around to ebb the flow of milk as it quickly spread across the tablecloth and down onto those sitting nearby. Pandemonium reigned for the next five minutes as servers and busboys rushed to assist, and the embarrassed parents apologized profusely to anyone within earshot. It reminded Lori of watching a three-ring circus. There were too many things going on to hold your attention in one spot for any length of time. Then her gaze fell on the single older woman at the far end of the table. She sat quietly, watching the drama unfolding in front of her, a faint grin playing at her lips. She was clearly enjoying the show.

The woman glanced toward her right and caught Lori's eyes. Lori shifted her gaze away, embarrassed that she had been caught staring at her. Though, after a few moments, she ventured another look and once again noticed the woman looking at her. The woman's eyes communicated her pleasure in all the fuss, and it gave Lori the feeling that it was okay with her to laugh at the comedy playing out before them. Lori smiled back, feeling a brief moment of connection. Something about her seemed familiar, but she couldn't quite put her finger on what made her feel that way.

The server came between them, and the smell of pesto filled Lori's nose. Feelings of comfort filled her as the big bowl of steaming pasta was set on the table. It was Jack's favorite dish, and although she was never quite as fond of it as he, Lori had taken to eating it whenever she felt particularly lonely. She had consumed her share of it this holiday season.

She supposed she should've flown home this week to be with her mother, but a holiday celebration just didn't feel right, or even possible. She didn't want to deal with all the well-meaning questions and expressions of worry and concern. Twirling the pasta around her fork, Lori contemplated on what to do with the presents she had bought for Jack.

She had found the perfect how-to book for photography, a hobby he was just starting to take up. The perfect tie to go with that hard-to-match green shirt she had bought for his birthday. And a small rock that had "I Love You" carved into it. Hardly gifts she could give to someone else. She pushed her plate back, as the thoughts of Jack had ruined her appetite. When the server came, she ordered another glass of wine.

Needing a diversion, Lori decided to go to the restroom before her wine arrived. Glancing at her watch, she found it hard to believe that two hours had passed. But there was no reason to hurry back to an empty house. As she touched up her lipstick in the mirror and brushed her hair, Lori noticed the subtle lines around her eyes and on her neck. Had she actually changed this much in just the last three months? Tonight, her forty-five years felt like sixty. Shaking her head in disbelief at her reflection, she went back to her table.

The family had departed, and the merlot had arrived in her absence. She could now drink it in peace. As she pulled out her chair, a piece of paper fell to the floor. Thinking it was the dinner check, she picked it up to look at the total. She sat back hard in her chair when she saw her name in neatly printed letters. What followed made her heart stop and the dark liquid get caught in her throat.

> **Lori, I have proof that Jack's death was not an accident. Meet me tomorrow at noon at the fountain in Booker Park. You'll recognize me.**

Lori gripped the seat of her chair in astonishment, reading the neatly handwritten words once more. *Who would be so cruel?* Jack's death was an accident. The police had confirmed that his car flipped over the guardrail and fell into the river when his tire blew. The autopsy showed that he was presumably unconscious from hitting his head on the steering wheel before he drowned. Lori took a deep swallow of the dark liquid from her glass, trying to calm the thoughts running in a thousand directions in her head. She summoned the server.

"Did you see who left this note on my chair?"

"No, ma'am. I didn't see anyone at your table. But I have been very busy tonight. Perhaps you have a secret admirer?" The server grinned as he left. *You couldn't be more wrong.*

Lori read the note over and over, clenching the napkin in her lap. The letters blurred through her silent tears. She was now in a place where she could think about Jack without completely losing it. She was starting to focus on more of the happy times, not on how lonely the house felt without him there. Now this?

The idea of Jack being killed was ludicrous. He wrote gaming software programs for a company that had employed him for twenty years. Jack was an ordinary man who lived a simple and happy life, with a smile and laugh that were infectious. A sports fanatic, he played on the community center's volleyball team and coached little league baseball in the spring. His latest goal was to train service dogs for blind people. Who would possibly want to kill him?

By the time she finished her wine, she had nearly convinced herself that this was simply a terrible prank by some sadistically cruel person.

Lori clutched the note tightly in her coat pocket as she walked home from their favorite restaurant through the small town's familiar streets. She would always think of Café Amore as "their" restaurant, as it was where they had first met at the bar and had their first date. Café Amore was where Jack proposed, where she told him the bad news of her infertility, and where he told her that she was all he ever needed anyway. Now their restaurant would also be the place of the mysterious note that would forever change how she viewed Jack's death.

CHAPTER

4

THE MORNING LIGHT came early after terrifying dreams of knocks on the door and Jack calling her name, begging her to save him from the cold, dark water. Lori woke with a start. She lay very still, clearing her head of the leftover merlot and the endless variety of nightmares about Jack's death.

It wasn't only the bad dreams. The content of the note was settling in again. She clenched her robe tightly around her waist as she made her way to the bathroom. *Who left that note?* Lori debated with herself about what to do. She was angry and curious at the same time. Should she go to the meeting at Booker Park? A part of her wanted to go, but another part of her argued that Jack was dead, and nothing was going to bring him back. The possibility that he had been murdered still seemed as ludicrous as it had the night before.

She had envisioned the horror of his death too many times. Murder provided opportunities to imagine even more terrifying possibilities. Besides, if Jack really was murdered, what could she do about it anyway? Was she willing to put herself through even more pain? Accidents happened. They were sad and unfair, but they were a part of reality. Murder, however, was a totally different ball game. It required a different mindset; one Lori didn't know if she possessed.

Looking at her reflection in the mirror, she knew she would go to the Booker Park fountain. How could she ever rid herself of this absurd idea if she didn't go? The note had put this in motion, and it didn't matter if she believed it or not; she had to see where it led.

Fastening the watchband around her wrist, she saw there were four more long hours to wait. She pulled on a pair of jeans and her warmest oversized sweatshirt, and she scrunched her auburn hair into a short ponytail at the base of her neck. Padding down the stairs in thick wool socks, the thought of hot chocolate seemed an appropriate way to start the morning. Lori breathed the soothing scent deep into her lungs. A sigh escaped her lips as the sweet warmth flowed down her throat and into her stomach, warming her hands around the big mug.

Wandering aimlessly around the living room, she stopped at a bookcase to rearrange items on the shelves, then fluffed the pillows on the sofa. Anything to pass the time. She set her drink on the mantle above the fireplace while arranging the logs and kindling to start a fire. Like the hot chocolate had warmed her on the inside, the fire worked its magic on the outside as she felt its warmth on her hands and legs.

She eyed the picture on the fireplace mantle next to her hot chocolate. It brought back memories of her early years with Jack. They were standing in front of their first apartment, and she was clutching Jack's arm like a young woman newly in love. They married in their second year of college. Lori closed her eyes and stepped into the picture. She could feel Jack's arm in her hand, and she could hear him tell her how he'd always love her. She felt her body flush when he kissed her in front of their friend while he was taking the picture. The feeling of love was intoxicating. Twenty-five years had passed so quickly, and then the unimaginable had happened. At forty-five, she was forced to contemplate a life on her own.

She loved that picture. It had marked the start of a real-life Cinderella love story. *I should take it down*. Now it served as another reminder that what had been given could be taken away in an instant. Lori was no stranger to love and loss.

Cassie was her identical twin, and just as twin stories go, they were inseparable. Even at five, they could read each other's thoughts, finish each other's sentences, and tell their mom what the other one wanted. They liked the same foods, loved books and music, and could color like there was no tomorrow. They put on dances and shows for their parents. Life was all about the laughter they always seemed to share. Lori looked over at the framed coloring book page on the bookshelf. It was the last picture Cassie had colored and given to her. Her mom had saved it for her until she was strong enough to look at it again, and that was well after she had married Jack. The picture had an instant effect.

She and Cassie were kicking the ball back and forth in the front yard. They were singing and laughing and having so much fun making up one game after another. Mom was sitting on the stoop, leaning back against the brick pillar, enjoying the warm sunlight while her girls were playing. Lori kicked the ball. It snuck between Cassie's legs, and she immediately turned to run after it. The driver of the car coming down the road never saw the tiny girl as she followed the ball into the street.

Lori's tear-filled eyes jolted open at the memory of what happened next. Like the nightmares about Jack, her little girl dreams were filled with that vision for months on end. She was still amazed at the vividness of the memory after all these years. The emptiness from the loss of her twin, someone who felt like a part of her very being, could never be filled. Lori spent her adolescent years feeling lonely and believing that Cassie's death was her fault.

Drifting off into her thoughts once more, Lori thought about her life in 1983. Her Dad was serving in the army during the invasion of Grenada, an operation that today no one remembers. He was on his last tour as part of an army intelligence unit. Finally, the man that Lori adored most was due back in less than two weeks. This time, he would be coming home for good. He had written that he was excited that she had decided to postpone her birthday party until he got home. He said it would be a celebration to be remembered—his military retirement and the beginning of Lori's teen years.

Lori would never forget looking out the window and seeing the black sedan pull up in front of their house just two days after her thirteenth birthday. Then there was a knock on the door. She noticed the chaplain's collar on one of the three uniformed men who were dispatched to give the dreaded news. Her mom, pale and shaky behind her, sent Lori to her room. Though Lori couldn't make out the men's muffled words through the closed door, her mother's sobbing was unmistakable. She gripped Cassie's teddy bear and sobbed for her dad and for Cassie until the men left. Finally, her mom pulled herself together enough to come into her room and give her the news she already knew in her heart.

Her mom was never given the details of her husband's death for security reasons. By mistake, she received a letter saying that the casket that was shipped home was empty. The transponder that he wore had stopped transmitting. They never found his body. Real closure never came for either of them; and once again, her nightmares continued for a very long time. Finally, at sixteen, when her grades plummeted, and it was more than obvious that she was depressed, her mom insisted that she go into therapy. Two months later, her mom decided to do the same for herself. Lori felt that seeing a therapist had saved them both.

These events took their toll during her formative years. Many years had passed before she healed, but Lori gradually gained the confidence to trust that she and Jack would be together forever. *And how did that work out for you?* So much for the Cinderella story. She opened her eyes. Lori felt certain that the love that she and Jack had for each other only happened once in a lifetime. And for the third time in her life, she had lost someone she dearly loved. Maybe it's better to live the rest of my life alone.

No matter how hard she wanted to believe that Jack's death was just an accident, life had taught her that the truth was always easier to deal with than the scenarios your own mind could make up. I need to know the truth. It's the only thing that will make the nightmares stop so I can move on with my life.

CHAPTER

5

IT WAS NOW ten minutes before noon, so there was still ample time for the five-minute walk to the park, but she couldn't wait any longer. Lori pushed her arms into the long, purple wool coat with the fur-trimmed hood. She fumbled as she secured the button hooks on her UGG boots. She dropped one glove, then the other. *Jeez! Calm down. This whole thing will just turn out to be a terrible joke, and everything will go back to normal.*

She pulled up her hood, securing it beneath her chin. No matter how hard she tried to ignore it, the question was still there. What if it's true? Even the shock of the ice-cold wind as she stepped out the door couldn't numb that thought.

As she started down the sidewalk, Lori looked back at the house. She and Jack had bought it twenty years ago when Cooperville was starting to grow. They loved being close to the center of town, as most places were within a reasonable walking distance. On good weather days, they both would walk to work. SpringWare was just beyond the newspaper's office.

Since Jack died, she walked to work no matter the weather, allowing the cold and snow to numb all unpleasant thoughts.

The closer she came to the park, the more detached she felt from her body. It was as though she was watching a character in a scary movie just before something bad happens to them. Was this really happening to her, or would she wake up in her warm bed and realize that all of this had been another nightmare?

This was a road she knew she must travel, but she sensed that dark things awaited her along the way. She shivered, and chills ran down her spine at the thought. She pushed her hands deeper into her coat pockets and tucked her chin under the fur that framed the hood of her coat. Her freezing nose reminded her that this was, indeed, very real. Too real.

Usually crowded on a Sunday, there were only a few people in the park. Certainly, the bitterly cold weather was keeping the sensible people indoors. *You'll recognize me.* Lori anxiously surveyed each face she saw, but she was unable to identify anyone that passed by.

She circled the fountain; ten minutes passed, but it seemed like hours to her. Her watch showed five minutes after twelve. No one was coming after all. *Five more minutes and I'm out of here.* Even in the cold, her curiosity was strong enough to hold her there a bit longer. But she longed to dash off to the safety of her home, and the innocence she enjoyed before that note had arrived.

Hearing someone clear their throat behind her, Lori froze. Slowly, she turned and looked into the very eyes that had seemed familiar last night. The woman immediately sensed her confusion.

"Let's get something warm to drink, shall we?"

Lori followed her without a word to a secluded booth in the back of the diner across the square.

CHAPTER

6

"RITA," LORI REMEMBERED at last. "I didn't recognize you last night. You look . . . so different."

"Yes. I wasn't so gray and fat the last time you saw me." Rita chuckled. "What's it been, more than two years?" Rita's eyes dropped slightly, unable to look directly at Lori. She continued, the pain obvious in her voice. "For months, I've been trying to decide if I should reach out. I feel so bad about not talking to you after the funeral."

Rita looked up again, struggling to find the right words to say. "Jack . . . was like a son to me, and I didn't handle his death very well . . . time passed and then, I don't know, it just felt too awkward to call you. I'm so sorry, Lori." Rita absently tapped her fingers on the table, pausing for a long time. "Then, as fate would have it, there you were last night in the restaurant. I took it as a sign that I was supposed to share what I found with you. I'm sorry to make you wait so long in the cold, but I had to be sure no one was following me. I had to make sure it was safe for us to meet here."

The server interrupted to take their order. They asked for hot tea and waited until it arrived, both of them deep in their own thoughts. Lori stayed silent as she watched Rita's fingers tremble on the paper placemat. Her own hands felt heavy and detached from her body as they rested in her lap, her mind held captive in a thick fog. She sipped the hot tea, hoping to dissolve the knot in her throat, but it still prevented her from speaking. She nodded her head for Rita to continue.

Rita glanced around to be sure no one was close enough to hear their conversation. "Jack was working on a software program for the NSA—the National Security Agency. It was a database program designed to organize information they keep on suspected terrorists. It was to be delivered within a couple of weeks after Jack's accident."

Lori nodded, but she was confused. *The NSA?* Jack had never mentioned they were clients of SpringWare. *Why would they be clients? I thought they just made games?*

Lori knew Jack was forbidden to talk about the details of his work. Competition was fierce in the gaming software industry. Because secrecy was of the utmost importance, employees were required to sign nondisclosure agreements. He rarely discussed more than the information given to the general public about any of the products he developed. Was she naive to think that new games for Xbox and Nintendo were the only things Jack created? It never occurred to Lori that a government agency like the NSA would be clients of SpringWare, much less that Jack would be designing software for them. The thought of the powerful intelligence agency's involvement struck a bad chord deep inside of her.

Rita continued her explanation. "Anyway, I wouldn't have known about any of this, but a few days after the crash, Jack's assistant had to leave town for a week. The deadline was pending, and Mason needed someone to get the project ready to be delivered. Because I'd worked with Jack for so many years and knew how he ran his office, Mason asked me to help. From everything I've found, I'm fairly certain that Jack and Mark Mason were the only ones who knew the NSA was the client."

Lori felt flushed. She loosened the tie of the sweatshirt around her neck, though the flow of cool air didn't seem to help. "Okay, but what makes you think that Jack's death wasn't an accident?" Lori asked, finding her voice, but suspicious about the veracity of what she was hearing.

"Well, I was familiarizing myself with the project so I could get everything ready for Mason. I started looking through Jack's calendar and his files—anything that pertained to the software deal. When I found the project data on the computer, there was an encrypted file in it. It stood out because it had the same name that Jack and I used for sensitive projects. I thought it was unusual, so I opened it. Inside were copies of emails between Jack and Mark Mason.

"Jack thought that the software he had created had been altered. The emails took place over a period of about a month. The messages detailed his discoveries and how concerned he was about what they meant. But the emails didn't say exactly what the alterations were. Maybe he didn't want to put it in writing . . . I don't know. But it was Mason's responses that puzzled me. He seemed to dismiss Jack's speculations. He had different explanations for the concerns Jack expressed, but quite honestly, even I didn't think his excuses made sense. In

Jack's final correspondence, Mason flat out told Jack to finish the project and deliver it by the deadline. Period. No more discussion. But I don't think Jack did that."

"Why do you say that?" Lori had been studying Rita closely. She could see that Rita believed every word she was speaking.

"I've spent the last two months gathering every piece of information I could find to piece all of this together. When I had more time to go through the CD, I found a second encrypted file. I haven't been able to open it yet because I can't figure out the password. But I think I know where I can find it. There's a small space hidden in a false back in Jack's credenza. I'm probably the only one who knows it's there. I'm willing to bet that he hid the password for that second file in there."

How can any of this be true? It was a lot to handle, coming at her from out of the blue. And from the look on Rita's face, she had more to say. And Lori knew she had to hear it all. *Why would she be making all of this up?*

"I have a copy of the files I found on Jack's computer. Here . . . " Rita looked around, then reached into her purse. She pulled out an old Matchbox Twenty CD and slid it across the table to Lori. "Put this in a safe place. I think it's best for more than one person to have a copy."

Lori stared at the CD case for a moment, as if it were a poisonous snake about to strike. With trembling fingers, she hesitantly put it in her coat pocket. She reached up and tightened the strings of her sweatshirt, drawing it up around her neck once more, hoping it would make her feel warmer and more secure. It didn't.

Lori knew how tight security was at SpringWare. She couldn't imagine how Rita had managed to smuggle the CD out of the building. *That was a big risk.* A part of her appreciated the fact that she cared so much about Jack to do this, but it just made her feel more apprehensive.

A hiding place in his office? Why didn't Jack tell me any of this?

As if reading her mind, Rita said, "Lori, Jack never wanted you to worry about anything at work. Honestly, most of the projects were harmless enough. And when Mason came on board, he shifted the company's focus strictly toward the gaming market. It's why I was so surprised to find out that the client was the NSA. But as I thought about it more, there *were* some projects that seemed odd. Jack usually oversaw projects from start to finish. But certain projects became segmented. There were things that didn't seem to fit within the company mission, and it deeply concerned him. As a result, Jack decided to start keeping certain files from those projects that felt off to him. Just in case."

Just in case what? Those words hung heavily in the air between them. And if that wasn't enough, Rita had more bombs to drop.

"Lori, it isn't just this that gave me reason to think Jack was murdered." Lori saw that her teacup was shaking, ever so slightly, in her hand. "A few days later, I found something else."

Lori felt the tears swell in her eyes. *What more could there possibly be?* She saw Rita's face turn pale and her forehead tighten. Lori imagined that she was also feeling the enormity of this discovery and telling someone else for the first time. She braced herself for what was to come as Rita took a deep breath before she continued.

"Mason is an old-school person in some ways. He likes me to keep written phone messages as they come in. You know, the old-fashioned, spiral-bound book that makes duplicate copies? He also keeps a written calendar for his appointments. At the end of each day, I take the phone message log to him so he can review the day's calls. The next morning, he returns it to me, along with his calendar. I tear off the original call message, so he knows I've dealt with it, then I record it on his physical calendar. I input any entries from his calendar into my computer, so I know when to schedule his appointments. Then I give his calendar back to him. I've followed this routine every day for the past two years.

"After I found the emails in the file from Jack's computer, I looked further back in the phone message book to see if there were any more clues . . . Lori, there was some writing on one of the carbons. It was faint, like he must have been writing on a piece of paper he had set on top of it, but I could read what it said:

Carl, Jack can't expose. Do whatever it takes. M.

"It was written on the sections that would have been two days before Jack's death . . . when I looked at his calendar and compared the entries with the ones that I made on my computer, I also noticed that Mason had two lunches that were not documented. He *always* notes who he ate with on his calendar so he can expense it to the company. In the two years I have worked for him, he has never once had an undocumented lunch out of the office. Both of them were during the two days before Jack died."

Lori tried desperately to take in this information, connecting the dots in her mind. *Is she saying Mason had Jack killed? That just can't be!*

"I have to decipher that second file. I know it has the answers, but I don't know how to get into Jack's old office to look in his credenza. George works in there now, and I'd have no reason to be there. If I'm right about all of this, I can never let Mason know that I suspect anything. If he did murder Jack, he must have important secrets to keep."

And you'll be next? Though she couldn't verbalize it, the look on Rita's face let her know that she was thinking the same thing. The deluge of information was incomprehensible. At that moment, Lori felt too overwhelmed to be as terrified as she should be.

Rita called to the server, and they ordered another drink, this time something stronger than the hot tea they had barely touched. Lori absently twirled the spoon in her cup while Rita tore pieces from the edges of her paper placemat, both quietly assessing the seriousness of the situation. The server delivered the wine, and each of them took a long drink. Finally, Rita spoke.

"Lori, I can't even pretend to know what you are going through right now. I'm sure you have a lot of questions, and honestly, I don't know how many of them I can answer for you. But there are two things I do know for certain. Jack loved you more than anything. He was dedicated to his work, and he never, ever would have done anything even remotely dishonest or illegal. That's why I think he didn't let this rest when Mason told him to. Jack must have believed that whatever was altered on that software had to be very important. And I think he paid for it with his life."

"But why kill him? Why not just find a reason to fire him?" Lori knew the minute the words were out of her mouth how stupid they sounded. *Of course, they had to kill him.*

"Lori, the NSA project had to be worth millions to Spring-Ware. If there was something wrong with the software, it would make the NSA very unhappy, and I don't believe that Mason would ever jeopardize SpringWare's profits.

"But then, I'm also pretty sure that no one was supposed to know that SpringWare was developing this program. From what I can tell, only five people in the company were involved in creating or handling this project in some way. They were all assigned bits of the design and probably didn't know what those bits were connected to. I think Jack was the only one that figured out the scope of the project and the identity of the client. From the tone of his emails, I think he discovered something he was not supposed to see. I ended up as the sixth person to be involved because Mason needed me at the last minute."

Lori felt sick to her stomach. She took another long sip of her wine, hoping to dull the accompanying headache. She couldn't find the words to articulate all of the wild and random thoughts tumbling around in her head. She rubbed her eyes, but it didn't help her see this any more clearly. "I . . . I have a lot to think about."

The involvement of the NSA made her cringe. It took her right back to her thirteen-year-old self and her reservations and wariness of the military or any organization that resembled it. Her dad had been in an army intelligence unit. The distrust she held of organizations like the NSA made it hard for Lori to believe that she and Rita could ever stand up to them. *Even if all of this is true, it would be impossible to prove.* They had the power to spin any story to make sure they came out unblemished.

"Lori, I understand if you don't want to get involved in

this. But I'm going to find a way to get into Jack's credenza. I can't stop now. Use this phone if you want to talk to me. Call this number and let it ring once, then hang up . . ." Rita slid a burner phone across the table. "The calls at SpringWare are monitored. If Mason suspects that I know anything, he'll find a way to tap my personal phone. Obviously, he has connections to the NSA who could do that. I have one of these phones too. I'll call you back as soon as I can, but remember that I won't be able to take this phone with me to the office. Security would immediately question why I have two phones."

With that, Rita put some money on what was left of her placemat and handed Lori a slip of paper with the phone number. She stood up, and as quietly as she had appeared at the fountain, she disappeared out the back door of the diner.

The dimness of the restaurant allowed Lori's tears to fall unobserved. The story seemed too incredible to be believable. But in her heart, she knew Rita had no reason to make any of this up. She was older, but certainly not senile. Rita was right about one thing, though. The ship had sailed for Lori's desire to ignore the fact that Jack had been murdered. Now she had to decide if she was going to get on that ship, or if she would let Rita go it alone.

CHAPTER

7

LORI TOOK THE long way home from the diner, aimlessly wandering the empty streets of her small town, immersed deeply in her thoughts. Rita's words replayed over and over again in her mind as she tried to make sense of it all. Numb to the cold wind and falling snow, she hadn't realized that it had gotten dark until the neon lights of Café Amore flashed in front of her. Her growling stomach reminded her that she had not eaten today. She couldn't think of a place that could make her feel safer, so she opened the door.

The aroma of Italian spices stimulated Lori's senses, and she felt as if she were stepping back in time to happy memories and feelings of security. A comforting warmth spread through her, punctuating the feeling of cold in her extremities that had gone unnoticed for the past few hours.

Bruno, the maître d', greeted her fondly. "Your usual table, Signora Crawford? What a delight to have you with us two nights in a row." His warm smile helped to further calm her rattled nerves.

"Thanks, Bruno. I think I'd prefer a booth tonight." Lori needed the perceived safety of something surrounding her. A protected place where she could continue to be with her many thoughts.

Lori watched Bruno's slow, short steps as he led her to a quiet booth, carrying the menu tucked under the arm of his red uniform jacket. Bruno had been hired shortly after the restaurant had opened over twenty-five years ago, already a seasoned maître d'. He had a way of making his guests feel at home the minute they walked in the door. She felt fortunate to be able to come here and reminisce when she felt the need. Being here somehow connected her to Jack, and she sensed that Bruno understood. She warmed at the memory of his tears and his gentle touch on her hand when she came here the first time without Jack.

Lori sipped the glass of cabernet as she watched Bruno seat guests at table after table. One of the few nice restaurants in town, Café Amore had a great reputation, so it was usually busy. Though it was still early for most diners, the dining room was slowly starting to fill up with guests, and she could already hear the commotion in the adjacent bar area. She found herself automatically playing the guessing game as she had the night before when Rita had arrived as a member of the party of ten. It provided a respite from the overwhelming information she had heard today.

Two men in particular caught her attention as they entered. One man, most likely in his sixties, had a close buzz cut and a stiff, formal gait. Definitely military. *Can I not get away from this for even a minute?* The other man wore a striking, gray Armani silk suit, but Bruno was in the way as he escorted them to a table nearby, so she couldn't see his face.

Armani man chose the chair that allowed Lori to see only a small part of his profile, facing mostly away from her toward the door. For some inexplicable reason, an uneasy feeling came over her, and Lori instinctively sank lower into the cushion of the booth, sliding her body slightly toward the wall. The men's voices were low, but the restaurant was still quiet enough that Lori could hear pieces of their conversation. It was mostly small talk as they decided on their entrée. Lori was beginning to tune them out as she nibbled on the pasta that she hoped to finish this time. Then the military man said something that caught her attention. She shifted slightly toward them in the booth, sliding her eyes in their direction as if to hear them better.

"I've got the software installed and am almost ready to implement the project. I'm still waiting for top level security clearances for the two people I want to handle the more unique part of this program. With Jack out of the way, who should they call with any issues they might encounter with the software? I want to stress again that confidentiality must always be of the utmost importance."

Hearing Jack's name startled Lori. Her hands suddenly felt like putty, but she maintained enough composure to set her fork down quietly before she dropped it. Her feet felt cemented to the floor.

"Jack was the primary designer on the project, but George Packwood will be able to handle any questions or problems. And Carl, I'm fully aware of the importance of confidentiality, so don't worry," said the man in the Armani suit.

The hair on Lori's neck raised as she suddenly recognized that voice. Armani man was Mark Mason. Her hands twisted the napkin in her lap as she decided what to do. She had spoken to Mason at every company Christmas party. Their paths had crossed in town when she had been with Jack. He had offered his condolences at Jack's funeral. If Mason saw her, he would conclude that she had heard their conversation. Lori had heard enough to confirm that Rita's suspicions were correct. Her heart was pounding so hard she could barely hear anything else. Her body felt glued to her seat. *I have to get out of here!* But that meant having to walk right by their table.

Her eyes shifted to the front door where a party of six had entered. She looked at Bruno, silently begging him to seat them on the far side of the men's table. Her prayers were answered; Bruno led them across the restaurant toward the other side of Mason's table.

The party's loud conversation attracted Mason's attention as everyone was removing their coats and taking their seats. Mason looked up at them from his appetizer. *It's now or never!* Lori knew this might be her only chance. She laid two twenties on the table and silently made for the front door. She didn't dare look back to see if she had caught their attention. With the loud shuffling of chairs and plenty of bodies between the door and the two men, she was relatively confident Mason hadn't noticed her.

Lori ran home as fast as she could, tears freezing on her cheeks. *With Jack out of the way* echoed in her ears. *What else could it possibly mean?*

As she threw the dead bolt, her legs buckled under her. She sat in a heap on the floor, sobbing uncontrollably. They *had* killed Jack. The unthinkable was true.

CHAPTER

8

MASON SAT IN the freezing car, waiting for the heat to defrost the frozen windshield. *This has gotten crazy.* Things were going so smoothly. No one was supposed to know about any of this. *Dammit Jack! Why couldn't you just leave it alone?* Yet a part of Mason understood Jack's passion for his work.

When he had arrived at SpringWare, he was young and ambitious. He was passionate about becoming successful, and he was well on his way. He never doubted that he was just the person the struggling software company needed to take it to the next level. Mason wanted to play with the boys in the big leagues, and he had plans to do just that.

He was born to hog farmers in rural Iowa. Throughout his young years of slopping, shoveling, and butchering, Mason's father told him he should be proud that they were feeding America. Mason felt that idea was as shitty as the stuff he was forced to shovel. His parents had always followed the rules, and they had little to show for it but debt and blood-stained clothes that smelled like manure. There was no way he was following in his older brother's footsteps to continue the family legacy.

He didn't waste a single day after his eighteenth birthday in getting out of there. His present to himself was a one-way Greyhound bus ticket to New York City. Mason didn't have much of a plan other than to stay with a friend of a friend who had lived in the city for a couple of years. Smart, confident, and with an ego the size of Manhattan, he planned on fulfilling his big dreams. Entertaining the thought of returning to Iowa was never a part of the plan. Twenty years later, he had yet to go back, even for his father's funeral.

Gifted with quick thinking and the ability to sell ice in the Antarctic, Mason talked his way through a series of promotions at several marketing firms, all without a college degree. As soon as local colleges started teaching software development, he enrolled in night classes. Once his skills were proficient, he sought jobs in the software industry. He had several attractive offers in Silicon Valley, but Mason wanted to be a big fish in a little pond. His head hunter found the opening for the position of vice president at SpringWare, located an hour from Washington, DC. He was certain that this was where he wanted to go. At SpringWare, he could develop serious relationships with powerful people. Six years later, he was all over the business news, and SpringWare had become a force to be reckoned with in the software industry.

He had never planned to leave SpringWare. All he had to do was to fulfill his end of the deal, collect his share, and continue as if nothing had ever happened. But Jack found out and other things cropped up. Now all he wanted was to stay under the radar, stay out of the news, and get out of the country as far away from Carl Baxter as possible. *Alive.*

CHAPTER

9

FOR THE SECOND day in a row, Lori woke up hoping that the day before had been a dream. Still fully dressed from the night before, she rubbed her swollen eyes. It took her a moment to orient herself. Groaning as she maneuvered her body into a sitting position on the too-soft sofa, she grabbed her aching back. Her arm had yet to wake up. Massaging feeling back into it, she couldn't recall how she got from the foyer floor to the couch.

Jack was murdered.

Amidst the harsh reality of that all-consuming thought, an alarm went off in her mind, reminding her that it was Monday. *I have to go to work.* Rubbing her neck, she pulled herself off the sofa, hoping that work would help clear her head and provide a distraction for a while. She suddenly craved something normal to remove her from the lead role in this bad movie she felt she had abruptly been thrust into. Perhaps work would be the solution.

After the conversation she had heard at Café Amore, there was no doubt in her mind that she had to act on what she knew.

Her eyes focused on the picture of her and Jack on the fireplace mantle. *You are NOT going to get away with this!* Ignoring this would make her feel complicit in Jack's death. But she couldn't answer the most obvious, nagging question: How would she and Rita prove that Mason and the NSA had killed him? Just the thought of the NSA made Lori shiver, even under normal circumstances. And nothing about this situation was normal. *I need coffee.*

A shot of caffeine was just the ticket for clearing her head. Her mother had brought some French Vanilla when she came for Jack's funeral. She had neglected to take it back with her when she left. Lori sighed as the scoop scratched across the bottom of the metal tin. This would be her first and last cup. It was for the best. It had taken her months to rid herself of the cravings for caffeine. The last thing she needed now was for a bad habit to return. *I promise not to buy any more, Jack.* She inhaled the sweet aroma as she walked upstairs to the bathroom. The warm liquid slid down her throat, pacifying her for the moment.

The hot water from the shower ran over her shoulders, soothing her stiff body. The French vanilla taste still lingered in her mouth. Lori sighed as she lathered the shampoo in her hair, recalling the bet Jack had made with her a few years ago. She had tried many times to stop drinking coffee. He promised her an extended weekend in Jamaica during the winter if she'd quit for three months. Travel to a warmer climate was appealing, but it was the whispered promise of certain intimate activities that motivated her even more. Even after all the years they'd been together, Jack was still quite imaginative in the bedroom. It was that part of the bet that had given her incentive to kick her coffee habit and never look back.

Wrapping her arms around herself, she was transported back to the resort's massive marble shower. Scene after intimate scene flowed through her mind. She could smell him, feel him. She always felt so secure in Jack's arms. *Never again. I'll never have that again.* Lori collapsed onto the teak shower stool, her tears carried away by the gentle cascade of the hot water. If only the water could wash away the dull ache in her heart.

Time was a fickle construct. There were days when it felt like Jack had been gone for a long time. Then there were days when it felt like it was yesterday. Memories would resurface in her mind out of nowhere, and sometimes those trips down memory lane were comforting. But not all of them were pleasant, and many of them felt much too real.

She heard the knock on the door. The state trooper stood on her front step. The look on his face told her everything. She felt paralyzed. Time stopped.

She had replayed that knock on the door every night in her dreams for a month. Then the nightmare came less frequently. It had been only a short time that she could finally say Jack's name and not fall apart. Lori felt like she had traveled through all the five stages of grief, but now here she was, back at stage two.

She stared at her hazy reflection in the steamy glass. Someone she didn't recognize looked back. An internal heat started to rise inside of her. The hair on her arms and neck rose. Her jaw tightened and her fists clenched. It was a force bigger than her sadness and fear. Pure, raw anger flew from her lips.

You took him from me! You killed him, you bastards!

An emboldened woman emerged from the shower.

CHAPTER

10

WALKING TO WORK, Lori dialed Rita's number on the burner phone, hoping she was still at home. Where this decision would lead her was unknown, but she was certain of one thing. Justice would be served for Jack's death. He would have done it for her, with no doubt and no questions asked. She let it ring once, then hung up. There was no turning back. She drew in a deep breath of ice-cold air, but even the cold weather couldn't put out the fire she felt inside of her body.

Over the past fifteen years, the *Town Herald* had become her second home. Her coworkers had been very supportive after Jack's death. Even Joe Delacourt, the usually crotchety editor, had shown his softer side. Lori thought that if she immersed herself in her research work, perhaps she could escape this new reality in her life—at least for a little while.

By the time Lori opened the office door, Joe was already barking out orders to his department heads. When he said jump, everyone asked how high. It wasn't unusual for Joe to get stressed so close to deadline, which was tomorrow, but this was a bit over the top, even for Joe. Something must be going on. Her suspicions deepened when she rounded the corner to her cubicle and Nathan Schilling was sitting on her desk.

"Hey, Lori. My printer's down again. I emailed an article to you for tomorrow's edition, so I'd have it when I got here this morning. Can you log in and print it for me real quick?"

"Yeah. No problem, Nathan." Lori set her coat and purse on her chair as he hopped off the desk and moved out of her way. She thought it was ironic for a homicide reporter to be nearly always happy. Nathan's personality never jived with the gruesome subject of the articles he wrote.

I wonder how you'd write about Jack's murder?

Lori trembled slightly and tried to focus her attention back on Nathan, who was still busy talking.

". . . and so I'm glad you weren't late. Joe's been on a rampage already this morning. Schilling! Where is it? Schilling!" Nathan mockingly imitated their editor's face and body language. "He's had to ask that like a hundred times already. And I've only been here twenty minutes!" Nathan grabbed his head like it was in a vise, faking a groan and laughing uncontrollably. "He's got to proof it in his hands, not on the screen you know, or he's not happy. Joe must own stock in some company that sells paper and red ink."

Nathan laughed out loud again as he stood behind her. Lori opened the document in the email and hit the print button.

The old machine started sputtering loudly. Lori knew it was on its last legs, and she considered asking Joe to spring for a new one. She watched as the paper slowly inched out into the tray as the document printed.

The headline Nathan had written peeked out first: "Woman Found Dead in Apartment." Lori dropped the pen she was holding when she saw the face printing out below it.

Nathan's voice seemed to fade as he continued babbling behind her. She struggled to regain her composure while the rest of the article printed. She vaguely felt Nathan at her feet, retrieving her pen. As the printer groaned to a halt, she braced herself and turned around with the best smile she could muster. It felt plastered on her face. "Here, Nathan. Go put Joe out of his misery."

Nathan handed her the pen. "You okay, Lori?"

"Uh, yeah . . . I'm just cold and tired. Didn't sleep too well last night," Lori honestly added. "You look like you could use some sleep too." His rumpled clothes, bloodshot eyes, and scruffy chin were obvious clues that he hadn't slept.

"Yeah, I was getting ready for bed around midnight when I heard the call on the scanner. I'm running on empty after working on this story all night. I hope Joe won't have too many rewrites." Lori raised her eyebrow in mock disbelief, and Nathan laughed at his comment. Joe always had lots of rewrites.

"Thanks, Lori!" Nathan waved the papers over his head as Lori watched him hurry down the hallway of cubicles to appease his waiting editor.

Lori collapsed into her chair. Her blood felt like ice in her veins as her body shivered in dread. She glanced down both directions of the hall. Satisfied that no one was near, her fingers quivered as she anxiously opened Nathan's email to read the entire story.

> **The police reported that the woman must have surprised a burglar when she arrived home after a late dinner. Neighbors called the police after hearing a gunshot, but no one saw anything. There was no trace of the burglar by the time the police arrived.**

Normally, this would have been just another murder, but Lori couldn't take her eyes off the picture.

CHAPTER

11

KARLA PHILLIPS HAD been Jack's assistant. Lori's hands shook on the keyboard as she deleted the email.

This can't be a coincidence! The plot of this bad movie had just gotten more complicated. *But how complicated is it, really?*

Lori pieced it together in her mind. Jack created software for the NSA. Something was wrong with it. Mason wanted it delivered. Jack was killed. And now Karla was dead. The sequence of events was pretty obvious to Lori. But who was behind this? Mason? Military Man? The NSA? What was it about that software that was so important?

Lori jumped in her chair when the ringing phone yanked her out of her ruminations. She took a deep breath, hoping Delacourt wasn't on the other end of the line. She didn't have the energy to focus on what he might want of her right now. She lifted the receiver to her ear. "Hello." Nothing. The phone rang again.

Lori's eyes darted around her office. By the fourth ring, she realized that it was the burner phone. She fumbled around inside of her purse, trying to find it before Rita hung up. The familiar voice on the other end focused her attention.

"Meet me in the archaeology section of the library at 5:30."

"I've got to tell you—"

"Not on the phone." The silence echoed loudly in her ear. Rita wasn't taking any chances, even on the burner phone.

So much for work being a distraction. Lori had no idea how she would get through the day.

CHAPTER

12

THE AIR WAS damp and bitterly cold as Lori walked to the library. Christmas lights reflected off the buildings in the wet snow. Any other time, it would have been a pretty sight. Tonight, Lori barely noticed. She was completely preoccupied with Rita, Jack, Karla, and what she had heard last night at Café Amore. In fact, the entire day seemed like it had happened in a slow-motion fog. It was a good thing that Delacourt was preoccupied with Nathan and his story because she had accomplished next to nothing today.

The library turned out to be the perfect place to meet. People were on their way home from work. Students were getting ready for dinner before they came in to do their homework. The place was nearly empty at that hour.

She appreciated the warmth of the library's beautiful main room, full of grand tables and floor-to-ceiling bookshelves. Old ladders sat upon rails that spanned the length of the walls. For a small-town library, it looked very impressive. A few patrons were sitting quietly, heads buried in books or laptops.

Breathing in the aroma of the books, she silently slipped off her coat and hung it on the coat rack just inside the door. Library rules. Lori certainly didn't want to draw attention or a reprimand from the librarian, who kept a close eye out for theft. Coats were required to be removed upon entry, as putting them back on in an open area made it harder to smuggle anything out. *Are book thefts really that common?*

Lori cringed when she heard her footsteps echoing in the profound silence as she climbed a short set of stairs. Walking softer on the wood flooring that led to the archaeology section, she wondered how Rita was handling the stress she must certainly be feeling. It was impossible for her to imagine what it would be like to work every day in such close proximity to a man that she suspected might have played a role in Jack's murder. Lori didn't think she would be capable of doing that.

She understood why Rita had avoided her after Jack's death. *I should have told her that in the diner yesterday.* Rita had been protective and supportive of Jack, in a motherly kind of way. Though they had worked together for a very long time, Rita always made sure that the relationship with Jack and Lori stayed professional. Jack had wanted Rita to continue to work with him when he was promoted to his new position, but he was equally happy to see her receive a nice promotion and pay raise when Mason decided that Rita would now work for him. Lori noticed that it was much harder for Jack after she left.

Rita was already waiting for her near the back of the small room, seated at the solitary oak table. Oddly, Lori felt relieved to see her. She quickly pulled out the chair next to her and mentally tried to prepare herself for all that she had to tell Rita. She immediately felt appreciation for how hard it must have been for Rita to tell her all those things in the diner yesterday.

"Rita, something happened last night that made me believe you are right. Jack's death was not an accident." Lori whispered as she leaned in closer to Rita. She proceeded to relate the conversation she had overheard in the restaurant, watching to see how Rita reacted. "I know Mason called the other man by a name, but I can't remember it. I think it began with a K or a C, but I'm not sure."

"The name written on the phone log was Carl. Was that it?" Rita asked.

"Yeah, it *was* Carl. He was military too. He had the look. You know, the haircut and that 'at attention' posture. We need to find out if there is someone named Carl with the NSA."

"Lori, the director of the NSA is Fleet Admiral Carl Baxter. He was in the Navy for thirty-five years. Six years ago, he retired, and the president appointed him director of the NSA. Do you think you'd recognize him if you saw a picture?"

"I'm sure of it. But Rita, the *director*? Do you really think that the person in charge of the most secretive intelligence agency in the world is involved in this? With SpringWare? In a murder?" She was truly dumbfounded by this notion. But the more the idea of the NSA being involved rolled around in her head, the more she started to realize that she should be more fearful than dumbfounded.

"I don't know. It does seem pretty absurd that he would be involved . . . But if it is true, then we need to be especially careful. They covered their tracks so well that no one ever thought Jack's death was anything but an accident."

She could see Rita was processing all of this while she nervously kneaded her fingers in her lap. Lori tried to assess Rita's emotional state of mind, as the next bit of information would be hard on her. "Rita, I'm afraid I have more bad news . . . Karla Phillips was found dead in her apartment, shot by a burglar."

Rita's face paled and her hands clenched tightly. She stared down at her hands and remained quiet for quite some time. When she finally spoke, it was with an intensity that sent a chill through Lori. "Now I know I have to get into that credenza in Jack's old office."

Lori observed Rita carefully as she put her thoughts into words. "Do you really think they killed her, Rita? Was there anything you found to indicate that Jack told Karla about this?"

"I can't imagine that Karla would have known anything. Jack would never have put her in that position. But that doesn't mean that Mason, or the NSA, didn't think so. Lori, it may be a few days, but I'll be in touch." Visibly shaken, Rita looked as though she just couldn't take any more conversation. She stood up and vanished around the corner, the sound of her footsteps fading quickly.

Lori sat there, not really knowing what to do next. She was worried about Rita taking the risk of getting into Jack's credenza. *What if she gets caught?*

Even though Rita was determined, Lori could also see that she was extremely stressed. She assumed Rita was in her midsixties. Lori didn't consider that old, but in just a couple of years, she had gained weight and visibly aged to the point where Lori hadn't immediately recognized her. *I need to keep an eye on her.*

Lori put those thoughts aside and decided that as long as she was here, she could do some research. She quickly made her way to the periodical section.

CHAPTER

13

THE PRESIDENT HAD been in the news a lot lately. *The New York Times* ran a story about him issuing an executive order for the NSA to wiretap US citizens suspected of terrorist connections. An executive order bypassed Congress and the courts. The order was being challenged because it was thought to violate the privacy of American citizens. It was prompting spirited debate around the issue of national security versus civil liberties. There were also rumors that the phone companies had turned over records of millions of calls made by their customers to government agencies. Massive legal battles were brewing. Lori was sure this topic would keep lawyers, politicians, college professors, and students arguing both sides of the issue for a long time.

And, of course, Lori had her own personal issues with intelligence and military groups. She had not been able to get full closure around her father's death because of so-called national security issues. It made her angry because her father had devoted much of his life to the military, missing out on much of her childhood. Had her mother not received the letter about the empty casket by mistake, they would have never been the wiser that the casket was empty.

Maybe they would have had more internal peace if they didn't know the truth, that his body was never found. But what if her dad had been captured? Did it mean they weren't even looking for him? No one would ever answer those questions. Lori still held on to her distrust of military agencies and the governments that ran them. As such, it was no easy task for her to be objective on this research issue because of her father, and now because of what she had discovered about Jack's death.

As she read through the articles, she noticed that even though the NSA was the agency involved in this major controversy, very little was said about it. It's no wonder why people joked that NSA stood for "No Such Agency" or "Never Say Anything." She discovered only a few sidebar articles about the NSA and what was written on Wikipedia. Lori finally found an article in *Newsweek* that had a picture of the director.

She drew in her breath as she stared at the face of Fleet Admiral Carl Baxter, the man she had seen in Café Amore. The picture sent a feeling of raw terror through her. Lori clenched her abdomen, feeling sick to her stomach. What was it about that software that would cause these people to kill over it? As she sat back in her chair, she found herself asking the same question. *How? How can we stand up to the NSA?* While Mason was most certainly involved, she knew that the real threat was Carl Baxter. Mason was simply a tool, a means to an end.

Lori suddenly felt very vulnerable in the library. She put the periodicals back, grateful that no one had been in this section and seen her reading about the NSA. She quickly grabbed her coat and headed out, not caring that the librarian was eyeing her nervous behavior. She desperately needed to feel the safety of her home. The shivering that had started when she looked at Baxter's picture wouldn't stop. She tried to convince herself it was the twenty-degree weather outside, but it was of no use.

Breathless from the freezing four-block walk at breakneck speed, Lori locked the door behind her, her frozen fingers pounding at the keypad to set the alarm. Still trembling, she grabbed a blanket off the sofa, wrapped it around her, and crossed the living room to the fireplace. As she put a match to the kindling nestled in the carefully placed logs, she wondered what Jack would do.

He'd stand up. He'd find a way to make this right.

Jack always had such a thorough, straightforward way of looking at problems. He obviously had some sort of plan in mind. He had documented the things he found at SpringWare and kept copies of his correspondence with Mason . . . *copies.*

Where was that CD Rita had given her? Lori bolted up the stairs and dumped the contents of the purse she'd had with her that day on the bed.

It wasn't there.

She ran down to the laundry room to search the pockets of her sweatshirt. No luck.

Leaning against the dryer, she tried to clear her head and not let fear paralyze her. She took a deep breath in, and another. *Where did I put it?*

My coat! She pulled the long wool coat she had worn yesterday out of the foyer closet and searched through the pockets. Finally, her fingers touched hard plastic. She let out a big sigh and rested against the closet door. The jewel case shook in her hand. Lori took in another few breaths and felt her body relax ever so slightly.

She had to find a safe place to put this disk. *Think!* Jack had always said that things in plain sight are sometimes the hardest to see. Scanning the living room, she spied the rack full of CDs that Jack had loved so much, right next to the stereo and shelf of record albums that he'd had since college. She put the Matchbox Twenty CD in the proper place, alphabetically, just like Jack had arranged them. It blended in perfectly with the other hundred or so cases on the rack.

Lori went into the kitchen and poured a glass of wine. She grabbed some dip and veggies out of the fridge and headed for the comfort of the living room sofa and the warmth of the fireplace. She took a sip and cradled the glass in her hands as she tucked her feet under the blanket. Eyes closed, she listened to the crackling of the flames. On another day, when she wasn't as overwhelmed, she would summon the courage to look at what that disk contained, but that would not be today.

The picture on the mantle of her and Jack attracted her attention. Somewhere inside, she knew she'd find the courage to do what needed to be done. How they would avenge Jack's death wasn't clear, but she wanted to believe that anything was possible. Lori shifted her focus to the food and wine in front of her and thought about happier times. For the moment, she just needed to be. The flickering flames had a hypnotic effect, allowing herself to find comfort in knowing that Jack would approve of her resilience and cleverness.

CHAPTER

14

AS USUAL, RITA arrived at the office on time. The morning's headline and picture in the newspaper deeply affected her, even though she already knew about Karla's death. Two of the six people with possible knowledge of the NSA project at SpringWare were dead.

Her instincts told her they had both been murdered.

Stop it! She chastised herself for thinking about this right now. It was essential to maintain a normal demeanor and to stay focused on her job when she was around Mason.

She hung her coat on the rack and laid her wet gloves on the radiator to dry. *I should have driven the car.* The temperature hadn't risen above forty for the past week. It was so damp outside that Rita felt like *she* needed to sit on the radiator to dry out, but she opted for her chair instead.

The photo of her daughter and grandchildren on her desk caught her attention. She imagined the kids playing in the pool this morning after breakfast, and she felt a touch of envy toward their life in such a temperate climate. It saddened her to think that she was closer to her neighbor's family than her own. It was nice of them to have invited her to a holiday dinner with them the night she saw Lori, but it made it even more clear how estranged she felt from her own daughter. As she ran her finger across the top of the picture frame, she made a mental note to dust the office later today.

Through the door, she could hear Mason talking on the phone in his office. She had been rehearsing her normal responses to his commands all night, watching herself in the mirror to see if her face would reveal anything. *You can do this. You have to if you want to get justice for*—She jumped as the intercom buzzed.

"Rita!" Mason snapped.

She took a deep breath and glanced one more time at the smiling grandkids. Rita pasted on her best "ready to work" demeanor before she walked through his door. *I can do this.* She crossed the large room and sat in her usual chair to take notes. Predictably, there was no "Good morning." The look on Mason's face was strictly business as he gave her nothing more than a quick glance. Mason was charismatic with people when he had something to gain, but when it came to rank-and-file employees, he couldn't care less.

"I'm sure you saw the paper this morning." Mason looked down at his notes and continued without waiting for a reply. "A tragedy. Send flowers to Ms. Phillips's family. Compile a list of qualified replacements within the company and pull their personnel files. We'll review staffing options this afternoon to fill her position. After you get that in motion with HR, check her desk to see if there are any assignments that need immediate attention."

He continued with a slightly perturbed tone in his voice, "George Packwood is also out today. He must be devastated by the news. Even though Ms. Phillips had only worked with him for a short time, he seemed quite fond of her. Check George's desk for any loose ends as well. I suspect he may be out for a few days." Mason opened a notebook on his desk. She was dismissed.

Coldhearted SOB. Just business as usual. Rita sat at her desk, thinking about his odd comments. Relationships weren't something she thought Mason would normally pay attention to. Had he heard the rumors that George and Karla were having an affair? Rita imagined that they'd probably had dinner together that night. It was lucky that George didn't go home with her.

Rita was relieved to be done with Mason for the moment. It was hard to be in the same room with him and keep her composure. She was grateful that he had made little eye contact and that he had little desire for conversation, other than giving her directions. His behavior enabled her to keep her comments to a minimum as well, so there was less chance for her to show emotion. Now she thought it for the best that he had never once inquired about her or her personal life. There had never even been a "How was your weekend?" kind of question. It made it much easier for her not to have to lie, or act like all was well when it definitely wasn't. She could remain her stoic, professional assistant self. *Maybe this will be enough to keep me safe.*

She took the next hour to check the phone message log and Mason's calendar thoroughly. Even the smallest of details might provide more clues. Finding nothing of interest, she picked up the calendar and rapped softly on his door. He gave the okay to enter with a soft grunt, and she walked the calendar over to his desk. "I've finished the usual morning tasks, Mr. Mason. I'll be going to Karla's and George's offices now to see what I need to do there," Rita told him.

Mason nodded, barely looking up from his paperwork. "I'm leaving soon for a doctor's appointment. I'll be back around three," he added. Rita managed a weak smile of acknowledgement, then headed out his door.

Rita walked down the long hall to her old office that Karla now occupied. *Did occupy.* This was the opportunity she was looking for. If Karla knew something that might have gotten her killed, perhaps she'd find it. Even if Karla had no knowledge of Jack's death or the NSA software, she might have information that would help Rita connect more dots. Clues could be anywhere, and she didn't want to miss them. This was also her chance to get into Jack's old credenza.

Her heart was beating so fast that it felt as if it would leap out of her chest.

CHAPTER

15

MASON SAT AT his desk, rapidly tapping his pen. Baxter had just texted that he was tied up in a meeting and couldn't meet until later. He sent the location of the meeting place and set the time for one o'clock. Mason was agitated with this change in plans. *He wouldn't stand for it if I changed our plans at the last minute.*

From the beginning, Mason had tried to position himself on equal footing with Baxter, but it was always tenuous at best. He had come to realize that Baxter had a way of making you think you were in control, then you'd suddenly realized he was playing you. Most people would say that the president is the most powerful one in our country's government, but in Mason's eyes, it was Baxter. Because the NSA was so secretive, he was hardly ever in the spotlight, and that made him all the more dangerous.

Looking back now, Mason didn't have any specific plans for how Baxter might serve his career when they had met at a performance at the Kennedy Center a few years ago. *Couldn't hurt to be tight with the director of the NSA, right?* Mason cultivated the relationship, conveniently running into Baxter at charity events or on the golf course. Mason chuckled to himself. *He may be a super spy, but he sucks at golf.*

Eighteen months earlier, Baxter invited Mason to his home for a dinner party with a small group of very influential people. Mason was in his element among these movers and shakers. Later in the evening, Baxter invited him into his study to introduce his idea for the software program.

Could I create it? Ha! Mason didn't think Baxter fully appreciated the skill set of his team and the power he held at SpringWare. Carl presented his motives in a patriotically flattering manner, but ego was only part of what motivated Mason. It was the financial benefits that Baxter offered that sealed the deal.

He gets to save the United States and restore her to her righteous glory, and I save myself by getting very rich. Mason had always viewed their arrangement as a symbiotic relationship. But since the time of Jack's death, Mason was beginning to understand that Baxter did not share his point of view. Hindsight now provided the proof that any control he thought he had was simply an illusion. Carl Baxter was, and always had been, in command.

Mason laid the pen down on his desk. *But he did need me.* It would have been too risky for Carl to call on the people within his organization to design the software. *No one else in the industry would have created this for him.* And there was no one else that Carl could trust as much as he had come to trust him. That made him an essential component in Baxter's plan. *I'm going to remind him of this at our meeting today.*

No more killing. He didn't sign on for murder, and though he'd never admit it to anyone, he was starting to feel a little vulnerable himself. He'd have to find a way to get Baxter to agree that everyone with knowledge of the software was gone, and that implementation should be the priority. He chuckled at the irony. *Now I'm the only one left to troubleshoot the software.* This new realization gave Mason some confidence that it made him a little more indispensable.

He sat back in his leather chair, looking around his spacious office at all he had accomplished. *I may not head the NSA, but right now, I'm the only path to your holy grail.*

CHAPTER

16

KARLA HAD BEEN assigned to work with Jack in another wing of the building when he was promoted. After Jack died, Mason had George Packwood take over Jack's position and his office. George's assistant had left on maternity leave about the time Jack died, so it was a smooth transition for George to have Karla stay in her office and start to work with him.

Rita held her breath as she entered the office that she had once occupied for so long. Of course, Karla had put her personal touches in the space; there were knickknacks on the shelves, a few family pictures on the wall, and a picture of a dog on her desk. *I wonder what happened to the dog?*

Shrugging off that thought, Rita sat at the desk, thoroughly checking Karla's calendar. She found a few handwritten notes and to-do lists, then she searched her desk drawers and filing cabinet. She found nothing particularly noteworthy. There were a few phone calls to be relayed to George and some filing to catch up on. It appeared that Karla had been a very efficient assistant. Rita was disappointed. She was going to need every scrap of evidence to support her theories, and there didn't seem to be anything of value here.

She turned on Karla's computer and entered the password the tech department had given her. Rita scrolled through the files, making notes of different projects in varying degrees of completion.

The company email system provided an array of messages that needed to be returned to her work list. As she was glancing through the sent messages, she noticed an unusual number of emails to George. After reading two or three recent ones, there was no doubt that the two were having an affair. *Pretty careless.* It was surprising to Rita that the two of them would send such things through company email, as they had to know that SpringWare monitored all employee communications. *Maybe they notified HR of their relationship and that's how Mason knew about it, or maybe Mason had accessed their emails through the company monitoring program?*

Rita never put anything on a SpringWare computer that she wanted to keep private. Her fingers hovered over the keyboard. She wondered if they would know if she tried to access more of Karla's emails that were earlier than the past week. *I better find out before I go snooping.* She was desperate to see if she would find something that would indicate Karla knew about the software, but Rita also had to stay under Mason's radar. *I can't figure this out if I'm dead . . .*

"I'm going now, Rita. Did you find anything that needs immediate attention?" Mason's voice jolted Rita out of her contemplation. She looked up to see him standing on the other side of the desk. She had not heard him come in.

Rita ran her finger down the notes on her notepad to give herself time to recover. "Uh, I don't think so, Mr. Mason. There are some loose ends, but nothing that seems to be urgent. Some messages to be relayed to George, some emails to be returned to a few vendors and clients."

She looked up from her checklist to find Mason studying her. Not sure what to make of his stare, she held his gaze as best she could and quickly added, "I'll put together a list of things that need to be done. You can let me know what tasks you'd like me to handle. I'll also have the list of potential replacements put together by the time you return this afternoon."

Mason nodded and turned to leave, allowing her to let out the breath she had been holding. *Did he see the emails I was reading?* She couldn't be sure, but one thing was for certain. *I better be more vigilant.*

Rita had learned quite a bit from Jack. Jack had entrusted her with many kinds of tasks over their years together. She doubted that Mason would ever think she had knowledge of encrypted files or anything other than the typical Microsoft Office applications. He had never given her any challenging tasks to do or any extra responsibility or privileges. In his mind, she was just an assistant, a lowly secretary.

Right now, that suited her just fine. *Let him think all I know how to do is keep schedules and answer the phone.* But then, if Mason thought that was true of Rita, she wondered why he wouldn't think the same thing about Karla. Why would he think it necessary to kill her? The link had to be George.

Rita remembered Lori saying that Mason had mentioned George's name to Baxter as the person to go to with questions or problems. If Mason knew about the affair, maybe he suspected that George had confided in Karla about the software. She couldn't imagine George or Jack ever putting their assistants in that dangerous position, but people like Baxter and Mason obviously didn't hold the same ethical standards. Of course, they would make that assumption if they knew George and Karla were in an intimate relationship.

Do they think Jack told Lori? A shiver went down Rita's spine. That was another thought she'd have to save for later.

Rita wondered if Jack had been creating this software while she was still working with him. It was certainly possible, as these kinds of projects could take years to develop. It made more sense, though, for the work to have started after Jack got his promotion. *Maybe that's the reason I was promoted to work with Mason.* He may have been concerned that Jack might disclose information about the project because of the trust they had built over all the years they had worked together.

She felt confident that there was nothing more to be found in Karla's office that would indicate she knew anything about the NSA project. As she turned her attention to George's door, another thought crossed her mind. *Is George in danger too?*

CHAPTER

17

RITA STILL FELT very much at home in these adjoining offices. Even so, she stopped at the threshold as she opened the door and looked in. There were no more pictures of Jack and Lori. She wondered who was given the unpleasant task of returning them to Lori.

Mason had moved George into Jack's office shortly after the funeral. SpringWare had installed new carpet and painted the walls a pale shade of green. George had hung his own collection of modern art on the walls. Other than the furniture, there was nothing left to remind her that Jack had once worked in here. Her gaze stopped at the credenza behind the desk. And that gave Rita's heart occasion to race once again.

She moved inside, partially shutting the door behind her. She didn't want to be caught unaware of anyone entering, as she had been in Karla's office when Mason surprised her. Rita knocked George's inbox full of papers off of his desk, scattering them onto the carpeted floor. She kneeled down between the desk and the credenza, facing the office door. She'd gather the papers in a moment, but for now she turned her attention to the bottom door of the credenza.

Quickly opening the door, her left hand slid along the back until she felt the small notch cut out in the corner. She put her fingernail in the slot and pulled her hand to the right. The false back opened, just as she remembered it would. Her hand felt a thin object. It was a jewel case. Rita quickly took it out and tucked it into the oversized pocket of her sweater. She closed the false back and the credenza door just as she caught the movement of the office door opening. Quickly turning toward the direction of the papers strewn across the floor, she started gathering them.

"Rita, I won't be going out as planned. The doctor's appointment was moved to . . . later in the day." Mason looked inquisitively at her on the floor.

"I knocked George's inbox off the desk when I came around the corner," Rita explained as she looked up from the floor. "Well, I've got to look through all of these papers anyway." She hoped the look on her face seemed one of frustration rather than nervousness.

Unexpectedly, Mason bent down to pick up several papers that were at his feet. "I'll be eating in today, so call for my usual lunch." He handed her the papers he had retrieved.

"I'll do it right away," she said as she struggled to get up off the floor. "I have to go through George's planner and these papers, then I'll be finished."

He left without a word, leaving the door open wide behind him. Rita didn't care. She already had what she came for. The papers on the floor had proven to be a useful idea to camouflage her actions, but it was a close call. She sat for a minute at George's desk to let her legs and hands stop trembling. If Mason had noticed her shaking hands, she hoped he chalked it up to her being a clumsy old woman, crawling around the floor to clean up her mess.

Jack's old office had never had bright enough lighting for Rita, even when her eyes were better in her younger years. She got up to open the blinds closest to her. Sitting down at the desk once more, the light hit the open planner on George's desk. Something caught her eye on the corner of last week's page.

It had been written in pencil, then erased, but she could still make out the name Baxter. Rita's heart beat faster. Something else had been written under it, but Rita could only make out what looked like a "k." Could the word have been Jack? Maybe George had put two and two together and figured things out. *How could I be so stupid!* If Mason had indeed killed Karla, of course, George would be in great danger. She had to figure out how to warn him, but she couldn't do that while she was at work without the possibility of Mason finding out. She'd have to find his phone number in the company directory and call him as soon as she left work and could get to her burner phone.

Rita put her head in her hands. The emotions of the past few days caught up to her. Tears tried to swell over the edges, but she fought them back. *Keep it together, Rita!* She couldn't risk Mason returning to see her crying. Bringing Lori into this situation had helped her feel less alone and bolstered her confidence. At the same time, Rita knew she had also endangered her. But Rita was fairly certain that none of them were safe. She rubbed the sleeve of her sweater across her eyelids and nose and sat up straight in the chair.

She looked at her watch. Frowning at how much time had passed, she picked up the phone. "Hello, Kelly? This is Rita over at SpringWare. I need to order the usual for Mr. Mason." She had been ordering from the Corner Deli for nearly two years. Kelly knew what Mr. Mason liked because he always wanted the same thing. Pastrami on rye with mustard. Rita suspected it reminded him of his days in New York City. She thought it oddly humorous that a sandwich made him feel nostalgic. "Actually . . . make one for me too." Rita smiled at her own cleverness.

Rita flipped through the rest of George's planner, but found nothing more. She sorted through the papers from his inbox. Still nothing. What she really needed was to access George's computer, but that was not going to happen. Rita had noticed that Mason had not authorized her to get George's computer password from IT. She sighed heavily as she pushed herself up, using the arms of the chair to go close the blinds. *God, I feel old.*

The sound of something hitting the carpet was barely audible, but it was enough to catch Rita's attention. She looked down to see a small gold key on the floor under the desk. Her leg must have knocked it loose as she stood up. Rita picked up the key and slid it into the pocket of her sweater with the jewel case. She ran her hand underneath the top of the desk as far back as she could and found the piece of tape that had been holding it in place. It was pure luck that she had found this key. There was no locking drawer in this desk or in the credenza.

Now I've got to figure out what it unlocks.

Rita gathered up the notes she had made for Mason and closed the planner so no one would notice what she had seen.

She quickly scribbled some words on a piece of paper that she put in her pocket with the jewel case and key. Making a right out of Karla's office, she headed for the Human Resource department to pick up the personnel files.

Hearing someone call her name, she turned to see Chris, the deli delivery man, walking up behind her with a smile that stretched ear to ear. "Hey, Rita. It's been awhile."

"Yes. Mr. Mason has been eating out more often lately. Thanks for getting here so quickly, Chris." Rita glanced around to be sure they were alone in the hallway. "Just leave one order here. I need you to do me a favor with the other one. It's my friend's birthday today, and I thought I'd surprise her with lunch. Her name is Lori Crawford, and she works at the *Herald*. Would you mind taking it over there?"

"Anything for you, Rita!"

"Great, thanks." While Chris was hunting through his receipts for the two orders, Rita slipped the piece of paper from her pocket into the bag for Lori. She thanked him again as she handed it back and watched him head down the hallway.

Where there's a will, there's a way. And that thought buoyed Rita's mood ever so slightly.

CHAPTER

18

COOPERVILLE SITS AMONG the plains and rolling green hills of Virginia about fifty-five minutes west of Washington, DC, if traffic is light. Before SpringWare arrived, it was farming and horse country. Barely a speck on the map when it was settled, less than three hundred residents were spread out over a relatively wide area. The main street consisted of a feed store, a general store, a gas station, and two taverns. The town took its name from the talented coopers who lived there in colonial times who made animal troughs and farm tools. Twenty years later, with not a cooper in sight, it had completely transformed. Because it still remained distant from neighboring towns, it appealed to people who were trying to get away from the DC area and the cities of Alexandria and Fairfax.

SpringWare, the largest company in Cooperville, grew to employ 1,900 people locally, across the US, and recently, internationally. Other ancillary companies were born when SpringWare moved its headquarters here twenty years ago.

Sandwich shops, couriers, graphic designers, printers, and a few new tech companies that fed off SpringWare's success soon arrived. Ground was recently broken to house a manufacturer of joysticks for gaming devices. An unlimited and ever-changing array of businesses continued to be established, catering to the various needs of the influx of people.

As additional jobs developed, the population increased to nearly twenty thousand. Incomes rose, increasing the average person's standard of living. Residents were eager to invest in their growing community. A library, a modest art museum, and a small movie house were built. There was talk of extending the light rail from DC closer to this area. Cooperville was rapidly becoming another popular suburb for people to get away from the busy political life of the capital. As the town developed its positive aspects, the disadvantages of a larger population were also starting to originate in the way of crime. And of course, that meant a local newspaper was needed to report it all.

Lori was not even twenty feet inside the paper's front door when Delacourt handed her a thick stack of papers to read on the series he wanted to run. She flipped through them as she walked back to her desk, looking at the topics they covered. *Great. The NSA. So much for separating home and work life.*

The *Town Herald* was a locally grown paper that started in 1941, mostly as a form of communication for the surrounding farmers. It had never employed a crime reporter until ten years ago, when it hired an enthusiastic Nathan Schilling from Atlanta. Unfortunately, his title quickly evolved into the more specific Investigative Homicide Reporter. Cooperville, while still maintaining a quaint image, was rapidly becoming like most other American cities.

As the *Herald*'s Research Specialist, Lori's job involved researching facts and information for Joe and the staff reporters, and compiling ideas for articles and series. She had learned a lot over the past fifteen years about a wide variety of topics and current events that had crossed her desk. Occasionally, the research was boring, but for the most part, her job was always fresh and challenging.

She hung her coat on the hook inside her cubicle and tossed her purse on the floor under her desk. Sighing loudly, she began reading Joe's notes about her latest assignment: the legalities of the president's actions concerning the NSA's monitoring of US citizens. He wanted to run a series of informative articles to educate the readers about the law and past executive orders and precedents that had been set by other presidents. *Ugh.* She knew the articles would be written in a way that would be interesting to the reader. What she didn't relish was the idea of sifting through stale law journals at the library to dig up the boring, but necessary, information that the reporter would need to craft them.

The coincidence that the NSA was a focal point in her exploration of the subject matter seemed especially cruel. With everything that was happening around her, she worried that her ability to maintain the correct focus would be difficult. She was much more interested in its director, Carl Baxter, than in laws and precedents. *Well, a deeper understanding of what we are up against can't hurt.* She typed NSA into the browser search box and got ready to take notes.

For an organization that was founded in 1952, like in the library the other night, she was amazed at how little information she could find on the NSA even with a deep dive into the internet. But what she did find truly frightened her. It was involved in data collection, monitoring, espionage, and cyber-attacks. It coordinated with all of the other government intelligence agencies, performing the work they were not allowed to do. The list covered pretty much every kind of clandestine activity you could imagine. She was certain that what was on this list was only a small accounting of their capacity as an organization. *The tip of the iceberg.* She scratched her scalp with the tip of her pen. *Perhaps the world isn't ready to know about everything they do.*

The more she read, the more discouraged she became. If the NSA was involved in Jack and Karla's murder, it was ludicrous to think that she and Rita could ever bring this information against them to light. *They are way too powerful.* Lori sat back in her chair, her arms folded against her stomach.

Depressed, anxious, and eyes burning from three straight hours of screen time, Lori sat back in her chair, completely exhausted. She needed a break. Lunch outside of the office felt like the perfect solution, even if, especially if, it meant going out into the cold air. She was putting her purse over her shoulder when she was surprised by a young man entering her cubicle with a bag in his hands.

"Lori Crawford?"

She nodded.

"Happy birthday," he said cheerfully as he put the bag on her desk and walked out.

"Thanks?" said Lori, a perplexed look on her face. It wasn't her birthday. She peeked in the bag and discovered that now there was no need to go out. Mysteriously, lunch had come to her. The puzzle was solved as she opened the folded slip of paper that sat on top of the sandwich and chips.

We have to meet. 7 p.m. at Café Amore.

Rita was certainly full of creative surprises. Ripping open the bag of chips, Lori knew that time would crawl until then.

CHAPTER

19

NATHAN SCHILLING CHEWED on his pencil while he looked at the police report. There was something nagging at him, but as he scanned the papers for the fifth time, he still couldn't find it. Yet, his reporter's instinct was telling him to be on alert. He had been born with this sixth sense, and it had rarely failed him.

Schilling had dreamed of being a reporter for as long as he could remember. Even now, his mother still reminded him how he used to carry a pad and paper around, interviewing people and pretending to take notes before he even knew how to write. All he had wanted for his seventh birthday was a tape recorder. He drove his family crazy, shoving a microphone in their faces at every opportunity to create his next news story. His young friends wanted to be like Superman, but he had no aspirations of being a superhero. Nathan dreamed of being Clark Kent, a simple newspaper reporter covering exciting stories.

His first job, at seventeen, was as an assistant to the lead crime reporter at the *Atlanta Journal-Constitution*. It sounded like an important title, but in reality, he ran errands, did some occasional research, and most importantly, kept his boss's coffee cup filled. That experience taught him invaluable lessons on how to do the job, though. In the thick of it all, he watched and listened, learning everything he needed to be successful. He became proficient in observing people and situations, and he learned the importance of being objective, of not showing your hand too soon, and of making connections and nurturing strategic sources.

Nathan propped his feet up on the desk as he recalled when his first article on a drive-by shooting was published. He had made it to the big time. He was a little fish in a big pond, but he was swimming nonetheless. That changed dramatically as the years went by. Nathan received two prestigious awards during his time at the *Constitution*. The Goldsmith Prize for Investigative Reporting honored him for his work in exposing police corruption in a precinct in Buckhead. The affluent neighborhood outside of Atlanta was filled with upscale shops and bars that provided a lively nightlife. It also served as a conduit for a major drug trafficking ring that sold primarily to local clientele. A tight-knit community of police officers in the precinct turned a blind eye to the drug business in their midst, and they made sure the buyers and sellers were never apprehended.

His second award was the Robert F. Kennedy Journalism Award for his reporting on the lack of health care in the poor communities of Atlanta and the effects it had on the disease and death rate in the community.

Neither of these accomplishments was listed on the resume he submitted to Joe Delacourt when he applied for the job at the *Herald*. Nathan was naturally humble when it came to his career accolades. He never rested on previous laurels, so Nathan left it up to Joe to delve into his career history if he chose to do so. He did this job because he loved it, not because he wanted to be famous or important. Mostly, he wanted to be a good reporter with integrity. Ultimately, he wanted to help improve the communities for which he wrote.

Now he was the lead homicide investigator in Cooperville. He wasn't at a big city paper like he was in Atlanta, but he had the title and the experience for which he could take full credit. Perhaps one day he'd apply to the *Washington Post*. He was getting closer, even if only geographically.

The crackling of the police scanner on his desk brought his thoughts back to the work at hand. He heard the dispatch sending units to a possible suicide. Nathan scratched the address on a piece of paper, grabbed his coat from the back of his chair, and sprinted toward the door.

Though he served as the homicide reporter at the newspaper, he monitored the police radio for any types of deaths. Joe gave him lots of leeway on stories as long as they related to crime. After all, they weren't a huge newspaper, so many staffers pulled double duties. Nathan thought suicides were especially interesting cases. They often went hand in hand with other intriguing information that could prove to be news in hiding.

Nathan had grown up with Cooperville over the fifteen years he had worked here, so he was familiar with the gated community where the call had originated. *How can people with money become so depressed that they would take their own lives?* Surviving on a reporter's income made it difficult for him to relate to the stresses that came with managing wealth.

As he drew up alongside the guardhouse, Nathan offered his press credential through the half-opened window. The frigid air almost took his breath away as it blew in the window. The security guard frowned, but he was resigned to the fact that it was going to be impossible to keep the press out today. He'd rather have them accounted for by letting them in the gate than having to worry about them scaling walls to get in through someone's backyard. Events like this in Cooperville usually drew reporters from smaller neighboring towns who had much less activity to write about. The guard pressed the button to open the heavy iron gate, and Nathan drove through.

Reaching across the front seat, Nathan flipped open the cover on his laptop. Most subdivisions like this were filled with wireless computer networks, so it was easy to hop on the internet from the street in front of any house emitting a decent signal. There was usually someone nearby who hadn't yet learned to put a password on their internet service. Maybe his luck would hold and he could get a head start on this story without using his phone as a hotspot. This old car didn't have a phone charger, and he never risked his phone battery going dead. It was his lifeline for many things.

Nathan assumed he wouldn't be getting details from the police any time soon, so he'd settle for a few pictures of officials going in and out of the house. He found an unprotected internet connection and Googled some background information on the victim while he waited and watched.

After twenty-six years of reporting, Nathan had learned how to find the stories behind the stories. Though, unlike other reporters, he had managed to resist the temptation to create news if nothing of real interest was to be had. Suicides weren't always indications of something bigger; sometimes, they were simply very sad events. He was sensitive to the fact that unexpected and bad things happened to people who never dreamed that their private lives would become public knowledge, so he did his best to respect the family's privacy. It was easier to maintain that integrity here than it had been in Atlanta. There, the juiciest story was always the one that got printed. It's why he left, and perhaps that's why he still hadn't applied to the *Post*.

Parked across the street, he counted two police cars, the unmarked car of a high-ranking detective, and the medical examiner's van. Nathan noticed that one of the patrol cars belonged to a strategic source he had nurtured over the years. Officer Matthew Abernathy was good for information if he knew there would be something offered in exchange.

This was a good omen for Nathan. He pulled out his notepad and pencil while he waited for the online search of the property's address to finish. Although most of his work was done on the computer nowadays, he still carried his trusty pad and pencil for notes and interviews. Old school still worked for him.

The weak Google connection finally yielded the tax records and identity of the homeowner. He searched that name as well. He hoped that the homeowner was of some importance, as that would make for a better story. In this neighborhood, the odds were good. Though, at this point, he didn't know if the homeowner was the victim.

Sure enough, a few news articles surfaced with the owner's name briefly noted in them. He had lost his wife to cancer not very long ago. But it was the third item that really caught his eye. The article mentioned that George Packwood was a software developer at SpringWare. It didn't take but a second for Nathan to recall the events of the night before. Karla Phillips was an employee of the same company. Nathan's experience led him to believe that there were no coincidences in life. Events like these were often connected.

Nathan stared at the house with a new perspective. This might prove to be a very interesting afternoon, after all.

CHAPTER

20

THE DARKENED WINDOWS of the limousine offered no possibility of discerning the identities of the people who sat inside. Carl Baxter and Mark Mason were deep in discussion behind the privacy screen, shielding them from the driver's curious eyes and ears. It wasn't every day that the driver took Baxter to meet with someone in the back of an auto salvage yard. Needless to say, he found that very curious. But Carlos knew not to question anything that concerned Carl Baxter or the NSA. It was best to keep your head down and do what you were told. He had found enough trouble in his life, and for some unknown reason, Baxter had made them disappear. He owed Baxter, and he knew that was why he had been hired.

"I'm very nervous about how everything is proceeding," Mason said, sweating even in the cold weather. "This makes the third SpringWare employee to die in the last three months.

Two of them in just two days! People are bound to get suspicious." Mason struggled to maintain his composure. "This is moving way too fast, Carl. I'm the one they are going to come after for answers." Mason didn't like it when he wasn't calling the shots.

"Calm down, Mark," Baxter said in his commanding voice. "There's nothing to worry about. Our steps have been carefully covered. The plan's in place, and it's rock solid. Besides, no one will think Jack's death is connected. It was three months ago."

"This is out of control, Carl. I know we had to do something after getting those emails from Jack. Obviously, he could've figured out everything. But Karla and George? I'm not sure they even knew about the program."

"Maybe that's true," said Baxter. "I know you think that Jack was the only one who could piece everything together and figure out what was going on. But we can't take the chance that anyone will expose this. There were enough subtle things in those emails between George and Karla that made me believe that George knew *something*. Stay calm. Karla was killed by a burglar they will never find alive, and George was a lover overcome with grief who killed himself. No one will suspect anything different. Is there anyone else that had knowledge of anything to do with the software that I need to know about?"

Mason paused before answering, internally questioning Baxter's motives. "Yes. Jacob Browning and Rita Johnson, besides myself, of course. Jacob helped with minor pieces of the design work, but I made sure that he would not be aware of the scope of the project. He was involved with two segments, both of which he was told were for two completely different projects. He's not a particularly ambitious person, so I doubt he'd question anything.

"I promoted Rita to my office when I promoted Jack to design the software so she wouldn't know anything about what Jack was working on. After Jack's death, I had Rita finish the logistical aspects of the delivery. There is no way she would have known what the project was, or that you were the client. She's a competent assistant but getting near retirement, so I think she's pretty much on autopilot. There were no accounting issues because, of course, I didn't run this through Spring-Ware. I handled the final delivery directly to you. That's it. No one else was involved."

Baxter almost pointed out that he'd become a very rich man using SpringWare's labor, but he decided to keep it to himself.

"We still have to decode the last encryption in the file. Normally, it wouldn't take so long, but I can't let anyone in the agency know about this either. I'm just waiting for the final security clearance on the two men I'm bringing in to work on this. Then we'll be able to see if there's anything else in that file to be concerned about before we launch the project. In the meantime, I'll assign a man to tail Browning and Johnson for a couple of weeks until we make sure this matter is resolved."

Baxter made a mental note to hire three men, one extra for Mark Mason. When he said he couldn't take a chance on anyone exposing this, he meant anyone.

Mason nodded and crawled out the passenger's back door. He'd hoped he would feel reassured after this meeting, but it hadn't changed anything. Baxter was running this show, and things were now beyond his control. *And I hate not being in control.* There was one thing he didn't doubt, though. *You don't cross a man like Carl Baxter.* Mason watched the limo carry him into the shadows of the falling snow. *You can never trust a man like Carl Baxter.* And he was beginning to doubt Baxter's trust in him. It was becoming crystal clear to Mason that everyone at SpringWare was expendable.

He didn't sit in his car too long, as he needed to return promptly from his "doctor's appointment" to meet with Rita. Mason had to be sure that he had sufficiently covered all his tracks. He also had some travel plans to make. It wouldn't be long now until the final payment was made to his account.

CHAPTER

21

RITA HAD NO doubt that Chris would deliver the lunch to Lori as she instructed. But before she could think about Café Amore, she wanted to examine the things she had taken from George's office. The only place she felt safe doing that was in the women's bathroom.

Rita bent down, looking for feet under all four stall doors as she walked by them. Confident that the bathroom was empty, she carefully locked the door of the handicap stall at the end of the room. She removed the disk from her pocket and a Lady Gaga CD case from her purse. She slid the disk between the pages of the multi-folded cover of the case, then placed it back in her purse. It felt slightly heavier than a normal CD, but she had done this before to get the file she copied from Jack's computer out of the building. If she distracted the guard at the employee exit with enough conversation, Jerrod would never notice it when he checked her purse. Being an old, lowly secretary had its rewards. *No one suspects you of anything.*

Removing the small gold key from her other pocket, she examined it closely. It looked like it might be a safe-deposit box key. *This must belong to George, because Jack would have kept it hidden in the credenza.* Rita assumed that George would only be out another day. She and Lori would have to figure things out quickly tonight so the key could be returned before George came back. *I'll figure out how to do that later.* She placed the key on her key ring next to the one for the front door of her house. It would set off the metal detector if it was in her pocket when she left, and she didn't want to draw scrutiny to it. No one would pay attention to it on her key ring. *Where there's a will there's a way.*

Satisfied that her plan would work once more, she was ready to go back to her office. Rita sighed as she looked at herself in the bathroom mirror. In the twenty years she had worked at SpringWare, she never would have dreamed that she would be smuggling out information. Even more unthinkable was that she would be working for someone she was confident was a murderer. The face of that nearly sixty-three-year-old woman staring back at her was someone she didn't recognize. But in some strange way, she liked what she saw: a frightened but very determined woman who wanted justice. She wasn't going to let anyone stop her from getting justice for Jack and Karla.

Rita left the bathroom and retrieved the two personnel files from her desk. She considered them suitable replacements for Karla. She knocked on the door for her meeting with Mason to give him her recommendations. Life at SpringWare marched on, no matter the circumstances. And she needed things to go on as normally as possible to stay alive.

CHAPTER

22

NATHAN WAITED UNTIL he saw Abernathy come out of the house and walk toward his patrol car. He sidled out of his ten-year-old Mazda Miata and swiftly maneuvered through the maze of cars that seemed to be growing by the minute on the street. He took a few bills out of his pocket and rounded the trunk of Abernathy's car just as he plopped in the driver's seat.

"Hey, Abernathy. Anything interesting for me?" he said, squatting down by the open door.

"Ha." He snorted. "Not surprised to see you hovering like a vulture round here. Depends on what *you* have that's interesting."

"I think you'll like my news," Nathan said, dropping the cash into his lap.

"Guy hung himself with his own belt. No note, but lots of letters and emails lying around from that Phillips girl last night. Figure he was really hung up on her and couldn't live without her. Sorry for the pun." Abernathy laughed at the joke he had made, convincing Nathan that he really wasn't very sorry about it. "This one looks pretty cut-and-dried. Nothing else out of the ordinary. Sorry to disappoint you, but no big sensational story here, Schilling." He started the patrol car and drove off.

There's always more. Nathan snapped a few more pictures of the house and police vehicles and headed back to his car. The battery icon on his computer was flashing as he closed the lid. He'd have to finish this column at his desk. He wanted to go back anyway. Two dead SpringWare employees. He needed to get there before Lori Crawford went home.

Nathan had wanted to ask Lori if she knew Karla Philips when she printed the draft of the article yesterday, but he wondered if it was still too emotional for her to talk about anything related to Jack or to SpringWare. She hadn't commented on the article's picture or headline, but the look on her face had seemed unusual. It made him wonder. Now, after Packwood's death, he had to find a way to bring it up with her. Maybe she knew something that would help him make sense of this. The death of three SpringWare employees in three months was certainly piquing his interest. *There are no coincidences.*

Ten minutes later, he was turning into the paper's parking garage, just in time to see Lori getting into her car. Nathan pulled into the first space he could find and ran toward her car. She jumped and let out a little scream as he rapped on the passenger window.

"Oh my God, Nathan, you scared me!" she said as she rolled the window part way down. She looked really shaken.

"I'm sorry, Lori. I need to ask you something before you leave." Lori nodded and unlocked the passenger door so he could get in from the cold.

Nathan didn't know what it was about Lori that occasionally caused him to lose his reporter's keen questioning skills, but his usual knack for tactfulness suddenly left him. He found himself looking at Lori, feeling nervous and uncomfortable. He stammered a bit as he said, "I just came from a suicide case and I . . . I think you might know the guy."

Nathan paused, noting the puzzled look on her face. Then, against his better judgment, he decided to just dive right in. "Do you know George Packwood, from SpringWare? It looks like he was having an affair with Karla Phillips and may have been distraught over her murder." As soon as the words left his mouth, the look on her face told him he'd gone about this completely wrong.

Nathan's words hit her like a hard punch to the stomach. Her hand gripped the steering wheel tightly as she labored to keep herself together. *Breathe, Lori, breathe!*

"I . . . I didn't know Karla that well." She stammered, struggling to find her voice. Her vision blurred with tears, her forearms now hugging her stomach. "George . . . George reported to Jack for about five years. Jack recommended him for his position when he was promoted. A few months after George took over for Jack . . ." Lori's voice broke again. She took a visibly deep breath. "His wife died unexpectedly from cancer. It was a late-stage diagnosis, and the cancer . . . it was all over her body . . . he was so lost." Tears fell steadily now. Nathan resisted the urge to reach over and hug her, to console her somehow.

"We invited George over for dinner about once a week, and I . . . I think it helped him get through it. He was very introverted . . . didn't have a lot of other friends. I know . . . he appreciated our support." The familiar feeling of grief finally overwhelmed her, and she covered her face with her hands. "He was a good friend." She choked out the words, and she sobbed softly for a minute before she could continue.

"Jack's death was hard on George. He couldn't talk to me about it afterwards, and he kept his distance for quite a while. I knew it must have been hard for him . . . all that loss so close together . . . I understood." Lori was fighting to get the words out. She dug in her purse for a tissue, using those few moments to get the next bittersweet words out. "So it surprised me when he called last week and said he wanted to have dinner. He said he had some happy news." Even in her grief, Lori was putting things together in her head. "If what you say is true about him having a relationship with Karla, I bet he wanted to tell me about her." Lori started crying again, but more softly.

The reporter in Nathan wanted to question her more to find out about Packwood's role at SpringWare. But the man, looking at Lori with her face in her hands again, her body softly shaking with each uneven breath, could clearly see that she was much too distraught for more questions.

"I'm sorry, Lori. I had no idea you were close to him." Nathan studied her carefully. She was in too much distress to be behind the wheel of a car. "Can I drive you home?"

Nathan watched her start to form an objection, but she stopped. If he could have used his sixth sense to read her mind, he would've understood the confusing look that came over her face.

I don't want to be alone. Other thoughts, very scary thoughts, were creeping into her head. Fear was rapidly settling in next to the grief. *Things I cannot share with Nathan.* Was this a suicide, or did they have George killed? Mason had told Carl Baxter that George was the contact person if there were problems or questions about the software, so it was a real possibility that they killed him too. *Three murders?*

"I don't live too far," Lori acquiesced. He could see that she felt too vulnerable to object. And, at the same time, she looked utterly petrified.

"Good. I'll drive you home." *What is she so afraid of?*

A few minutes later, they were pulling into her driveway. They made their way to the front door through the thick snow that had fallen on the sidewalk. After a few attempts of trying to get her key in the door, Nathan gently reached around and took them from her. The door swung open, and she stepped inside.

"Can I get you a cup of hot chocolate?" Lori said with a shiver. Any kind of distraction would do at that moment.

Nathan almost said no, but he could see she needed some company. The snow was really coming down now, so maybe it would be a good idea to wait until it let up before he had to walk back to the office.

"Tell me where it is and I'll make it." He gave her his warmest smile, afraid to say anything that might cause her to cry again. Looking completely defeated, she still managed the briefest of smiles in return for his offer. Right now, Lori needed a friend, not a colleague, and Nathan would be there for her as long as she wanted him to stay.

CHAPTER

23

RITA RAN THE damp cloth over the edges of the frame that encircled the smiling faces of her daughter and grandkids. Kyle was going to be five, and Jackie was almost seven. *I'm glad that these kids are growing up in a better environment than their mother did.* It was an assumption she had to make, as she knew very little about her daughter's relationship with her husband. Rita looked at Natalie's face and felt so much regret. *Why didn't I have more courage back then?*

Rita had started working at SpringWare just after she turned forty-two, not long after her twenty-year marriage to her alcoholic husband had finally come to an end. Twenty-two years later, her daughter Natalie still hadn't come to terms with the divorce. Or maybe she couldn't understand what took Rita so long to do it. Even though so much time had passed, Rita didn't think Natalie would ever get over it. Even so, she held out hope that one day they could bridge the gap that had widened between them. Her ex-husband had never touched Natalie, but she had witnessed the physical and verbal abuse he gave Rita nearly every day. The memories of the drunken rampages, the fights, and the beatings were hard to forget. For both of them. She sighed. How could she expect Natalie to be able to figure out why she stayed when she couldn't reconcile it for herself? She had failed Natalie, and she had failed herself.

She presumed Natalie only stayed in touch because she wanted her children to know their grandmother. She'd make the obligatory calls on holidays and her birthday, but Natalie would quickly turn the phone over to the kids. Rita would like to see them more often, but California was across the country, and she could only afford the flight once a year. Maybe then she'd move a little closer in a couple of years when she retired so she could see them more often. It pained Rita to think that she felt closer to Jack than she did her own daughter. She didn't know if her relationship with Natalie could ever be repaired, but she knew she could do something for Jack. It was time for her to stand up for something to make her feel better about her own personal failings.

Rita picked up her employee of the month plaque from last July and rubbed the letters with the rag. *Mason seemed distracted when I suggested Karla's replacement.* He was never very friendly, but this was something else. She had strongly recommended one particular applicant, even though she knew Mason didn't like the woman. She actually dropped her pencil out of shock when he mumbled his approval with no argument. Was Mason showing signs of stress? Maybe he wasn't the one running the show. *Oh, poor baby.*

It was growing too late to stay at the office any longer, and Café Amore was waiting. She gathered her purse and coat and took the elevator down to the lobby floor.

All employees were required to pass through security when entering and leaving the building. This helped minimize theft and the selling of secrets to competitors. Employees at Spring-Ware never took work home to finish. In fact, other than Mason and the company's CEO, Rita had never known anyone to carry a briefcase. One wouldn't be needed if you couldn't take anything out of the building. At one time, there had been talk of forbidding purses coming into the building. There were so many complaints from the female employees that management had to take that idea off the table. Instead, screening devices and tighter security checks were put in place for purses, lunch boxes, umbrellas, and the like. Nothing went through these doors in either direction without being scanned.

Rita emerged from the elevator on the main floor. Now it was time to execute the plan she had practiced so thoroughly. *I did it before; I can do it again.*

"Hi Jerrod," Rita said, trying carefully to appear jovial and calm. "Are you ready for the holidays?" Rita knew Jerrod had three children.

"I don't know, Miss Rita. My wife said she had it taken care of, but I have a feeling I'll be putting a bike together on Christmas eve." He laughed a deep, hearty laugh.

She put her keys in the little bowl and her purse on the conveyor belt of the X-ray machine, then waited for the green light so she could walk through the metal detector. "Well, I hope you are good at that." He shook his head in the negative and laughed again. Rita could feel that her armpits were soaked under her heavy coat, and she knew it had nothing to do with being too hot. As expected, Jerrod asked to look in her purse when it came out of the other side of the machine. She nodded her consent.

When he took out the CD case, earphones, her antiquated Walkman CD player, and flip phone, Rita managed a laugh. "If it wasn't for my grandchildren, I wouldn't have a clue who Lady Gaga was. But I have to admit, I really like some of the music they send me. I still can't get into that rap music, though."

Jerrod laughed. "I know what you mean, Miss Rita. May I suggest you trade in this old flip phone for a smart phone? It's 2015. You could carry a lot smaller purse and not have to haul all of this stuff around!"

"Maybe I will, Jerrod. I really enjoy listening to music on my walk to and from work. Are those smart phones expensive?" Rita's conversation was distracting him, and she was sure Jerrod was laughing inside at the older woman's inability to come into this decade. He started to put it all back in her purse. *Let him think what he wants. I'm getting what I need!*

"Too much for my wallet. Will set you back 800 big ones," he replied.

"Wow!" Rita laughed. "I think I'll be carrying a big purse for a while."

Jerrod wished her a good night and handed her the purse and keys. She let out a big breath as she felt the cold wind on her flushed face when she went through the revolving door. *I did it!* Now to solve the mystery of the key and find out what was on that disk. *Maybe Lori can help.*

CHAPTER

24

THE SKY FORETOLD the coming of more snow, even though the weatherman had not predicted any. Rita wondered if the bleak weather was a foreshadowing of other things to come.

She was out of bread and coffee, and she needed both for breakfast in the morning. The small downtown grocery store would be closed by the time she was done eating, so now was the time to pick them up. Glancing at her watch, it was still a little too early to meet with Lori. She'd might as well use that time to stop at the electronics and music store. The iPhone that Jerrod had told her about did make her curious. But even if she could afford one she wouldn't buy it. *I may need the cover of carrying those CDs for a while longer.*

Rita was fully aware of how ironic it may seem to others that she still carried a flip phone and a Walkman while she worked for a company that developed software. But working there had only caused her to become more entrenched in her electronic past, resistant to upgrading her technology.

She had been trying to help her friend, Madeline, get out of an abusive relationship with her alcoholic boyfriend. He'd been using her cellphone to track her movements. He remotely deleted her emails, messages, and calls, and routinely scoured through her social media feeds and photos. One day, he put Maddie in the hospital with broken bones and internal bleeding. His behaviors triggered terrible memories of her volatile relationship with her ex-husband. Though Rita wasn't currently in a relationship and understood that her feelings weren't logical, it was those old emotions that kept her from upgrading to technology that might allow something like that to happen to her in the future.

Being able to walk everywhere was one of the advantages of living in the old city center of a smaller town, but the weather was so bad that she really should have taken her car today. Rita thought she'd be the only crazy person out walking in this miserable weather until she saw a man in a long coat standing against the building across the street as she entered the store.

The young sales clerk easily impressed her with the features of the popular iPhone. She had to admit that the things you could do with it sounded amazing. But even though the sales pitch was good, the cost, coupled with thoughts of Maddie's boyfriend, wouldn't permit her to even consider buying it. Instead, she settled for an old Johnny Mathis CD. Her budget could handle a fifteen-dollar purchase, and his soothing, sexy voice was sure to help her escape some of the stress she was feeling, even if only for a few minutes.

The snowfall was heavier as she rounded the corner toward the grocer. It was already thick enough to hear her footsteps crunch on the deserted sidewalk. A new display in the window of the home improvement store caught her eye, and she stopped to take a look.

She could see her reflection in the shiny pots and pans sitting on the new kitchen cabinets they were selling. Rita reflectively touched her hair. It was nearly all gray now, and it made her look old. No wonder Lori had not recognized her in the restaurant. *Maybe I should color it.* As her fingers moved to tuck her damp hair behind her ear, she caught the reflection of a long trench coat across the street. It was the same man she had noticed outside of the electronics and music store.

Rita continued to pretend to look at the display, suppressing a powerful urge to run. Finally, she started in the direction of the grocery store, doing her best to walk at a normal pace. *Is he following me?* She could think of no other reason for someone to be loitering outside in this abominable weather.

The grocer greeted her by name when she entered. She jumped as the wind caught the door and slammed it behind her. She nervously smiled a hello in return and proceeded to look around the store as casually as possible. She circled a display of pasta sauce and positioned herself so she could look out the window without being seen from the outside. *There he is!* The man had walked into the alley across the street and was watching the door. If she hadn't known to look for him, she would have never seen him there when she left.

She didn't dare go to Café Amore now. She dialed Lori's number on her flip phone, but stopped before pressing the send button. If they were following her, it was likely that the NSA was monitoring her cell phone calls. She always had her flip phone with her in hopes that Natalie might call out of the blue, and besides, Jerrod would certainly question her having a burner phone.

She casually walked over to the register, wondering if trench coat man could see what she was doing. "Bob, my battery's dead," she said, holding out her old flip phone. "Can I use your landline for a minute?"

"Sure, Rita. Here you go. Maybe it's time for an upgrade." He chuckled and handed her the store phone.

Rita dialed Lori's number. She carefully positioned the phone away from the view of the window. She hoped it would appear that she was talking to Bob. When she answered, she simply said, "We need to change the time to ten tonight. See you then."

"Thanks Bob. It's a good thing people have answering machines, or you'd never get to talk to anyone these days!"

Bob grinned as he rang up her bread and coffee. "Try to stay warm, Rita. It's pretty miserable out there tonight."

The five-block walk home seemed like miles. With each step, she wondered if he was just watching her or if he was waiting for the right opportunity to harm her. She listened carefully for him approaching as she walked, but heard nothing other than her own footsteps. With two blocks to go, she pretended to slip on the wet snow and dropped her groceries. As she bent down to pick them up, she covertly looked behind, but could see nothing in the darkness.

As she took off her wet, heavy coat, she felt relieved to be behind the locked doors of her home. Still, she heard her shallow breath and felt her heart beating in her chest. *Act normal. Follow your normal routine.* Opening the front door again, she picked up the morning paper from the table on the covered porch where she had set it before she went to work. Discreetly glancing around, she spied the man in the dark shadow of a moving van parked two houses down the street. Her living room, kitchen, and bedroom all faced the street at the front of her home. He had a good view from there, and he would be able to see her lights going off and on as she moved around the house. She double-checked the lock when she went back inside.

Rita felt sick with fear. *I wonder how long he's been following me? Days? Weeks?* She mentally retraced her own actions over the past few days. It couldn't have been very long, as she would've noticed him when she watched carefully for twenty minutes before meeting Lori at the fountain. *This changes everything.* She'd need to scrutinize all of her behaviors to appear as if nothing out of the ordinary was happening.

Rita headed to her bedroom to change her clothes. She paused in front of the sheer curtain so he could see her getting dressed for bed. If he had been watching for a while, this is normally what she would do. She was, however, putting her nightgown on over her clothes, as she had every intention of going out later.

For the next ninety minutes, Rita sat in front of the television where she would have normally eaten her dinner. Tonight, she settled for a shot glass of Sambuca. She couldn't recall a single image on the television that flashed before her eyes during the entire time she sat on the sofa. Her brain kept replaying the events of the past few months, searching for a solution to the trouble she had found. There were no specific answers yet, so she had to maintain the faith that they would be made clear.

Over the past couple of months, she had compiled quite a dossier on Mark Mason. There were multiple clues from

Mason's and George's planners, and the file from Jack's computer with the emails and encrypted files. Along with some other unexplained bits of information, she was sure she'd find more that would help her understand what was happening. Along with Karla's death and the conversation Lori had overheard in the restaurant, everything pointed toward Mason and his connection to Carl Baxter and the NSA. But they would need an airtight case to prove that they had murdered Jack and Karla.

The NSA? What have I gotten into? Rita had been so caught up in her search for the truth, she had yet to think about what she was going to do with all of this information. Now, with the realization that she was being followed, everything suddenly seemed complicated—and very dangerous.

When the living room clock chimed nine times, she made sure the bathroom light stayed on just long enough before she pretended to crawl into bed.

Rita crept to the kitchen through the darkened house to peek out the window. Twenty minutes passed before trench coat man appeared from behind the moving van. He was on his cell phone, walking down the sidewalk toward her house. She tightened her body against the wall so he couldn't see her through the slit in the curtain, even though she knew that wasn't possible. A wave of nausea came over her. She held her breath as he passed by on the sidewalk and moved on toward the corner.

Rita padded softly, but quickly to her corner bedroom, where she had a better view of the direction he was going. He walked halfway down the next block and drove away in a dark red SUV. He must have presumed that she was tucked in safely for the night. *Perfect.*

Rita quickly removed her nightgown, grabbed her coat, and headed for the back door. She walked the small back alleys of the town she knew so well. She found her way to Café Amore, unseen by anyone who may have happened to be out in this miserable weather.

The man in the red SUV dialed the number he was given. A strong, firm voice answered. He could tell the man had military training from the sound of his voice and the language he used. He was also certain this was someone he should not disappoint.

The money was excellent for what he was tasked to do. Follow an old lady and report in at the end of the day. Or if anything seemed unusual. Piece of cake.

He reported that nothing seemed out of the ordinary. She went to work, did some shopping, and came home and watched television. Then, she was in bed at nine.

The man seemed satisfied and told him to arrive early before she went to work the next day.

If only more jobs were like this.

CHAPTER

25

SHE OPENED THE door of the restaurant a few minutes before ten. Bruno helped her with her coat, and then he led her over to where Lori was anxiously waiting in a booth in the back of the dining room.

"Can I get you a cup of coffee to help you warm up tonight?" Bruno asked, placing a napkin in Rita's lap. She responded with a warm smile and a nod.

Bruno turned to Lori. "No thanks, Bruno. I'll have a pinot noir tonight."

She waited until Bruno was out of earshot before launching into the events of her day. Rita told Lori about the emails to George she had found on Karla's computer, then about getting the disk from Jack's credenza and almost getting caught by Mason. She passed the disk to Lori under the table. "Damn. I forgot to make a copy of this."

Rita went on to tell her what she had found in George's planner and about finding the key. She slid it discreetly under her hand across the table to Lori. Then, she dropped the final bomb. "I'm being followed."

Apprehension spread over Lori's face and her body seemed frozen in her seat. She could barely get the words out. "Are you sure?"

The server came with the wine and coffee and took their orders. Once he left, Rita relayed what had happened from the time she left SpringWare until she arrived at Café Amore.

"I felt like I came by way of the yellow brick road." Rita described the path she had to take to get to the restaurant, somehow managing a strained chuckle. "But this changes everything. It means they have suspicions about me. I'm not sure the man was sent to harm me, because he could have easily done so when I walked home. Maybe they are just keeping an eye on me . . . to see if I know something."

The server delivered the risotto they had both chosen. Rita could see that Lori had something on her mind as well. *I don't know how much more I can handle today.* But she knew she had to hear whatever Lori was about to say.

"Rita, I have some news too. It's been a terrible afternoon. Nathan Schilling, the homicide investigative reporter at the paper, told me that George Packwood committed *suicide* this morning."

Rita could hardly register the words she had just heard. *No! Not George too.*

"I can't believe it!" Rita whispered through her tears. She wiped her eyes as she saw the server coming to confirm that they were satisfied with their meal. "I'll have a glass of cabernet now," she told him.

Rita was the first to speak as he walked away. "Mason said he thought George would be out for a couple of days. I wonder if he knew? If he did it?"

"This is a nightmare. I can't even believe this is happening. I'm scared, Rita." The fear in Rita's eyes conveyed the same feelings Lori had used words to express. "Do you think we should go to the police?"

"And tell them what?" Rita shook her head. "What? What can we actually prove at this point? We need more information . . . more proof . . . before we can even think of getting anyone to believe us."

"I know you're right. It's just that it seems impossible for us to think that we can challenge someone like Carl Baxter. These agencies are run just like the military. They operate on their own terms, they keep secrets, and they have powerful ways of spinning things to be someone else's problem."

"I know how you feel, Lori. Hell, I didn't think that *you'd* believe me when I told you. I was afraid that you'd think I was a crazy old woman . . . we've just . . . we've just got to get more information. We can figure this out. I know we can." They both sat quietly for a long time, as they were hardly able to digest the situation they were in, much less the food in front of them.

Lori nervously fingered the key in her lap. Finally, she broke the silence. "I don't think this is a key to a safe-deposit box. I have a box at People's Bank, and they don't look like this." Lori seemed to be talking to herself, absently pushing the risotto around her bowl. Suddenly, Rita saw her eyes light up.

"Rita, I know what this is! It's for one of those storage lockers at the mall in Denton." Brightening a little, Lori managed a bite of food. "About eight months ago, I was getting my car serviced at the Toyota dealership near there. They dropped me at the mall to shop until it was done. I bought too many things to carry around, so I rented a locker to put the packages in until they came back to get me. I'm *sure* this is what the key looked like!" She looked down at the key in her lap and saw the number "27" etched into the side of it. "I'll drive out there and see if I'm right . . . It's too dangerous now for you to go."

"I was worried that we had to get that key back under the desk tomorrow before George came back," Rita said sadly, tears playing in her eyes again. "I guess we can take all the time we need now." Rita put down her fork, having barely touched her meal.

Lori reached across the table and gently squeezed Rita's hand. "We'll figure this out, Rita. I know we can." She hoped she sounded more confident than she felt.

"I don't think we should meet in public like this again. I know I'm being followed, and I don't want them to see me with you. They might already think that Jack shared secrets with you. If we were seen together, it would confirm their suspicions about both of us. You need to figure out if they are following you too. Only go to that locker if you're *sure* you are not being followed."

"I understand," said Lori.

"Now, I need to tell you what to do with that disk. I've been giving this a lot of thought about something Jack told me when I still worked with him. I didn't see the advantage of it at the time, but I think it will be useful now. Do you still have your old Mac laptop?" Rita asked.

"Yes, I still have my Mac and Jack's PC. They are both pretty old now. I can't even update the operating system on my Mac anymore."

"Even better. I'm willing to bet the CD I just gave you from Jack's credenza has instructions for how to open and decode the encrypted file that I couldn't get into." Rita paused for a minute while she tried to remember the instructions Jack had explained to her. "This is what I want you to do. Copy the files from both CD's I gave you onto your Mac. Then copy the files from your Mac onto one CD. Don't open any files until they've been copied to the CD. If you open them before you do that, it will be time stamped with that date and time. So, in case it *is* found, it won't look like you've ever opened them. I have not had a chance to make a copy of this, so be sure to hide the CD in a very safe place where it won't be found.

"Then you can look at the files on your computer. After you've seen what's on them, put all the files you copied to your laptop in the trash. Go to the menu bar at the top and look for something that says Secure Empty Trash. Jack told me this overwrites the data many times and makes it impossible for anyone to restore what you've thrown away. No one will be able to tell it was ever on your computer or that you may have seen the files. Burn the original CDs in your fireplace."

Lori shook her head, vaguely recalling this function that Jack had also explained to her a long time ago. Rita was right. She could clearly see its usefulness now. They could look at the files, and if the CD or the laptop were discovered, it would be as if she hadn't seen them.

"I don't think we should use our cell phones for communication. Let's stick to the burner phones, and we should only use them if there's no other way. After doing all this research for Joe on the NSA, I'm not even sure if using any device is really safe. I'll find a way to let you know when I've gone to the locker and decoded the file."

Rita would be thinking of a way to give her newly discovered watch dog the slip again.

CHAPTER

26

CARL BAXTER STOOD up from his chair for the third time in an hour. He looked at the tall grandfather clock. *One o'clock. Another sleepless night.* He circled his home office once again, stopping in front of the dark mahogany medal display case his wife had given him as a retirement present.

As Fleet Admiral of the Navy, Baxter had enjoyed a long and successful career. He had been decorated with nearly every medal possible in his long tenure. Some harbored memories he'd like to forget. Especially the Navy Cross and the Purple Heart. A two-for-one that left him walking with a slightly awkward gait. He had accomplished more than even he could have imagined, even though that fifth and final star that he so coveted had eluded him. But in the end, he realized that he was now in a more powerful position than the star would have ever provided for him. No one in his entire family had come close to what he had achieved in his career.

He stepped toward the right, stopping at another gift, this one from his mother, given just before she died ten years ago.

Baxter's eyes traced the family military tree. He followed the list of names all the way back to the American Revolution. Every male on his dad's side had served in some branch of the military, as well as most of the men on his mother's side. Red, white, and blue ran deep in his blood. Baxter's smile quickly faded. For all of his many accomplishments, he was the end of this proud lineage. This was something his father had reminded him of until the day he'd died. Baxter had no children to carry on the family tradition. The salt in the wound was that he had no one to blame but himself, for it wasn't his wife who had the problem.

His father was correct in that he had left no bloodline to continue the family heritage. But he was wrong that there would be no legacy. Baxter could hardly believe his good fortune when the president appointed him head of the NSA. It was the perfect post for a man who thrived on power and ambition. He was determined to use the power of his position to make sure that this country remained safe from all enemies, foreign or domestic. There would not be another 9/11 while he was in charge. What he was creating would keep this country safe for decades to come. His plan was the ultimate family endowment to his nation.

Even though the NSA was the most secretive spy agency in the US government, it wasn't sanctioned to be involved in the operation he was planning. *This country is fighting a war on terror. My plan is essential to our nation's very existence. I will win this war and keep this country safe. It's the only way.*

The thought that he was operating outside of his boundaries never crossed his mind. He would do whatever he could to protect the country he so loved, at any and all costs. Vice

Admiral Baxter had never failed at any mission in his career, and he wasn't about to fail now.

Baxter could never have had this software created at the NSA. The controversy would have been too great, even within the ranks of an agency that was always on thin ice as far as civil liberties were concerned. No, he *had* to outsource this project. He chose SpringWare because of its proximity to Washington and because of Mark Mason.

He had gotten to know Mason through several charitable functions over the past years. Mark was ambitious, coming frequently to DC to market his company, bragging about his successes in the software industry. Silicon Valley be damned, he'd have his operations near the real seat of power in Washington. Baxter admired this bravado, his "nothing can stop me" attitude. *He reminds me of myself at his age.*

He thought Mason could handle the stress and complexity of dealing with such a covert operation. Now he wasn't so sure that Mason had the stomach for the necessary decisions he was making. Mason had convinced Baxter that he was a patriot, but now he was unsure in that regard as well. *The only thing that motivates Mark Mason is money.* And he was getting plenty of that.

Unfortunately for Jack Crawford, he had proven to be a man dedicated to quality control. He had discovered some design "flaws" in the program. Although Mason assured him that they were taken care of, Jack took it upon himself to keep probing. If he would have left things alone, no one would be in this position now.

Crawford had discovered the secret behind the software that only four people in the world were supposed to know: Mason,

Baxter, and soon, two NSA employees with top security clearances. Both of these employees were known for their loyalty to this country and were handpicked by Baxter. They would report to no one but him.

It was Mason who had discovered that Jack was keeping notes and files about the project. *He could've told someone else.* Mason's theory was that Jack might be keeping the files as leverage to blackmail him. From what Baxter knew about Crawford, that just didn't make sense. He was a straight arrow. And straight arrows didn't understand the world as Baxter knew it to be. What he did understand was that Crawford could bring down his entire operation.

Baxter was determined that under his command, the NSA would become the most influential and successful agency in the U.S. government. He would infiltrate terrorist organizations in a way no one had ever done before. *The nation's security depends on it. There's no way that a few employees of SpringWare are going to undermine that goal. Not on my watch.*

———

Lori Crawford glanced over at the red light on her house alarm keypad. *Still set.* She flipped the small gold key over and over in her nervous fingers. The flames in the fireplace reflected off the shiny silver disk that she held in her other hand—a disk that was endangering her life. She was sure it held the key to many unanswered questions. The information on that disk killed her husband, and perhaps the information in the locker that this key would open, killed George Packwood.

She was more afraid than she had ever been in her life, and the adrenaline rush was keeping her wide awake. It was very late, but she knew she wouldn't sleep until she looked at that disk. She opened her Mac laptop and slid the disk into the drive.

———

Mark Mason was normally a night owl, but these days, he was living on very little sleep even for him. The bottle of scotch was calling him for just one more late-night drink. It was flattering when Carl Baxter had approached him about this software idea, and it was an opportunity that would make him a very wealthy man.

He had taken extreme precautions in laying out the security measures for developing the software. The right people were placed in the required roles, a small team, but talented. The project was completed in stages, with everyone working on different segments of the final product so they appeared to be unrelated.

Mason promoted Jack so he would be working independently of the others. Jack was a dedicated, longtime employee of SpringWare and had proven to be trustworthy. Jack would bring all the parts together. Only he would see a completed product and be aware of who the client was.

Baxter and Mason were the masterminds of the underlying secret in the software. Mason coded those final touches after Jack had finished the project. No one should have been the wiser. It was this final version of the software that was on his desk, waiting to be hand-delivered to Baxter right after lunch. *Everything had gone so perfectly.*

Mason had underestimated Jack's commitment to the finished product, and that's what led to his demise. While Mason was out having lunch, it occurred to Jack that an improvement needed to be made to the record sorting aspect of the software. He came to Mason's office to retrieve the final copy of the program for one tweak and diagnostic test. Rita retrieved the disk from Mason's desk, unaware that it was a copy Jack should have never seen. It was then that Jack soon discovered a much larger problem. *And no matter what I said, he just couldn't let it go.* He downed the scotch and decided to have another.

When Mason realized what had happened, he carefully crafted a strategy to convince Carl that Jack had become a threat to the project. But it was his carelessness that had been the reason Jack discovered the truth. And this was a secret that Mason could never let Carl know.

For the first time in his life, Mason had met someone more ambitious than himself. And now, three dead employees later, Mason fully understood that Baxter was not only powerful, but ruthless. He knew he had sold his soul to the devil, and the devil was in the form of Fleet Admiral Carl Baxter. He had to see this to its end, or he'd be joining Jack in the river.

Rita Johnson woke once again from a fitful sleep, drenched in sweat. The red light of the digital clock screamed 1:30. *Thirty minutes of an endless nightmare.* It seemed that the dreadful scenarios in her dreams were becoming her reality. *Well, I'm not ready for that yet!*

After twenty years of living with an abusive, alcoholic husband, Rita knew she could survive this. She was a fighter. She had gotten up the courage to leave him, to change her life and support herself. She was close to her retirement dreams. No one was going to take that away from her. They had done it to Jack and Lori, and now to George and Karla. It made her even more determined to survive. Yes, she didn't want to die, but for twenty years she had faced death at the hands of her ex-husband. This was different, but it was not new to her. She would find a way to expose the people responsible for this and hold them accountable for what they had done. Perhaps she would even find a way to make Natalie see her differently. To make her proud of her mother.

———

Nathan Schilling was tired, but he still did his best thinking after midnight. He stared intently at the three names on the computer screen. He waited, silently asking for them to tell him something.

Jack Crawford
Karla Phillips
George Packwood

He was trying to put together a puzzle that was missing many pieces. These deaths had to be connected. Spring-Ware had lost three employees in the past three months. By themselves, they weren't all that unusual, but together . . . his instincts were telling him something else. He started typing, hoping the connection would appear on the screen.

Jack - 3 months ago - close friend and work associate of George Packwood; killed in a car accident

Karla Phillips - 2 days ago - assistant at SpringWare, lover of George Packwood; killed in a burglary gone wrong

George Packwood - 1 day ago - long-term employee of SpringWare, connected to two other victims; distraught lover commits suicide

George could have been distraught over Karla's death. But in Nathan's mind, it didn't fit. His wife of twenty years had died a sudden painful death with cancer, and he didn't choose the suicide option then. So why would he choose to do that over a woman he hadn't dated all that long?

This is not what it appears to be on the surface.

His gut was telling him something; he just wasn't sure what language it was speaking. Tomorrow, he would start delving into SpringWare, its management and these deceased employees. And he was sure he wouldn't be wasting his time.

Officer Abernathy stumbled through the door of his bedroom after another very late night at the bar. He thought time was supposed to make it easier to come home to an empty house. The more time that passed since his wife left him, the more he tried to avoid coming home at all. The booze made him numb enough to bear it; he just needed more and more of it to do the job.

He emptied his pockets on the night stand by the bed: gum wrappers, loose change, a cell phone, and a slip of crumpled paper. *Damn!* It was the note he wrote to remind himself to call Schilling about that suicide case. He owed the guy. *After all, he paid for the round of drinks I bought at the bar tonight.* And for many nights over the past few years. His last thought before he passed out on the bed was to call him in the morning to tell him about the unexpected development.

CHAPTER

27

SHE HAD GONE to bed fearful, frustrated, and exhausted. Lori woke up feeling exactly the same. The disk was password protected, an important piece of information Rita had forgotten to give her. After an hour of trying to remember all of Jack's previous passwords and strategies for coming up with them, she had finally given up and dragged herself to bed. She wanted a hot shower and a cup of coffee, and she knew that only the first wish would come true. At least it was Friday.

As the steam rose around her in the shower, her head cleared, and she started to regain some confidence. *There's a lot at stake here.* Rita was in danger, yet she seemed to agree to the risks she was taking. And she had made it clear that she was going to do this with or without Lori.

Lori had a hard time believing that Mason and Baxter might be suspicious of her. It had been more than three months since Jack had died. *Wouldn't I have already gone to the police if I suspected there was foul play?*

Nevertheless, she shouldn't take for granted that she wasn't in danger. *Just maintain my normal activities so nothing looks unusual. Easier said than done.* The weatherman said it would be cold, but no snow. She decided to walk and take the same route to work. That would be normal. She tried to recall the tactics used in every murder or detective show she had seen to think about how she might observe someone following her.

Lori dried her hair and dressed quickly. She was running late from oversleeping, and she needed time to make a stop. *Sorry Jack, I really need a Starbucks this morning. I know you'll understand.* It could be a considered a sign of weakness when she needed to be mentally strong, but being in such uncharted territory, she decided not to beat herself up about a simple cup of coffee. It was a small step in feeling like she had control of something.

Standing on her front porch, she adjusted the scarf around her neck, stealing a glance up and down the street at all the familiar cars in her neighborhood. There was nothing abnormal. She turned the corner onto the main street toward the *Herald*, where it would be easy for someone to follow and for her to be unaware of it. Lori reached into her purse for her makeup kit. She brushed on some blush, and then she stopped to apply her lipstick. All of these tasks required the use of her mirror, making it convenient to keep an eye out behind her. Rita wasn't the only one who could be clever. *I don't even know what I'm looking for.* People were on the streets going about their day. It would be impossible to know if one of them had their eye on her. She made some mental notes of coat colors and would see if they were still hanging around when she came out of the Starbucks.

Even though she didn't understand why, facing the possibility that she could be a target gave her a bit of confidence. While she didn't consider herself a risk taker, she had also never assumed the role of a victim, and she wasn't about to try out for that part now. *Just channel that fear into anger.* It seemed to give her the strength. *And I'm going to need all the strength I have to bring these killers to justice.*

Lori reached the door of the Starbucks and headed in for anything grande. As she tucked her lipstick into the pocket next to the one where her cell phone fit, an idea came to her. She could have mustered a laugh if she had known that Rita had used the same stroke of genius last night.

"My cell phone's dead, and I have to leave a quick message for someone," she said to the cute guy at the counter. "Could I borrow your phone for just a sec? Oh, and I'll have a mocha latte grande too." She gave him her best flirtatious smile.

"No problem. Just don't tell my boss!"

Predictable. It still puzzled Lori that some men could be so easily persuaded with a suggestive smile. She took the phone and quickly dialed Rita's burner number, hoping she was still at home. One ring wasn't going to work today. Thankfully, Rita picked up after a few rings. "I need the password," Lori whispered.

"Jamaica," Rita spelled. "Sorry, I forgot."

Lori felt a little guilty taking the coffee after hearing that password. She mentally kicked herself for not having thought of it herself. It made sense that Jack would have used that as a password. It was a trip they promised never to forget.

She took a seat at the window counter and took some time stirring her coffee, discreetly checking out the streets on either side of the building. The two front doors to the corner coffee shop exited to streets in either direction, so if she was being followed, the person would have to be in her view to see what direction she went when she left the building. She saw no familiar coats, no suspicious person, just lots of people on their way to work. *If someone is following me, it would be impossible to know.* She would stay alert and go about her normal business.

Lori took a long sip of the pacifying warm liquid, followed by a deep breath. Her thoughts were all over the place. *If I'm going to get through this, I have to gain more self-control.* She needed to be more present, especially if she wanted to spot anyone following her. She started to practice this mindfulness by focusing on the weather. The sun was peeking through the clouds outside. Maybe the local weatherman's prediction for no snow would be right after all, even if it was still freezing outside. She hoped the sun would lift her mood and at least bring the illusion of warmer weather.

She sat at the counter for as long as she could, but it was time to get to the office before Joe started his ranting again. Surveilling the street one last time, she slid on her gloves and scarf, and gathered up her purse and half full coffee. The caffeine had made a slight improvement in her mood. As her last task, she had the barista top off her coffee. *Sorry, Jack.*

The bright sunlight hit her face as she stepped out the door and prevented her from seeing the patch of ice. Her feet came out from under her, and she fell hard as she stepped down off the landing. Lori managed to save the coffee from her own clothes, but the person entering the store was not as lucky. She looked up to see Nathan Schilling wiping frantically at his pants.

"Nathan! I'm so sorry," Lori cried in recognition.

"It's okay. Lori, are you hurt?" Nathan looked concerned as he carefully lifted her off the sidewalk.

"No, only my ego is bruised. Come on. I'll buy us both a coffee."

They became a little self-conscious as they realized how many people were watching with amusement as they both slipped and skated through the spilled coffee that had already turned to ice in front of the doorway. Lori mumbled an apology to the employee who was headed their way with the salt for the sidewalk.

Inside, Lori felt unusually awkward when she realized Nathan's arm was still wrapped around her, supporting her at the waist. She turned toward him, casually freeing herself from his protective grip.

"What are you drinking? I'll get it while you go to the bathroom to clean up," she half-whispered to Nathan, motioning to his pant leg. When he gave her his order, Lori noticed how he smiled from the side of his mouth. *Just like Jack used to.*

She had regained her composure and taken up her corner post at the window by the time Nathan returned, stain-free but wet. She handed him his coffee, knowing he'd appreciate its warmth when his soaked pant leg hit the cold outside. After reassuring Nathan that she was fine for the third time, they left for the *Herald*'s office across the street. Nathan opened the door and gave the predicted little shriek when the cold air hit his wet pant leg. Lori couldn't help but grin.

The sound of Delacourt screaming at no one in particular greeted them at the door. Too many deaths in this town for him, Lori guessed. As soon as he saw her, he yelled across the room for her to come to his office. Lori took her coat off, put her coffee on the desk, and left Nathan sitting in her chair. They exchanged knowing looks, and she trotted down the hall to see what Joe wanted.

"Lori, how are you doing on that assignment I gave you yesterday?"

"Honestly, I didn't find much online that was useful. Law books are going to be better resources for what you want. If I don't find what I need at the Cooperville library, I might have to go to the one in Denton. They have a more extensive collection of legal works there."

"Well, get on it. I want the information to give to David this afternoon so he can start drafting the first segment. The series will appear in Sunday's edition."

"No problem, Joe. I'll leave as soon as I get things organized at my desk." Lori walked back to her office, wishing now that she would have driven her car. The library wasn't too far, but it looked like the weather outside was taking a turn for the worse. *So much for the sun. Never trust a weatherman.* Hopefully, she would find what she needed at the small local library without having to walk home to get her car to drive to Denton.

Nathan was still in her cubicle when she got back. "Hey, if you have a minute, I'd like to talk to you about SpringWare." Lori had been much too upset when he took her home the other day to ask her questions. The small talk they made over the hot chocolate had been uncomfortable for both of them. But today was a different day, and Lori knew that he wasn't going to wait much longer to ask his questions.

"I really can't now, Nathan. Joe wants me at the library right away. I've got a deadline to meet." SpringWare was the last thing Lori wanted to talk about. For a few moments, she had actually forgotten about the plight she found herself in.

"I'll drive you there. We can talk on the way," Nathan suggested.

Lori hesitated. She knew how persistent Nathan could be. It's what made him such a good reporter. She didn't relish answering more questions about George, but she knew it was inevitable. Nathan would be diligent in his quest for information. It was his job. Now, looking out the window at the falling snow, the invitation to a warm, dry car became much more appealing.

"Okay. I'd love the ride." He flashed her that smile again, and Lori wondered why she hadn't noticed it in all the years they'd worked together. She made small talk about the poor dependability of the local weathermen all the way to his car.

Her phone rang as she was buckling her seat belt. It was her mother. *My lucky day!* "My mother," Lori mouthed to Nathan as she held her hand over the phone's speaker. "I'll be just a minute." She knew better. Lori nodded her head and muttered "uh-huh" at the appropriate intervals. She rolled her eyes and looked at Nathan, and he laughed quietly. They only had one block to go before they reached the library when her mother finally hung up.

"Sorry, Nathan. She doesn't call often, so I hate to cut her off. I think she's still worried about me. Look, I know you wanted to ask me some questions. Maybe you'll be around when I get back to the office this afternoon?"

Nathan hesitated. "How about dinner tonight? I mean, just *business*. We can talk then."

Lori didn't know how to respond. It felt awkward. The look on Lori's face was like a mirror showing him that both of his feet were in his mouth. Especially after what she just said about her Mom worrying about her. *What am I, fifteen? I'm such an idiot!*

"I, uh . . . I understand if you're not comfortable with it. Sorry." It was nice of him to give her an excuse not to accept.

"No . . . it's okay. Dinner will be fine." Lori was as surprised as he was as the words came out of her mouth. *Did I really just say yes?*

"Okay, then. I'll pick you up at seven," he said, stunned and maybe a little too enthusiastic. *What's the matter with me?*

"See you then. Thanks for the ride." Lori got out of the car, bewildered at what she had just done. She heard Nathan's phone ringing as she closed the door.

CHAPTER

28

ABERNATHY WOKE UP hung over for the third day in a row. He started to get up, but he felt his stomach doing somersaults, so he sat back down, hoping the feeling would pass.

He'd be popping mints all day and still wouldn't be able to get that taste out of his mouth. His partner once joked that he should buy stock in the company that made those mints. Abernathy knew there was more to the comment. *I should lay off the booze.* Internal Affairs was looking for any reason to fire him. There had been too many incidents in the last year for them to have any more patience with him. Fifteen years on the force had taken its toll. With his elbows on his knees, he rested his head in his hands. *Ah, screw 'em.*

He'd been married for twelve years when Maria left. The first seven years of their marriage had been good ones. But he wasn't surprised when she grew tired of the drinking, the angry outbursts, the mood swings, the nightmares. *Killing a kid would do that. Messes with your head.* He remembered every detail of that evening five years ago, like it was happening all over again.

His partner had gotten sick that afternoon and Abernathy had taken him back to the precinct. He told the captain he'd just go solo for the last four of his twelve-hour shift. It wasn't like a lot happened in Cooperville anyway.

There was only an hour left before he could call it a day. The sun had set a while ago. Parked in the alley behind the used car lot, he was trying to catch some shut eye when the call came blaring over his radio. A clerk had activated the silent alarm button at the convenient store on MLK street. He radioed his response and requested backup. In less than three minutes he was at the scene.

As he sped into the parking lot, two armed men with ski masks came out of the door. There was no time to turn his car in the other direction to use it for cover. Instead, he slammed it in park and jumped out, using the door as a shield.

"Police! Put your weapons down!" he screamed through the open window.

The first perp got off five shots, peppering the car door with bullets. The last bullet connected with Abernathy's left shoulder. Abernathy returned fire, with two rounds hitting the first man in the leg. As he fell to the ground, Abernathy's third and last shot hit the second man, who was now exposed as the shooter went down. The round hit him in the chest, killing him instantly.

Abernathy ran over to the suspects, kicking the gun out of reach of the first man, who wasn't seriously injured, but certainly not going anywhere. The second victim was bleeding profusely from the chest, already surrounded by a big pool of blood. Abernathy pulled off his mask to find a neck pulse. It was a kid.

Nooooo!

The next few minutes still remain a blank. He might have blacked out momentarily. He was never quite sure. Another unit pulled up, and both officers were at his side, screaming orders for ambulances and cuffing the wounded suspect. Someone helped Abernathy off the ground and sat him on the sidewalk. His shoulder was bleeding profusely.

A kid. He was just a kid. He was only thirteen, and he was carrying a damn pellet gun.

The wounded suspect later told the investigators it was the kid's first robbery, and he wouldn't let him carry a real gun because he was so nervous. He didn't want it to go off in his pocket and have the kid end up shooting himself the first time out.

It was Abernathy's first time too. The first time he drew his gun on the job. The first time he fired it. The first time he killed someone.

Internal Affairs ruled it a good shoot, but he didn't care. It didn't make it any more justified that he was defending himself against real bullets. He had killed a thirteen-year-old kid. That was the only thing that mattered to him.

It took a couple of months before his shoulder was healed. In the meantime, he had physical therapy and saw a shrink, by order of the department. They said he could go back to work. In all of the time since then, he'd never had to draw his weapon again.

He fought with his wife about pretty much everything. Slowly, things fell apart. Maria tried to be patient with him, but as bad as he acted toward everyone else, he seemed to save the worst for her. At least that's what she said. *Hell, Maria was right.* More than anyone, he wanted her to understand what he was going through. But how could she, when he could never figure out why he tried so hard to push her away?

His career became just a job. Lax in his paperwork, moody and arrogant, it was no wonder that other cops didn't want to work with him. Sometimes, he slept in an alley when he had the late shift. He took a few bribes, and he let certain reporters "exchange" information with him. He told himself he should save the money because he knew he was never going to last long enough to see a pension. But mostly, he just drank it away.

Abernathy tried to stand up again. Swaying, he waited for the room to stop spinning. Then he waited for his stomach to stop doing more somersaults. He was getting this routine down.

Does the clock really say ten? He only had an hour to pull himself together and get to work. His eyes traveled in an uneven line to a slip of crumpled paper on the night stand. He picked it up and clumsily dialed the number on his cell phone.

"Schilling," he said, groggily. "Abernathy. Got some news. Your hanger from yesterday? The ME said he was strangled first, then hung. Marks on the neck were consistent with a ligature mark from a thin rope. Mark from the belt was laid over the top. Quote this in the paper before it comes out of our office and your ass is mine. Guess you got a story brewing after all."

CHAPTER

29

LORI HEAVED THE thick book onto the oak table. She wondered how many pounds of monotony made up this volume. She let out a big sigh and flopped over chunks of pages until she found the index in the back.

An hour passed and her exhaustion from this morning returned with a vengeance. For the first time in the fifteen years at the *Herald*, Lori did the bare minimum to satisfy Delacourt's research request. She simply couldn't concentrate anymore. She had found enough on the NSA after she met with Rita and enough on precedent today to give David a story to write for Sunday. It was all the effort she could muster.

On her way out, Lori stopped at the small bank of phones in sound proof booths near the front of the library. They had installed them a few years ago, so the paralegals and businessmen that frequented wouldn't bother patrons on their cellphones. She made a mental note that they might serve the purpose of a place to communicate anonymously. Rita was at work today, and she thought it would be difficult to trace a call made from the library through the main switchboard at SpringWare. Rita didn't think that calls were recorded, but Lori didn't want to take any chances with what she said.

"Hey, it's me," Lori said when Rita answered her phone. "I'm doing the electronics thing tonight, then heading out of town tomorrow. I'll catch you later." Lori hung up before Rita could say a word. She was confident Rita would understand what she meant.

Buttoning her coat against the gusty wind, she hoped that walking the few short blocks back to the office in the cold would reenergize her.

What was I thinking, making plans for dinner with Nathan tonight? There was real work to be done. The disk was waiting at home for the password she now knew. The key was burning a hole in her pocket, but the mall would have to wait till tomorrow. The stores would be busier on Saturday, and it would be easier to blend in with the holiday crowds.

The snow was falling continuously now, and by the time she reached the *Herald*, her hair was soaking wet. *Damn weatherman!* Lori saw from across the room that Joe wasn't in, so she took advantage of being able to set the research papers on his desk without having to discuss the meager information in them.

The hand dryers in the restroom weren't very efficient at drying hands, but it was all she could do with her wet hair. Swiveling her head under it, Lori glanced at her watch and saw that it was only 10:30. *There's still time.* She was feeling a little guilty about her poor attempt this morning, so maybe she would drive to Denton after all and do a little more research at the library there. She could eat a late lunch at the mall and find the locker. She'd still have plenty of time to get back to look at the disk before dinner with Nathan.

She hastily scribbled a message telling Joe she was going to the Denton library and left it on his desk. Then she headed home to pick up her car. Lori felt the adrenaline starting to work through her body. Locker 27 was calling her. She slipped her hand into her coat pocket and felt the coolness of the small gold key.

As Lori walked down the street, she saw Nathan running into the office from the neighboring parking garage in an obvious hurry. She thought he must be on to some hot news story and was sure he would fill her in on it tonight. Right now, she had more important thoughts on her mind.

The trip to Denton was normally a half hour drive. Because of the worsening weather, it was going to take longer, but the traffic was light. Lori kept an eye on her rearview mirror, and she was satisfied that she wasn't being tailed. It would have been easy to see someone following her with so few cars on the road. She wondered if there had been a time when she and Jack had been followed.

Lori's subconscious brought a memory to the surface. She had returned from the funeral home after Jack's wake. A few things had been moved around in the den and in the living room. She hadn't thought much of it at the time, as friends and neighbors had been coming by since the accident to help out. They would tidy up the house and keep her freezer stocked with food. At the time, she thought that one of them had been there in her absence. *Had someone been in the house looking for something?* But nothing was missing. *If there was something they wanted, they would've certainly taken it then.*

Her thoughts were interrupted by the exit sign for Denton. She watched carefully behind her, but no one followed her off the highway. Most of the roads in Denton didn't look as though they had been plowed yet, and it was nearly 11:30. Lori drove toward the library, but the street to get there was piled high with snow. Only the main road had been cleared. *Well, no library today.* Lori briefly wondered why the streets weren't plowed, but her mind quickly fixated on locker 27.

She continued on toward the mall, which was on the main drag. The full parking lot revealed that it was busy today. That struck her as quite unusual for a workday, even if it was just before Christmas. *The more people, the better.* She checked the rearview mirror as she circled the lot to find a parking space, but again, no one seemed to be following her.

As a final precaution, she took her time brushing the snow from her coat when she reached the inside of the mall, careful to leave her gloves on. She examined a store window near the entrance for a few minutes, but no one else came in.

Deciding to not waste any more time, Lori headed for the lockers located near the restrooms. Alone in the small space, she quickly searched for number 27. She turned the key a half turn to the left, and the locker door opened, revealing a brown envelope. Lori quickly removed it and stuffed it inside her coat, tightening the belt to keep the envelope in place. She rubbed the key all over with her gloved hands, then closed the door, leaving the key in the lock. She walked into the women's bathroom and selected the farthest stall from the door, next to a wall.

Taking the envelope out of her coat, she laid it on the back of the toilet. She wanted desperately to open it, but she knew she should wait for the privacy and safety of her home. Her fabric purse was just the right size, so the envelope fit inside nicely. Lori zipped up the purse and put the strap over her head, so the purse hung across her chest and under her arm.

Walking back into the mall, the smell of food drifted her way. Her stomach reminded her with a big growl that she hadn't eaten yet today. Against her better judgement, she turned right and headed toward the crowded food court. Lori made her selection by choosing the food vendor with the shortest line and ordered chicken teriyaki and a soda.

"The mall is really crowded today," she remarked to the lady taking her money.

"Yeah, the city workers went on strike yesterday. Guess they don't care it's Christmas. Most of the streets aren't passable, so the government buildings and a lot of small businesses are closed. Volunteers have been out plowing the major roads since our snowstorm yesterday."

That explained the unplowed streets and the busy mall. Now she had an honest explanation for Delacourt as to why she didn't go to the library after all.

Lori carried her tray to a table that was placed against the far wall of the food court. It gave her a full view of the horde of people eating in the dining area. The purse felt bulky under her arm, making the temptation to look in the envelope harder to ignore.

Everyone was busy eating. Kids were running around. People were checking items off their Christmas lists. This was her first Christmas alone. A distraction would keep her from going down the rabbit hole of sad emotions that were building inside of her. She pulled the envelope out of her purse and laid it in her lap. She stared at it for a few moments before deciding. *I think this will serve nicely.*

CHAPTER

30

"MR. MASON'S OFFICE. This is Rita. How may I help you?" Rita gave her automatic response as she answered the phone.

"Mark Mason, please. This is Nathan Schilling."

"May I ask what company you are with, Mr. Schilling?" The name sounded familiar, but she couldn't place it.

"I'm with the *Town Herald*," Nathan responded.

Homicide Investigative Reporter. She could see the tagline on the newspaper pages. Rita's mind raced. She had to find out what he wanted, but she was not letting him talk to Mason.

"And what is this in reference to?" Rita inquired as casually as she could.

"It's about an employee of his. A Mr. George Packwood." He had a feeling this woman was not going to let him talk to Mason, so he added, "I have information that he should know about his death."

Rita almost gasped out loud. *What could it be?*

"He's out of the office today. Give me your number and

I'll be sure to have him call you when he gets in on Monday." Rita wrote down the number on the message pad.

She hung up the phone, disappointed in herself for not getting more information from him. *What could it be? I don't think I can handle anything else.* Rita's anxiety was in full gear. She wiped the moisture from her forehead with the back of her hand, feeling the panic rising to the surface.

She punched the keys in frustration, taking three tries to dial the number for the *Herald* correctly. Her fist clenched around the handset as Lori's answering machine came on. *Damn it!* She slammed the phone back onto its base, somehow hoping it would undo the action she had just taken. She cursed herself for calling from her extension and letting the machine pick up. *What were you thinking, Rita! Lori used her name on the message, for God's sake!* Stupid mistakes like this could have big consequences. If they weren't already suspicious of Lori, they certainly would be now. The stress was starting to affect the clarity of her thinking.

She remembered Lori's call earlier today: "Hey, it's me. I'm doing the electronics thing tonight, then heading out of town tomorrow. I'll catch you later." The one-sided call may have seemed odd to anyone listening in, but there was nothing incriminating in it. Rita felt sick to her stomach over the mistake she had just made, but it was too late to undo any of it now.

Rita had to talk to Lori before she left work so she could tell her to ask Nathan about the information he had about George. *I need to find a way to bring that damn burner phone into this building.*

CHAPTER
31

THE FOOD COURT echoed with loud voices. Lori casually looked around at the crowd as she ate her chicken. For as far as she could see, everyone was engaged in some activity. In fact, she didn't see a single person eating alone. Normally, that would have made her feel lonely, but nothing about her life at that moment was normal. It made her feel better about what she was about to do.

Inside the envelope was a CD and some papers. The first several pages were copies of the memos she had already seen between Jack and Mason. It looked like George had read Jack's file too. She assumed that Jack's file was probably what was on the CD. *I wonder if George was able to get into the other encrypted file?* The next few pages had multiple series of numbers on them. Lori had no idea what they were, so she continued flipping through the papers. The last page was a letter:

My Darling Karla,

You have no idea how much the last five months have meant to me. I thought I was destined to spend my life alone after Carolyn died. I never dreamed I would be so lucky to find two women in my lifetime to love so deeply.

The tears came quickly to Lori's eyes, for George and Karla, and because his words swept her back to the familiar, raw feelings she still had for Jack. She read on:

I am terrified for both of us. Do not trust Mark Mason or anyone from the NSA. Keep these documents in a safe place. They may be negotiating tools for you if you find yourself in a situation where you need them.

I know that if you are reading this letter, it's because I have had to disappear or have been killed. I fear that they may find out what I know, or worse yet, that they suspect you know something. I pray that you stay safe. I love you so very much,

George (12/18)

George had written the letter last week, shortly before Karla was killed. Lori guessed that he didn't have time to tell Karla about the locker. She wondered if George had told her about the software. *I guess it really doesn't matter.* Lori stuffed everything back into the envelope and pushed it into the purse under her arm. She had lost her appetite.

The snow was falling as Lori ran to her car. Sitting behind the wheel, she absently watched the wipers push the snow back and forth across the windshield. She hoped that George and Karla had kissed and told each other how much they loved each other the last time they were together.

Jack and Lori had never had that opportunity. She had stayed up late the night before, finishing a research project for the newspaper. Jack didn't have the heart to wake her when she slept through the alarm. He reset it for an hour later and went off to work. They had tried to reach each other several times during the day, but never connected. Lori still kept two of his messages saved on her cell phone. Sometimes, it was comforting, but most of the time, it was painful to listen to them. She wasn't sure if she'd ever erase them, but she listened less and less frequently.

The honk of a horn brought her back. Someone wanted her parking spot. Lori put the car in reverse and headed back to Cooperville. She called the receptionist at the *Herald* and told her that the weather was really bad in Denton and the library was closed. Joe had received the information she left. Lori wasn't really worried about anything because if Joe was unhappy, she would have heard from him by now.

One o'clock. She couldn't wait any longer to see what was on that disk. She was going home. Patience was no longer a virtue.

CHAPTER

32

NATHAN WAS FRUSTRATED that he had failed to get by Mason's assistant when he tried to reach him on the phone. He had been confident that Mason would have called when he heard the topic of the message. He hadn't heard from him yet, and he didn't want to wait until Monday to talk to him. Publishing an article in tomorrow's paper might be a way to get him to call, but he was unsure of how to proceed with the story.

There was no official information he could use from the ME or the police department about George Packwood. Even though he knew that it was not a suicide, after Abernathy's warning he couldn't print that yet. Certain that Karla's death was not the result of a burglary gone wrong, he wondered how long it would take for the police to reach the same conclusion.

Nathan decided that the column for Saturday's paper should describe the two incidents and speculate on them being related in some way. Nathan knew that he would have to sell Delacourt on this idea, though. Joe believed the paper should report only the facts, not print innuendoes. He carefully crafted an article recapping the events of the past few days. It was factual, but it was the headline that invited speculation:

"Two SpringWare Employees Dead!"

It was short, simple, and true.

It took three revisions and a strong assurance that Nathan's source on the homicide, not suicide, was for real before he finally won Delacourt's approval.

Most importantly, Nathan was certain that this would get Mark Mason's attention.

CHAPTER

33

LORI RESET THE house alarm, tossed her coat on the sofa, lit a log in the fireplace, and went right to her computer. She slid in the first disk, entered the password, and copied it to her computer's hard drive. Following the same steps with the second disk, she recalled Rita's instructions not to open any of the files until she copied them to a new CD. *Done!*

Now it was time. With trembling fingers, she opened the second disk. She was petrified, yet curious, to see what the file contained. Part of her wanted to believe that if they didn't know what Jack had found, this would all go away. She and Rita would be safe again. But her logical part knew that would never be true. They had to know what this was about if they were ever to going to punish those responsible.

A file and a document appeared on the screen. Lori swore in frustration. She couldn't open the file. *Dammit, Jack!* The document, however, proved to be exactly what they needed to make sense of what was happening.

Though he wasn't completely sure without digging deeper into it, Jack described the potential ramifications of the hidden program he found embedded in the software. Lori was not an expert about how software worked, but Jack's words were straightforward. It didn't take an expert to comprehend the consequences if he was right. Lori's icy hands shook in her lap, yet her cheeks burned red hot with anger. If what Jack thought was true, it was crystal clear why the NSA would want to keep it a secret. Lori had no doubt that they would kill—and continue to kill—to keep this secret from being disclosed. She could no longer deny the extreme danger they were in.

They were keeping an eye on Rita. Lori was pretty confident that she wasn't being followed yet. *But it's only a matter of time.* Her stomach somersaulted, and her body tensed as the adrenaline kicked in at full speed. To hell with phone tracing and tapped phones. Every fiber of her being told her to act *immediately*. Rita was in much more danger than she knew. She needed to get her away from SpringWare and Mark Mason, now!

Lori picked up her burner phone and dialed Rita's work number.

"Hey stranger. It's Gloria! I bet you didn't think you'd ever hear from me again."

"Hi, Gloria," Rita answered, puzzled. *What is Lori doing?*

"Listen, I was just in town for a short meeting in DC and don't have to leave until later tonight. Can you sneak on down that magical yellow brick road of yours and meet me for some tapas and margaritas somewhere? Oh, never mind tapas, I know Cooperville is still like living in another universe! Tea will probably have to do. It's been too long, girl. I just gotta see ya!"

"Gloria," Rita played along. "It's been, what, four years? It's so good to hear from you. Yeah, I think I can get away. Give me an hour."

"Great. I can't wait to see ya, girl. I'll head your way now!" Lori hung up and hoped that she got her message across.

Lori had one hour to do what she needed to do. Suddenly, an idea came to her. *Brilliant!* A few minutes later, she emptied the files from her hard drive to securely empty the trash, just as Rita had instructed. She tossed the original two CDs in the fire and put the new one she made back in the empty spot in the rack. She stuffed George's disk and the papers from the locker into her purse.

Lori stood in the middle of the room, hands on her hips. She reviewed all the steps she had taken to be sure that she hadn't missed anything. Satisfied, she was out the door to meet Rita. There'd be no walking this time. She definitely needed her car.

CHAPTER

34

THERE MUST BE something very important that Rita needed to know about right away for Lori to take the risk of calling her at the office. Rita went over a few excuses for leaving in her head. She knocked on Mason's door and went in when he granted her permission to enter.

"Mr. Mason," Rita said, measuring her words carefully. If they were listening to her calls, she'd give them what they had heard. "I had an old friend call just now that I haven't seen in a few years. She's passing through town today. I wondered if you would mind if I took the rest of the day off to go meet her? I'm all caught up on my work."

Mason paused for a moment. Tuesday was Christmas, so why not let her have one last present? Mason knew Baxter was having her tailed; and in a few days, none of this would matter anyway. He really didn't care anymore. "Sure, Rita. Go ahead. Look, I'm not sure if I'm coming in on Monday, so why not just take it off too. I'll see you after the New Year. Merry Christmas."

"Thanks, Mr. Mason. Have a nice holiday." He responded by returning his attention to the paperwork on his desk. Dismissed. *What was that about?* He was never generous like that with anyone. And he never voluntarily missed work, even if Monday was Christmas Eve.

His behavior made her even more frightened than she already was. It seemed that with every passing hour, something new came up to make her fear grow. She needed some time away to regroup and figure out how to solve this dangerous dilemma before she had to return to work after the new year. To be in the same room with a murderer was getting to be more than Rita could bear.

Rita was on the elevator in a flash. She mentioned to Jerrod that Mason had given her the rest of the day off as he checked her purse.

"Well, that has to be a first. Do you think he finally caught the holiday spirit?" Jerrod's laugh was contagious, but she could barely manage a smile. Rita wished him a happy holiday and good luck with putting the bike together; after that, she was out the door. There was no time for small talk today.

She pulled her coat tightly around her as the wind tugged at it, trying to think of the best way to ditch her ever present shadow. *Lori said to meet for tea.* Then, at that moment, it finally made sense to her! Rita made a left toward the row of small shops that lined the main street. With only a few days left before Christmas, shoppers filled the sidewalks, purchasing their last-minute holiday gifts. People were smiling and getting into the holiday spirit. Rita was relieved to see that the downtown area was crowded, but the Christmas spirit was definitely not what was on her mind.

Two blocks down the main street, she entered the Tea for Two Shoppe. She walked over to a small display of teapots and feigned interest until she was able to spot the familiar trench coat across the street and two stores down. From his position, he wouldn't be able to see her in every part of the store, and he couldn't come any closer without making himself visible. *Perfect.* Rita picked up a box of tea and went to the counter to pay.

She kept an eye on the man in the trench coat as she waited for the two people in front of her to be taken care of. The store was very busy today, with people going in and out of the store regularly. Several shoppers were already lined up behind her. All of this activity would provide good cover for Rita in her attempt to sidestep her now familiar tail.

Rita had shopped in this store for years, but she didn't recognize the clerk behind the counter today. "Where's Layla today?" Rita inquired about the owner as she approached the register.

"Doing some last-minute Christmas shopping of her own. I'm Jackie, a friend of hers. It's hard for her to get away from the store, so I'm filling in for her for a few hours this afternoon."

"That's really nice of you, Jackie. Tell Layla that Rita said Merry Christmas." Rita took her change. Clutching her stomach and groaning, she said, "Mmm . . . I don't feel too well. Jackie, can I use the restroom in the back? I know where it is." Being old had its advantages. Not many people would refuse an older person who needed to use the bathroom.

"Sure. No problem." Jackie was already focused on the next customer.

Rita entered the small storage room in the back, but instead of opening the restroom door, she quietly opened the one next to it and stepped out into the alley. Today, it was better known as the yellow brick road. Lori smiled as she reached across to open the passenger door to let Rita in her car.

"Great impersonation, Lori," Rita said. "It almost fooled *me*."

"Glad you figured it out," Lori said, speeding through the alley toward the road that led out of town. Still glancing in the rearview mirror, she said, "Rita, I got the stuff out of the locker. We were right. George knew about the software, but I don't know if he told Karla. Here." Lori handed Rita the envelope to look at while she drove.

Rita carefully paged through the papers. "Do you know what these numbers mean?"

"Not a clue," replied Lori. "The last page is a note to Karla. I doubt she saw any of this."

Rita withdrew the last page from the stack of papers. Her eyes welled up with tears as she read George's heartfelt letter to Karla. "George must have killed himself after he saw the article in the paper about Karla's death. He was obviously in love with her." Rita wiped at her eyes with the collar of her sweater. "Have you looked at this disk?"

"Not yet. I figured it was a copy of the file that we have from Jack's computer. It must be where he got the copies of those memos between Jack and Mason. But none of this is why I felt you needed to get out of that office right away." Lori steered her car into the parking lot of the busy supermarket a few blocks from downtown. She chose a space with empty cars parked all around them. She unbuckled her seatbelt so she could turn in her seat to look at Rita.

"Rita, I was able to look at the two disks you gave me. There was a note that Jack wrote on the second one. He explained his theory about why that software program may be so important." Lori proceeded to give Rita a thorough review of what Jack thought the program might be capable of doing. "After reading it, I'm surprised that *anyone* who had anything to do with it is still alive."

Rita heard Lori's voice crack as she said those words. She swallowed hard and closed her eyes for a moment as she tried to regain her composure. "Oh my God . . . we really are in trouble, aren't we?" Rita's voice expressed the gravity of the situation that both of them were feeling. The two women sat silently for a while, contemplating the real danger they were in.

Looking at nothing in particular out the front window, Rita didn't realize she was speaking out loud. "We can't let them get away with this!" But though she expressed this with great determination, she had no idea how they were going to accomplish this. She turned to Lori once again.

"They aren't going to leave any loose ends. Actually, I'm not sure how I have survived this long. There's one more person who worked on this program. Jacob Browning, he's a software specialist at SpringWare. We need to warn him of the danger he's in before he becomes the next *accident*."

"Can you get in touch with him?"

"I'm sure he'll still be at the office. We've got to think of a way to get him out of there." Rita glanced at her watch. It was getting late in the afternoon. They'd have to move quickly to catch him at work because Rita had no idea how to contact him after he left. They took a few minutes to formulate a plan to contact Jacob.

As Lori backed out of the space, Rita remembered one more thing. "I almost forgot! Nathan Schilling called the office today to talk to Mason. He said he had new information about George's death. I told him Mason wasn't in. He asked if I would have Mason call him on Monday. What do you think that's about?"

Lori felt a shiver run down her spine. It couldn't be anything good. "I'm having dinner with Nathan tonight. He wants to ask me more questions about George and Karla. I'll find out what he knows." Lori guided the car out of the parking lot, turning back onto the main street toward Cooperville. "Did you tell Mason that Nathan called?"

"No. I was still debating on whether I should when I got your call. Now I'm glad I didn't. We don't need to add any more fuel to the fire."

"You're right about that." Lori glanced over at Rita. She looked as though she'd aged another five years since the last time she saw her. "Rita, maybe you should go out of town for a while. Visit your daughter?"

It made sense for them both to leave town, but Rita had already decided that she was in this until the end, no matter what that meant. "Lori, where could we go that the NSA isn't capable of finding us?"

CHAPTER

35

JACOB BROWNING'S FINGERS flew over the keyboard nearly as fast as his mind could perceive the letters. *Another one bites the dust.* His foot tapped to the rhythm of the music in his head. One more project completed well before the deadline. He popped the disk out of the tray.

He loved hearing the sound of the CD drawer opening. It always reminded him of his first computer. To this day, he still didn't know how his mom, single and working three jobs, saved the money for the used Mac desktop she gave him on his eighth birthday.

Computers were his first, and so far only, love. He preferred the company of his screen over people, and as a result, most people at SpringWare didn't know him very well. As a loner, that was fine with him. A quiet life is what he preferred.

Jacob swiveled his chair to the side to stretch his long legs. He thought about growing up in the projects near Oakland, California. Computers kept him off the streets and out of trouble, unlike a lot of the boys his age in the neighborhood. In fact, he did everything he could to avoid those boys, as they bullied him and called him a nerd. Twenty-five years after his eighth birthday, he had grown to a be a big man with a very soft center.

Pushing the tray back into the computer made him feel a bit melancholic. It wouldn't be long before CDs went the way of floppy disks. USB drives would soon be the norm. Jacob wondered if he'd forget the sound that made him feel so nostalgic, like he had easily forgotten floppy disks. He laughed out loud. *Everything changes but me.*

He'd been at SpringWare for five years, an unusually long time for a software programmer. Most of his other colleagues jumped around from job to job, or preferred working as subcontractors. But sending resumes and drumming up new business wasn't for him. Jacob liked the security that SpringWare offered. It provided the opportunity to use his skills and get paid well for doing something he loved.

Because he was efficient at his job, he found that he often had a lot of spare time. Today was no different. The holidays were coming up and SpringWare always closed during the week after Christmas. No new projects were slated to start until he returned after the new year. He had nothing to do for the rest of the afternoon but play video games or balance his checkbook online. *Decisions. Decisions.* He laughed out loud again. *Not a difficult choice.*

Jacob was aware that SpringWare monitored all the terminals in the building, so designing the "Shield" for his computer had been a brilliant idea. He'd love to find a way to market it, but coding was his specialty, not selling. Besides, he didn't think SpringWare would take well to his latest program. He had created it on their time clock, and it was meant to deceive them. It was skills like this that had almost landed him in jail.

He straightened in his chair and shook his head as he flashed back to his last year in California. His previous employer was a small tech company. Large companies would hire the gray hat hacking firm to break into their security system in order to discover and fix their vulnerabilities. But Jacob soon realized that these projects were just a cover for some major black hat hacking that was going on. Luckily for him, his ethical side won out and he quit. One day later, the Feds burst in and arrested everyone. Jacob was interrogated, and he disclosed everything he knew. Because he was cooperative and had not been involved in the more nefarious part of the business, he didn't face charges.

The East Coast was the solution to getting as far away from Silicon Valley as possible. He found SpringWare, and the rest was history. He recently bought a small house and finally felt settled. *Predictable and quiet. Just the way I like it.*

Jacob hit a few keys, and the screen registered just the faintest of quivers. That let him know that the Shield was up and running. Now SpringWare was being led to believe that he was still hard at work for them on his computer, when in actuality, he was loading his pirated copy of Counter-Strike. *Let the games begin!* He logged on just as the phone rang.

"Browning."

"Jacob Browning?"

"Yeah, this is Jacob."

"This is Officer Moreno. Do you drive a white Ford Mustang?"

"Yeah, why?"

"Someone has backed into your car. Could you come to the parking garage?"

"Sure. I'll be right down." *Really? Not just before Christmas!* Jacob moaned as he shut down the Shield and logged off his computer.

Five minutes later, after clearing security, Jacob entered the parking garage. There was no visible damage to his car, and no police were in sight. Instead, Rita Johnson was leaning against the trunk. He sauntered toward her, laughing.

"Rita? What's going on? This some kind of early April Fool's joke?" Jacob stopped short when his lighthearted manner didn't elicit a smile from her. The look of fear on her face caused his heart to skip a beat.

"Jacob, we need to talk. I know this is coming out of left field, but just trust me. Your life is in danger." Rita opened the door to the car next to her and motioned for him to get in. "Get in and I'll explain."

Every cell in Jacob's body tingled with apprehension. As he got in the back seat, he saw Lori behind the wheel. *Jack Crawford's wife? What the hell is going on?* Lori drove the car up to the top of the garage, where no one would be parked in this terrible weather.

"What's going on, Rita?" She answered by handing Jacob the memos from George's envelope. He scanned the first few pages and was now even more puzzled.

"What is this? Why are you showing me these?" Jacob's voice revealed the anxiety that was now churning inside of him.

"Jacob, I know this is going to seem unbelievable to you, and we don't have time to talk about the details right now. You worked on a portion of a program for the NSA, even though you weren't aware of it. Jack is dead because he discovered details about it that he shouldn't have known. So are Karla and George. The three of us are the only people left who might know anything about this software besides Mark Mason."

Jacob put his hand up to object. *This is craziness.* But Rita wouldn't stop.

"Jacob, every day I'm followed by a man in a trench coat, who drives a red SUV. It's likely that your phones are tapped, and that there's someone following you too. You have to trust me, Jacob! I know this sounds insane, but we have evidence that Mason is involved in these deaths. I'm afraid he thinks we know something about it." Rita paused, recognizing the fear and disbelief on Jacob's face. She hated to reveal this to him in this way, knowing how incomprehensible it was, but there was no time to waste.

"Look. I'll fill you in on everything tonight. Finish your day and act as if nothing is wrong. After work, go to your bank and withdraw as much money as you can in case we need to leave town."

Jacob could feel the beads of sweat on his brow. He was breathing fast and shallow. Her touch on his hand brought his focus back to what she was saying.

"Jacob, I need you to do one more really important thing. Go to George Packwood's office, and bring me his planner. It's sitting right on top of his desk. Lori and I will fill you in on everything tonight. If the guy tailing you works the same way as my shadow, he'll leave soon after he thinks you have turned in for the night. What time do you usually go to bed, Jacob?"

"Uh . . . about nine-thirty," he said, his voice shaking.

"Good. Just keep your routine the same. Leave your back

door unlocked, and I'll come in around ten. I'm sorry to spring this on you this way, but we're running out of time. The three of us are in great danger, and we need to come up with a plan to stay safe."

"Rita, I . . . uh . . . this doesn't make any sense . . ." Jacob couldn't find the words to express his confusion. He felt like he had entered some kind of time warp since he walked into the garage.

"I understand. I know this seems like a bad dream, but I promise it will make sense after we explain everything tonight. Now get back to your office before anyone gets suspicious. There will be plenty of time for questions later. Go!"

Jacob hadn't even noticed that Lori had driven over to the garage elevator door. He gave Rita his address and stumbled out of the car toward the elevator. He turned and watched them drive off as he waited for the elevator to arrive.

Once inside, he leaned against the wall to get his bearings before going down. *What the hell just happened?* His watch indicated that less than ten minutes had passed, but it seemed like it had been an hour. He forced a couple of deep breaths when he realized he was hyperventilating. Absently, he pushed the lobby button. He felt as if he couldn't trust what his brain told him had just happened.

The elevator door opened, and Jacob headed for the busy coffee shop. His mind was reeling with confusion and questions. He thought about the memos between Mason and Jack. But what did they mean? *So what if Jack had a problem with the software?* It was Mason who was ultimately responsible to the client. If he said nothing was wrong and there was a problem, it was on him. *How can Rita have proof that Mason killed Jack?*

And Karla? George committed suicide. None of this made sense. *We create gaming programs, not spyware for the NSA!* He just couldn't wrap his head around any of this. Maybe Rita was crazy. Was Lori Crawford involved in this because Jack told her something? *No way. Jack was a straight arrow. He would never violate his NDA, even with his wife.*

Jacob's mind went back to Rita. She was one of the first people he met when he started at SpringWare. He'd had frequent dealings with her when she worked in Jack's office, but not so much now that she worked for Mr. Mason. He liked her and trusted her, but this just seemed too absurd. *Someone was trying to kill him? All of them?* Sure, three people had died, but there were perfectly reasonable explanations.

His thoughts were temporarily disrupted by the barista asking for his order. He asked for a dark chocolate mocha. *Act normal? After that?* He felt like he had just met with Deep Throat in the parking garage. This was too cloak-and-dagger for him. *I design software for God's sake!* He paid for the coffee and a candy bar and went back through the lobby toward security.

"Hey, Jerrod," he said, setting his purchases down on the conveyor belt of the X-ray machine. "Couldn't resist the sweet tooth any longer." *Did that sound normal?* He certainly wasn't feeling very normal.

"Sugar *and* caffeine? You must be having a bad day, Mr. Browning. Pick up your java, and carry it through so it doesn't spill in my machine!"

"You wouldn't even believe. See you on my way out." Jacob grabbed his candy bar and turned toward the elevators. He almost froze when he saw Mark Mason waiting for one to take him up as well. Mason nodded in acknowledgment of him. There was no other choice but to ride up with him. *Come on, Browning. He won't murder you in the elevator!*

"Mr. Mason." Jacob greeted him with a voice that was as steady as possible. *Act normal.* "You ready for Christmas?"

"As ready as I'm going to be. Taking a sugar break?" he wryly joked as he eyed the candy bar. The door opened and Jacob followed him into the elevator.

"Yeah. Seems like this time of the day my sugar gets low. It's a sugar and caffeine kind of day today. Must be the stress of the holidays. I still have some shopping left to do, and I have no idea when I'm going to get it all done. Guess I'll be one of those Christmas Eve shoppers this year. At least I've caught up here though, so I won't need to feel bad about not working the week we're closed." Jacob heard himself rambling. *Shut up, you idiot!*

"Well, if you're almost done for the day, why don't you knock off early and get a head start on your shopping?" This was completely out of character for Mark Mason. Now he was more frightened than ever. Little did he know that Rita had the same feeling just a couple of hours ago.

"Really? Wow. That'd be great. Thanks, Mr. Mason." The bell dinged, and the door opened to their floor. "Have a nice Christmas." Jacob strode down the hall, trying to keep his pace leisurely, while every inch of his six-foot, three-inch body wanted to run. He wondered if Mason was watching him, but he didn't dare look back.

CHAPTER

36

WITH THEIR PLANS in place for tonight, Lori dropped Rita off in the alley at the far north end of Main Street. About an hour had passed, and Rita hoped that Trench Coat Man was still looking for her. Her plan was to appear that she had continued shopping and that he would assume he missed her coming out of the tea shop.

Rita went into the grocer, bought a few things, then headed back toward the Tea for Two Shoppe. She stopped at two more stores, quickly purchasing items in each, so she would have multiple bags.

She was relieved to have located Jacob, but she felt bad about giving him the news the way she did. She had felt the same way when she gave Lori the news about Jack's murder. At least this time, she might have prevented another tragedy by being able to warn Jacob. She was sure Jacob thought they might be crazy. *It's okay. He won't after I give him the details tonight.* At least in the meantime, he'll be on alert for anything unusual.

Rita ran into a few people she knew on the street and lingered to chat with them. She stopped to window shop occasionally, staying out on the street as long as possible in the cold to give her tail an opportunity to find her again.

When she reached the home improvement store, she said a silent thanks to those shiny pots and pans. It was brief, but Rita caught a glimpse of the now familiar trench coat. She was oddly relieved to see him, hoping that her strategy had worked.

CHAPTER

37

JACOB SHUT DOWN his computer and gathered his coat and coffee. He was about to bolt out of his office when he remembered that he was supposed to get the planner from George's office. *I wonder why Rita wants it?*

There were only a few offices in this corridor, and George's door was next to his. Jacob stepped into the hall and nervously looked around. He didn't see anyone, so he quickly slid into the opening for George's office. Without turning on any lights, he walked through Karla's workspace toward George's desk. The planner was exactly where Rita said it would be. Sliding it into his pants, he tucked it in the waistband of his underwear and under his shirt. He made a mental note that the plastic comb binding wouldn't set off the metal detector. Before stepping out into the hall, he peeked both ways. No one was in sight.

Jacob could hardly breathe as he waited for the elevator. He looked at his reflection in the shiny elevator walls to make sure the planner wasn't noticeable. His palms were sweaty as he adjusted the position of his coat on his arm to make sure it covered the bulkiness under his shirt. He wished he had a Shield for himself to make him invisible in case he saw Mason again. *What's taking this elevator so damn long?*

"That was fast," said Jerrod, as he saw Jacob come around the corner.

"Mason must be in the Christmas spirit today. He said I could go home early. Needless to say, I didn't argue."

"Must be. He said the same thing to Miss Rita just a short time ago." Jerrod lowered his voice in a whispered aside to Jacob. "Kinda strange if you ask me." The men exchanged knowing smiles.

Jacob nodded toward the cup of coffee in his hand that was also carrying his coat, an unspoken question to Jerrod if he could carry it through.

"Aww, go on through, Mr. Browning. I checked you less than ten minutes ago!"

"Have a good holiday, Jerrod." *The payoff for developing good employee relationships.*

Jacob got back into another elevator to take him up to his car. His legs felt weak, and his body was tired from the adrenaline rush of the last hour. His eyes darted around the parking garage, but he saw no one around. How could someone be following him and he not be aware of it? He backed his Mustang out of the space and drove down the ramp. At the street, he turned right and headed for the bank. He noticed a dark blue sedan pull out of a parking space on the street and fall in two cars behind him. *Just my imagination. Stop being paranoid.* As he pulled into the bank, he watched the sedan continue down the road. Jacob slid the planner under the front seat.

He entered the bank lobby with the ridiculous thought that this could be Rita's way of robbing him. *I withdraw a bunch of money, leave my back door open, and she comes and takes it.* He almost laughed out loud at the absurdity of a woman her age and half his size doing that. *But is the rest of her story any more believable? Mason involved in some murderous plot?* Everyone knows he is an ambitious jerk, but he definitely didn't seem like the type who'd kill to get what he wanted.

Yet, here he was, following Rita's instructions. His gut told him it was the right thing to do. He would at least listen to what she had to say. The money could always be redeposited on Monday.

Ten minutes later, he was back on the road toward Main street. The empty space in front of the Hallmark store was too inviting to resist. He really wasn't ready for Christmas yet and decided there was no time like the present to tackle the job. *Nice pun.* He was supposed to go home during his winter break, so he'd better have some gifts for his mom and younger sister. Besides, he didn't relish the idea of sitting at home for the next four hours thinking about murderous plots.

Five shopping bags later, Jacob was breathing easier, having immersed himself in his hour-long buying spree. He was heading back to his car when he heard his name called from across the street. It was his next-door neighbor. "Merry Christmas," he called and returned the wave, lifting the bags in the air to indicate what he had been doing. The neighbor lifted his bags in return, and they both chuckled. It was a nice way to end his hour of enjoying the Christmas spirit.

Jacob was scanning the row of cars looking for his car when he spied an empty dark blue sedan. Suddenly, he felt anxious.

Could it be the same car he had seen earlier? He continued walking toward his car parked a few spaces down the street. Opening the trunk, he casually looked around. The sidewalks were full of shoppers. If someone was following him, it could be any one of them. Shaking off the uneasy feeling, he drove home a bit faster than normal.

The attached garage was one of the selling points when he bought his house, as it meant not having to scrape ice or snow off his car on winter mornings. Jacob pulled into the garage and closed the door with the remote. He entered the kitchen through the door from the garage and plopped the shopping bags on the kitchen table. It felt good to be back in his home. But as he recalled the incident in the garage with Rita, the tightness in his body returned. *I'm sure it's nothing other than an old woman's imagination.* Still, he seemed unable to convince himself that his thought was true.

Jacob took a glass from the cupboard, and he noticed that the sky was darkening. More snow was on the way. He opened the refrigerator to get something to drink. As he poured some orange juice into the glass, his eyes caught the sight of a dark blue sedan going slowly down the street. The carton dropped from his hand as Rita's words rang in his head. *Your life is in danger.*

CHAPTER

38

DELACOURT NOTICED THE man in the dark suit as soon as he came through the office door. He had a clear view from his office to the front desk, where the man was asking the receptionist for Lori Crawford. When he was told she wasn't in, he demanded to see the editor. *Sure. Send him my way!* The hair raised up on the back of Joe's neck. He felt particularly protective of Lori since her husband had died.

As the receptionist walked the man toward his office door, Joe noticed Nathan Schilling peeking out of his cubicle, following the man's path. He could see that Nathan's instincts were also flaring red hot. Joe watched Nathan stroll behind the man at a safe distance and slide into an empty cubicle right outside his door. The receptionist didn't close the door behind him.

"Agent Simms. IRS," he said, flashing a plastic badge at Delacourt when Joe stood up. "I'm here to see Lori Crawford."

"What's this about?" The reporter in Joe sprang to life. He wasn't about to give this man any information until he knew what was going on.

"It's a personal matter about a previous tax return for her and Mr. Crawford."

"She's left for the day. You do know that Jack is deceased?"

"Yes. I'd like to be shown to her workstation."

"Sorry," Delacourt replied. "Everything in this office is considered confidential and is the property of the *Town Herald*. I'll be more than happy to show you to Ms. Crawford's office when you return with a warrant."

The agent, obviously annoyed, kept his cool. "I'll be back with the proper documentation." He gave Joe a threatening look and stalked out.

Joe followed the agent out of the office and watched until he left the building. Something about that man and his credentials didn't sit right with him. *Since when did the IRS send an agent out into the field concerning a tax return problem?* He'd had too many years of experience to fall for that story. *It'll be a cold day in hell before you harass Lori for no good reason.* And that was what was bothering him. He could think of no good reason for anyone so suspicious to be inquiring about Lori Crawford.

Joe turned his attention to the cubicle where Nathan Schilling was standing with his back to him, pretending to look busy. "What are you doing in there, Schilling?"

"Just looking for some paperwork, Joe," Nathan muttered.

Joe rolled his eyes at Nathan and gave him a stern look. He was well aware that he was eavesdropping on the conversation with the supposed agent. "Sure you were. Did that feel off to you?"

"Yeah. Everything about it." Nathan stared at the front door while a dozen questions ran through his mind.

Joe nodded in agreement. "Have you seen Lori today? She left a message that she was going to the Denton library to do some research."

"No, but if I run into her, I'll ask if the IRS has notified her of a tax issue." Nathan purposely didn't mention that they were having dinner tonight. He hurried toward the exit before Joe could say anything else.

Joe turned back to his office. He buzzed the receptionist and told him that if anyone came looking for Lori Crawford, they were to be shown to his office immediately. He made a mental note to tell Lori that she was to work only at home or at her desk until this was straightened out.

CHAPTER

39

ABERNATHY SAT ALONE in the empty interrogation room after his shift was over. Even cops didn't like these cold, sterile rooms. When occupied, they were stressful places, times filled with tears, yelling, or confessions of things most would rather not remember. But when he needed a quiet place to think, where no one would bother him, it was the perfect place. Though he was confident that he had missed all the chances he would have to make detective, right now his mind was operating like one anyway.

The two SpringWare cases were gnawing at his insides in a way that alcohol never could. He had been called to respond to gunshots at 11:25 p.m. and found the body of Karla Phillips, less than ten minutes after the shots were reported to have been fired. There hadn't been anything suspicious on his drive there, and he'd seen no one on the streets. The building itself was extremely quiet as he entered the lobby and the hallways inside.

It appeared as though the burglar had come and gone the same way, through the front door. It was open when he arrived, with no sign of forced entry. Either someone had a key or the intruder picked the lock. Abernathy wondered if the woman was home when the burglar entered, or if he was already in the apartment when she arrived home.

Abernathy popped an antacid, reviewing some scribbled notes on his pad from that evening. Picking a lock on a random second story apartment was unusual. Professional. All the typical valuables were there. Nothing had appeared to be looked through or even disturbed. Nothing appeared to be missing. *What was he after then?*

In his mind, this was no burglary. It was also too coincidental that her boyfriend had been found dead the next day. At first, Abernathy suspected that Packwood might have killed her. He ruled it out when they found his body hanging in his bedroom. In cases of murder-suicides, it was usually done in the same place, not in different locations on different days. There was also no suicide note. Another unusual detail.

Then the ME called to tell him that Packwood's death was staged to look like a suicide, but sloppily done. Perhaps the killer didn't count on the small town's previous mortician having gone back to school to be trained to have such keen skills.

He was ready to bet on his mother's grave that Phillips was murdered and that the two cases were connected by more than love. The common denominator was SpringWare. Tomorrow, he'd dig into that company to find out more about what the two victims did there.

Abernathy chewed on another antacid. This time his stomach was doing somersaults, not from a hangover, but from instincts. Maybe a drink would help calm his stomach and put things into perspective.

CHAPTER

40

LORI HURRIED HOME to get ready for her dinner with Nathan. She had no idea how she would be able to get through the evening after all that had happened today. *I shouldn't have agreed to this in the first place.* Her watch told her it was too late to call and cancel. Sighing, she double-checked that the house alarm was set and went upstairs to get ready. She must remember to find out why Nathan had called Mark Mason. But she couldn't figure out how she was going to do that without letting him know that Rita had told her. *Let's hope it just comes up.*

She stared at the clothes in her closet. *What to wear?* The red dress was too revealing. She felt a pang of guilt as she passed by the black one Jack had given her. This wasn't a date, and yet, it didn't feel like business to her either. The purple skirt and top held promise, but it wasn't very warm for this cold weather. Pass. *This should not be so difficult.* After eliminating three quarters of her closet's contents, she chose a dark sable mid-length skirt, a caramel-colored turtleneck, and knee-high brown boots.

She spent an inordinate amount of time drying her hair and applying her makeup. Lori looked in the mirror at her reflection, clicking her tongue in disgust at herself for making such a fuss about her looks. After one final inspection in the full-length mirror, she went downstairs to wait.

She was just about to go back upstairs to get a different purse when the doorbell rang. A look through the peephole hole revealed that Nathan was early. No time to change bags now. The shoulder bag would have to suffice. At least it was brown.

———

Mason had been trying to reach Carl Baxter all day but received no response. He reassured himself with the thought that Baxter had many other important things to deal with at the NSA besides this matter.

For the first time in any of his careers, he wanted to get out of the office. There was nothing here that he cared about anymore. He had a successful run with SpringWare, and now he was done. There was already more money than he could ever imagine in his account and more on the way. *Soon, I can start enjoying it.*

He plugged his phone into the car's console beside him and pulled out into the street from the office parking garage. He didn't notice the black 4x4 sliding in two cars behind him.

———

Jacob put the final bow on the gifts he had finished wrapping. The hands of the clock had ticked by ever so slowly.

He had checked the locks on the door every half hour. He was too nervous to leave the back door unsecured, so he set a reminder on his phone to unlock it a little before 9:30 so Rita could get in. There were no more stupid thoughts about her robbing him. Whatever this was, the blue sedan that was still parked a few doors away indicated that there was some credibility to her story. Still, the more he thought about what she had said, the more bizarre it seemed. *Murders? It can't be true.* That kind of thing only happened in the movies.

He turned down the heat, convincing himself it was the reason he was sweating. He flopped on the couch and turned the television on, hoping to get absorbed in the monotony of evening prime time. There was simply not enough to keep him distracted from the hundreds of questions and steady flow of thoughts in his head. Even his computer games couldn't hold his attention.

Jacob stared at the planner he had taken from George's office. He flipped through it, page by page, looking for something of interest inside of it. The guy had hardly made any entries, and the ones that were there seemed pretty benign. What was in here that Rita needed so badly that he had risked smuggling it out? Under the bright lights of the kitchen, he saw the pencil marks Rita had seen, but he had no idea of the significance they held.

For the fifth time, he walked over to the window and carefully peeked through the blinds. The blue sedan was still there.

Ten o'clock will be a long time coming.

CHAPTER

41

LORI OPENED THE door to see Nathan holding a bottle of wine. She waved him in with a nervous smile.

"Before you get any wrong ideas," he quickly said, seeing the look on her face. "The place we're going for dinner doesn't serve wine. I thought we'd go eat and enjoy ourselves, then come back here. A glass of wine might help take the edge off answering some of my questions."

Lori considered him for a moment. She understood that he viewed this night as an opportunity to discuss material for his story. At the same time, he seemed truly concerned about her feelings. It made her feel much more at ease. She took the bottle of wine, a La Crema Pinot Noir, into the kitchen. *A nice choice.*

"Thanks, Nathan. That's very thoughtful."

"Well, I'm glad you're not offended." He readily switched gears. "Come on, let's go before they get busy!"

"Where are we going?" Lori laughed. Nathan looked like an excited kid going on a new adventure.

"I can't divulge all of my secrets to you," Nathan teased as he helped her into her coat. "You'll have to wait and see." She searched for her keys in the bottom of her purse, realizing she still had George's envelope in there from this afternoon.

"Have you got the kitchen sink in there too?" Nathan laughed as he eyed the oversized bag.

"No, but I suppose it would fit. I forgot I still had all of this work stuff in here." She rattled the keys in her hand. "Okay, let's go. I'm starving!" She was surprised at how easily Nathan's excitement had rubbed off on her.

He opened the passenger door of his red Miata. Lori climbed in and immediately experienced a moment of internal conflict. She felt guilty for going somewhere in another man's car to have dinner, yet there was also a small twinge of excitement. She attributed the pleasurable feeling to the diversion from what had been happening these past few days. It was a welcome respite.

It seemed as if weeks had passed since she crawled out of bed this morning. The next few days promised to be even more stressful. *Just appreciate having a few moments to relax . . . at least until Nathan kicks into reporter mode.*

Lori was supposed to pick up Rita and Jacob at midnight. There was nothing to be done until then. For the next couple of hours, she would put those thoughts aside and concentrate on dinner. She turned slightly toward Nathan to focus on what he was talking about. *Something about his car?* Lori suddenly became aware of how handsome he was. Like his smile, she had never noticed that before.

Nathan exited the highway at the sign for Canterbury. Lori hadn't been here in many years, but she didn't remember there being much of interest in this small town. As if Nathan were reading her mind he said, "There's only one thing in this town that makes it worth coming here." As if on cue, he pulled into The *Original* Mel's Drive-In. "No one knows how original it really is, but they have the best burgers anywhere in Virginia!"

Once again, Lori allowed herself to tap into his excitement. "It's been years since I've been to a drive-in!" Nathan pulled into a space under the canopy. Before he could turn the car off, Lori watched a girl dressed in a snowsuit and ear muffs skate up to the driver's side window.

"Dining inside tonight or in your car?" She smacked her gum.

"In the car," Nathan replied. Before Lori could voice the protest on her lips, the girl handed him menus and a small portable heater for the dashboard. She could feel the heat immediately.

"That'll work." She smiled as Nathan passed her a menu. He pointed to his ear as "Rock Around the Clock" played on the speakers outside. Lori laughed, and it felt good. *This is just what I needed.*

"I'll apologize up front," said Nathan, not looking very apologetic. "I'm just a romantic at heart. These old diners were well on their way out when I was growing up, but my parents used to take me to one near our house. It was always a big treat. When I moved here from Atlanta, I couldn't believe my good fortune in finding this place. It's a feel-good flash from my past in more ways than one."

"I bet you take all the girls here," Lori said, immediately cringing at the cliché. She could tell that the comment had hurt his feelings by the look on his face. *Whatever possessed me to say that?*

"No, you're the first," Nathan said seriously.

She reached over and softly touched his arm. "What's good on the menu?" she said lightly. The smile quickly returned to his face.

"Would you like me to order for you? I promise you won't be disappointed." Lori nodded her consent.

The skater girl had reappeared at the window. Nathan rolled it halfway down. "Two of the usual. It's her first time here, so tell Mel to cook 'em just right." She grinned and skated off.

"So, you *are* a regular." Lori laughed. She could see that Nathan really enjoyed this place. "The heater's a great idea. I bet business would be terrible in the winter without them." Lori observed that there were a lot of people eating in their cars.

"You'd be surprised. This place really rocks all year round, inside and outside. I sit at the counter inside once in a while, but it gets loud when the dancing starts. If you want to have any kind of conversation, you're better off in the car."

"They have dancing, like with a band?" Lori asked, surprised.

"Oh, no. But there's a great jukebox inside with hundreds of the best oldies. People get up and dance around the tables whenever they feel like it. Mel finally took out a few booths in the back to make room for a small dance floor."

"Sounds like fun. Maybe next time." Lori surprised herself with the honesty of that remark. The mixed emotions she initially experienced had been replaced with a relaxed feeling of ease.

The food arrived quickly, and for a few minutes, they were both silent while they ate. Lori was famished. She had skipped or left many meals on the table since this mess started.

"I didn't realize how hungry I was," Nathan said between bites. He laughed as he watched her devour hers. "Looks like you were hungry too!"

"Mmmm. Yes . . . you weren't lying when you said they have the best burgers. This is incredibly good!"

"I've been trying to get Mel to tell me his secret recipe for a long time now, but he won't give it up. I have no idea how you can make a simple hamburger taste this good."

Lori looked him in the eyes. "Nathan, thanks for this. Really. I've been pretty stressed lately. This has been the perfect distraction for me."

"Well, I'm glad to share my little secret with you." Nathan assumed she was speaking of Jack. That was one topic he had hoped wouldn't come up tonight, but he guessed it was inevitable. "I know this must be awkward for you, after Jack's accident and all." He moved uncomfortably in his seat.

"Nathan, it's okay. That's not what I was referring to, but yeah, it was a bit awkward at first. You made it a lot easier, though . . . bringing me here. It's made me feel less pressured, and I'm enjoying myself . . . thank you. This has meant a lot to me." Lori smiled warmly at him. She was once again surprised at how honest her words felt. He was easy to be with. Nathan beamed like a little boy who'd been given his favorite piece of candy.

While they finished their burgers, Lori steered their conversation toward neutral subjects, like living in Cooperville and working for Joe. When the skater girl arrived again, Nathan grinned at Lori. "They make *the* most fantastic milkshakes. Can I interest you in something chocolate?"

"I couldn't take in another thing!" Lori said, rubbing her belly. "I want to save room for a glass of that wine you brought." She leaned back into the seat of the small sports car, feeling fully satisfied, physically and emotionally.

"Perfect. Then let's go." Nathan settled up with skater girl and returned the heater. They made small talk on the way back. Lori noticed that Nathan was keeping his promise of no business until the wine was poured. She smiled appreciatively. *A man who's true to his word.*

CHAPTER

42

AS THE MIATA pulled into the driveway, Lori noticed the front porch light was out. "I was sure I turned on the outside lights before we left," she said, walking up the sidewalk. When Lori attempted to push her key in the lock, the door opened slightly.

"I *know* I saw you lock that door," Nathan whispered, putting his hand on her arm and motioning her to stay by the door. Heart pounding, he pushed the door open and entered the dark foyer. Lori followed closely behind him. She turned on the lights for the living room.

"Wait *here*, Lori," he whispered again. Just a few more steps inside and he could see the house had been ransacked. Lori ignored his request to stay by the door and closely followed him inside. She grabbed his arm and gasped out loud when she saw her house in shambles. She kept her hand on his arm, hoping to keep it from shaking. Her legs felt like rubber.

Lori flipped on the kitchen lights as they walked into the kitchen on the left. She withdrew the two largest instruments from the knife block and handed one to Nathan. He nodded.

It was clear that she wasn't going to stay anywhere by herself.

"We need to call the police." Nathan kept his voice low.

"No!" Lori shouted in a whisper as she faced him. Nathan was taken aback at the intensity of her reaction. "Let's see if anyone is here, first."

"But . . ." Nathan protested.

"NO!" she said with even more determination, but clearly terrified. Standing silently in the kitchen, they listened intently for any sound that might indicate someone was still in the house. There was no creaking or rustling, no sounds at all. Frozen in place, two cycles of the heater turned on and off before they moved.

Finally, Lori turned toward the garage and opened the door. No one. They moved from room to room. The living room and den were a disaster. Everything appeared to have been searched; even the open closet doors had items thrown from them. Nathan had been on too many crime scenes to know this was not a robbery. *Someone was looking for something.* There was no one downstairs.

They had not checked upstairs yet, and both of them sensed how frightened the other was to venture up there. Visions of Karla filled Lori's head. Nathan pulled her behind him as they reached the landing. Lori pointed to her bedroom. Her stomach revolted each time a door was opened. Both bedrooms, the bathrooms, the closets, and the drawers had all been rummaged through.

It was clear that whoever did this was gone. Nathan's adrenaline rush was quieting, though he still gripped the knife tightly. Lori held hers out in front of her body as they walked back downstairs.

"Lori, we need to call the police," said Nathan.

"No, Nathan," she said resolutely, heading straight to the kitchen. She had to process what had happened. *This has to be the work of kids or vandals. Or was it them? It couldn't be them.* She felt completely overwhelmed and confused. She needed to sort this out in her mind before she could decide what to do next.

Even if Mason and Baxter were responsible for this, she had no proof. They had to have more evidence before involving the police. What they had was still mostly conjecture and circumstantial. She imagined the police rolling their eyes when she told them that the NSA had killed Jack, and Karla, and George. They would think that she and Rita were total lunatics. *I'm in the middle of it, and it's still hard to believe. No police. Not yet.*

Lori stared at the bottle of wine on the counter. "It's almost like they left this for us. I bet you never guessed how much we'd both need a drink when you brought it." The words came out laced as much with sarcasm as relief. The shaking slowly started to take over her body. She dropped the wine opener as she took it from the drawer. She attempted to cut the wrapper around the neck of the bottle. The opener fell from her hand again. Nathan gently took it from her.

"Here, let me help," he said softly. He put the bottle on the counter, then took her in his arms and held her tight. He let her cry until her body finally calmed and the tears stopped. *There is more going on here than a ransacked house.* Lori had seemed very tense when he arrived. *Was that IRS agent here earlier? Did he do this after we left?* "Do you want to call the police now?" he asked again.

Lori drew away from him and reached for some paper towels to dry her eyes. *I want to tell you, but then you'll be in as much danger as I am. I can't do that to you!* She blew her nose and fought hard to control her voice. "No . . . and please don't ask why." Her eyes pleaded with him.

"Okay. Okay . . . let's sit down for a minute and have some wine. I have a few things to tell you." Nathan opened the bottle and took the glasses she had removed from a cabinet.

Lori felt comforted as he guided her by the elbow into the living room. She stood silently as he righted the coffee table and put the cushions back on the sofa, motioning for her to sit. She stared blankly at the dark red liquid in the glass he held out to her as he sat down next to her. While she hadn't been looking forward to Nathan's questions, this was certainly not how she envisioned the rest of the evening playing out.

Lori peeked over the rim of her glass as Nathan sat quietly, sipping his wine. *Is he waiting for me to start this conversation?* She watched him look around the room. *I've got to come up with something to tell him.* She silently sighed with relief when he started talking.

"Lori, there are some things you need to know. This morning, I found out that George Packwood was murdered. It wasn't a suicide." He waited for her response.

Lori started to cry softly. She had already known it in her gut. After reading the letter George had written to Karla, she had wanted so badly to believe that he took his own life, that it was because he loved her so much, but she knew the truth. *They killed him too.*

Nathan took note that she asked no questions, or even seemed surprised by his announcement that George had been murdered. "I don't know the details, but it was confirmed by a source I have in the police department who saw the ME's report. Do you know anyone who would want George dead? Or Karla?"

Lori's mind went on high alert with this question. He assumed that their deaths were related. *What else does he know?* "I really couldn't say." Lori carefully chose her words and tried to keep her body from reacting. Her hand tightened around the stem of the wine glass.

Nathan noticed. *This has to have something to do with that fake IRS Agent.* He waited a few moments before he made his next statement. "Well, that's three SpringWare employees to die in the past few months."

She saw Nathan deliberately watching for her reaction, but she couldn't stop her body from tensing. He was including Jack in that remark, but she didn't reply. She took a long sip of her wine, stalling. Thinking. *He knows I'm keeping something from him.* Lori could see it in his eyes. She broke eye contact and stared into her glass.

"Another thing happened today that involves you directly, Lori."

She looked up at him, having absolutely no idea what he was about to say. *What else could there possibly be?* She braced herself against what was to come.

"A man came to Delacourt's office today who identified himself as an IRS agent. He said he was investigating a return that you and Jack had filed, and wanted to talk to you. When Joe said you weren't there, he wanted Joe to show him your office. Joe flat out refused. Neither of us believed his story, or that he was with the IRS."

Panic surged through her body once more. Her eyes darted from place to place around the room. She couldn't process this information and felt herself fighting to stay in control. Her thoughts kept jumping from one thing to another until she couldn't understand them anymore, like her mind was speaking a foreign language. *Keep it together, Lori!*

"Lori . . . Lori, do you know who this guy is?" He touched her hand.

Nathan's touch brought her back, even though she couldn't register what he had asked. Dread quickly turned to terror. *They went to where I worked. Boldly. In the middle of the day! They ransacked my house. Oh my God!* She had been disoriented ever since she saw her house in shambles, but now, clarity blasted through her like a bolt of lightning. *What did they take?* Her eyes shot to the CD rack by the stereo. *They're gone!* In an instant, she was off the sofa, headed for the den. Even through the tangled mess, she could see that both Jack's PC and her laptop were gone.

Nathan had followed her. He caught her as she collapsed and carried her back to the sofa. She hadn't fainted, but her eyes were glazed over like she was in shock. He held her close to him for a few minutes, finally feeling her body relax ever so slightly. Then, as abruptly as before, Lori jumped up, startling Nathan so much that he almost cried out.

"What time is it?" she cried. She spun in circles, looking wildly across the room. "Rita!"

"A quarter to ten," Nathan said. He took her by the shoulders and held her still. "Lori, look at me. What's going on? . . . Lori, who is Rita?"

What have we been thinking? She covered her face with her hands, sobbing. *We have no real plan.* They had no resources or powerful connections and no one they could trust to help them. Everything was unfolding so fast that she hadn't realized the depth of the denial they'd been in. The three of them were no match for these killers. It was painfully obvious that they were in great danger and would always be outmatched. They needed help to survive.

I've got no choice. She shifted her gaze from the wreckage of the living room to Nathan. She looked him straight in the eyes with an intensity and determination that she didn't know she possessed. Clarity had definitely dawned.

Lori grabbed both his arms. "Nathan. If I were you, I'd get away from me as fast as possible and pretend this never happened. I won't ever blame you. But if you really want to know what's going on, your life will be in great danger. It's your choice, but you have to make it right away, because I have to go somewhere *now*!"

Lori sprinted to the kitchen for her purse. Nathan was right behind her. She couldn't let this purse out of her sight now. The CD was gone. She swung around to face him, her eyes unwavering and wild with fright. "I have to know now, Nathan!"

"Where do you need to go?" he replied without hesitation.

CHAPTER

43

CARL BAXTER ANSWERED the private secure line in his study. He had been waiting anxiously for this call. "What do you have?"

"We did a thorough search, sir. We have two laptops and all the CDs in the house. The file in question was on a computer that obviously belonged to Mr. Crawford. The date on the file indicated it had not been opened since before his death, so Mrs. Crawford didn't look at it. The other laptop was hers. There were only a few old documents on it, and none of the information was on her computer. We did find a copy of the file on a disk hidden in a music CD. Again, the date stamps are the same as the one on his computer. He could have hidden it there without her knowing about it. Mrs. Crawford does not appear to have knowledge of the software."

"I'll be the judge of that," Baxter said curtly. "Permanently destroy all the evidence." Baxter hung up the phone. There was no way to open a file on a computer without changing the time stamp that showed when the document was last opened or edited.

Three months had gone by. That was more than enough time to come forward if she suspected foul play around Jack's death. Sending someone to her house tonight had been a big risk. He had intentionally avoided doing anything with Lori Crawford that might cause someone to become suspicious about a possible link between Jack, Phillips, and Packwood. Still, he had to confirm if she was a potential threat. All signs indicated that she wasn't, but something still made him feel unsure.

What Baxter didn't know was that his instructions for the search had not been strictly followed. It was supposed to look like a robbery, but the "thieves" hadn't taken jewelry or any other valuables, only the computers and the CDs.

CHAPTER

44

JUST LIKE RITA had predicted, the blue sedan left when Jacob pretended to go to bed. Now he was sitting in his darkened kitchen, waiting. His imagination was filling in all the gaps in his knowledge of what was happening to him. It wasn't pretty, and none of the endings were happy. He heard the back door open a few minutes after ten.

"Jacob?" Rita called out softly.

"Come to your left," Jacob whispered. "I'm in the kitchen." The dim light from the street lamp outside the kitchen window cast enough light to enable Rita to find her way. She joined him at the table.

"I've been outside for half an hour, watching your shadow. He left in a blue sedan a few minutes ago. Lori will be getting us out of here in a couple of hours, so we'll be long gone before he returns in the morning," Rita explained. "Just in case, do you have a room that doesn't have any windows? I want to show you some things, and we need light."

Jacob was about to answer when he heard the back door of

the house open once more. Even in the dark, Jacob could see the fear on Rita's face. He gripped the handle of the butcher knife in his lap even tighter as the adrenaline surged through his body. *Is it him?*

"Rita! Jacob!" whispered Lori.

"To your left," Rita whispered back to her. *What's she doing here? We said midnight.*

Jacob didn't like seeing the surprise on Rita's face. He really tensed when two people came through the doorway. *What the hell is going on?*

"This is Nathan Schilling. He works with me at the paper," Lori explained. Nathan nodded in acknowledgement, and Rita and Jacob returned the gesture. The two women fell into an embrace.

"Oh, Rita," Lori cried. The words rushed from her lips like water over a broken dam. "I was so afraid they might have killed you! They looked for me at the paper today and my house was torn apart tonight. The computers and the CD are gone! Nathan was with me when I came home to find it. And they did kill George. Oh, Rita, I'm so glad you're alive!" Fear punctuated every word that flew from her mouth. The two women sobbed in an unlikely combination of terror and joy.

Jacob watched them both intently, and from the look on Nathan's face, he could tell that he had no idea what was going on either.

"Lori was so focused on making sure we weren't being followed that she hardly said anything other than the directions to get here. I'm in the dark about what's happening, but can I assume that it has something to do with the SpringWare deaths?"

"I think we should start from the beginning. I'm Jacob Browning. I work with Rita at SpringWare." He reached his unsteady hand out to Nathan. "I have a lot of questions too. Let's go down to my office."

Jacob grabbed the flashlight from the table and led them to a door off the kitchen that went down to the basement. Nathan came last, closing the door behind them. It was only then that Jacob flipped on the lights.

They sat in chairs around a folding table. For the next thirty minutes, Jacob and Nathan listened as Lori and Rita took turns relating the chain of events from the time Rita discovered the file on Jack's computer until tonight. Both men were too stunned to speak, much less ask questions.

Jacob and Nathan were in awe of the courage these two women possessed. Jacob never imagined that Rita was so strong. Nathan was seeing a side of Lori Crawford that he had never witnessed before. At the same time, neither could understand how they believed they could deal with this on their own. This was the NSA they were talking about.

Lori reached for her purse while describing the theft at her ransacked home. She took the papers and the disk out of George's envelope and passed them to Jacob and Nathan. "I'm so glad you arrived early tonight, Nathan. I didn't have time to take this out of my purse after getting it from George's locker this afternoon. I'm sure they would have taken it too."

"What's on this disk?" Jacob asked. This was a subject that could soothe him from the fear of the incredible tale he had just heard. Putting it in the CD drive would make him feel even better. Right now, he'd be more than happy to escape to a keyboard and disappear into a video game. Jacob was keenly aware, though, that if he was going to survive, he needed to stay grounded in this reality. *Reality sucks.*

"I haven't looked at it. I assume it's the files that Rita copied from Jack's computer. It has to be where George got the copies of the emails in this envelope. They are what made her suspect that Jack's death wasn't an accident." Lori rubbed her eyes, clearly fatigued from crying.

"Even if that is what's on George's disk, we still don't have the codes to open that second file that was on the disk I took from Jack's credenza. Now that they've taken Jack and Lori's computers, and the disk she copied everything to, we may never know what's in that file. I'm sure it would have given us more information." Rita sounded dejected and exhausted. "Maybe all of this has been for nothing."

Jacob saw Lori's eyes absently wandering around the basement. They stopped at his desk and a smile began to spread across her face. "What are you smiling about, Lori?" Jacob asked.

Lori started fumbling around in the mess where she had dumped the contents of her purse on the table. She smiled even wider as she held up her iPhone and looked at the Mac sitting across the room on Jacob's desk.

"Jack always told me to have a backup plan in case things don't work out the way you hoped they would. Before I trashed Jack's files from my laptop, I not only copied it to the disk they took, but I also copied it to my cloud account! With all the excitement tonight, I totally forgot that I had done that. Seeing Jacob's computer made me remember."

Now Jacob was smiling from ear to ear with her. "Lori, that was good thinking!"

"I also emptied all of the messages, mail, and music off my computer, so no one would suspect that I might have another device or a cloud account that I might transfer or sync data to. I left a few old documents on it, so I hope they will think that it's so old that I don't use it anymore." Even under the incredible stress of the day, she had been able to think clearly enough to formulate a plan B.

"I want to look at what I helped create that has caused all of this," Jacob said as he stood up. "Lori, hand me George's disk so I can take a look at it." Jacob was in his element now, projecting a confidence that they had not yet seen. He asked for Lori's cloud account's username and password and started downloading all the information to his laptop. "The files are huge, so it's going to take a while." Jacob rejoined them at the table while he let his computer work away.

Nathan brought them up to speed on the things he had uncovered, but that he wasn't at liberty to disclose yet. "Tomorrow, there will be an article on SpringWare that I wrote. It was meant to get Mason's attention so he would feel compelled to grant me an interview." He glanced at Rita. He smiled, now aware that she was the gatekeeper for Mason that he had spoken with on the phone. "After hearing all of this, I have no doubt that he will call me."

"What is the article about, Nathan?" Jacob asked.

"It's not so much what the article says, it's what the headline insinuates. 'Two SpringWare Employees Dead!'"

"Oh, you *will* get a call," Rita responded. "Mason will be livid about SpringWare being viewed negatively in any headline.

"I think we should make arrangements to get Rita and Jacob out of town. Now that we know that both of you are on Mason's and Baxter's radar, it's the prudent thing to do. I'm afraid the article might serve to escalate their need to find you even more."

Jacob suggested they devise a Plan A and a Plan B. Just in case.

CHAPTER

45

THIRTY MINUTES LATER, their strategy was complete. Even though it was nearly midnight on the east coast, it was time to put their plan into action.

Lori dropped Rita off at her house after circling the block several times, but there were no signs of the red SUV. Rita called her daughter on her flip phone. She told Natalie she had a change of heart and would be leaving soon to come visit for a week after all. She would be stopping to pick up a friend who would be coming with her, and should arrive just after Christmas. Natalie hadn't seemed very thrilled, but the kids sounded ecstatic in the background. About thirty minutes after she made the call, the dark red SUV showed up down the street. Aware that she had company, she put her roller bag in the trunk of her car and headed west.

The break-in had to be reported, otherwise Baxter and Mason might be suspicious as to why Lori didn't call the police. Lori should have no reason to think that it was anything other than a burglary. She sat in her car and one more time went over exactly what she was supposed to do.

She opened the front door of her house. It was still as shocking as the first time. Once in the living room, she threw the sofa pillows back on the floor and picked up the wine bottle and glasses. Next, the bottle was wiped clean and thrown in the bottom of the trash can. The two glasses were washed and she dried out the sink. She cleaned the wine opener and the knife that Nathan had held. Anything he may have touched was wiped off—the coffee table and the door knobs. Then Lori put her prints on them. The police would check for fingerprints everywhere, and they didn't want Nathan's showing up.

When she was finished, she went back to her car and called Nathan from her burner phone. She told him that everything was done. Then she sat, waiting for Nathan's friend Abernathy to arrive.

———

Jacob made a late-night call to his mother's house in Florida. A night owl like himself, he told her he was getting on the road to come spend Christmas with her. If the weather wasn't too bad, he'd be there by Monday.

He left immediately after the call so that his tail couldn't possibly get back in time to follow him. He was certain the person in the blue sedan would wait awhile to watch for Jacob's car to leave. He intentionally left the blinds open on the side window of the garage, so he'd be able to look in and see that his car was not there. *I bet he'll dread letting his boss know that he had lost him.*

Thanks to a software program that Jacob had created, they would be able to track him by his credit card charges at different places along the route to Florida. Of course, he'd never actually be near any of them. Even still, Jacob made sure that no blue sedan, or car of any color, was following him when he left his house.

CHAPTER

46

ABERNATHY WAS WORKING the late shift when he got the call from Nathan. He turned his cruiser around and radioed in the address he had given him. Nathan was at nearly every crime scene, always looking for a scoop. Now crime had followed Nathan into his own personal life, to the home of a friend.

Another break-in. Luckily, this one didn't catch the perp in the act like that Phillips woman. Abernathy wondered if it could be the same perp. *What's happening to this town anyway?* He'd seen more crime in the last week than he'd seen in the last year. *That's progress for you.*

He was tired from drinking the night before, so he didn't think to ask Nathan why she hadn't called 911. At least Nathan had sense enough to tell her to not go in the house when she saw that the door was open. He pulled the cruiser in behind her car and walked over to the driver's window, shining his flash light in. She rolled it only part of the way down, unsure of him, even with the uniform and the squad car. *Definitely afraid.*

"Stay in your car while I secure the house and make sure no one's in there, ma'am." Lori nodded her assent. She watched as Abernathy pulled the gun from his holster and disappeared inside the front door.

The perp was certainly long gone, but he wisely held his weapon in front of him as he went from room to room. You just never knew. *Damn. This place is a disaster.* He knew right away that this was no burglary or vandalism. Vandals would have made as big a mess, but they would have also destroyed the television, maybe graffitied the walls, cut the cushions on the sofa. A burglar would have taken things that were of value. He wouldn't know for sure until the lady had confirmed what was missing, but the jewelry boxes, televisions, stereo, artwork, and collectibles were still there. Through his experienced eyes, it looked like whoever did this was looking for something. *I wonder if they found what they came for?*

Abernathy came out of the house, and the woman got out of the car to meet him. He led her back to the front door.

"Everything's clear, but I'll warn you, it's a big mess, Miss?"

"Lori Crawford." *Why does that name sound familiar?*

"I need to go to my car for a minute. Don't touch or move anything yet. I need to get a team out here to take pictures and dust for prints. Take a look around to see if anything valuable is missing." Abernathy watched Lori go into the house. There would be no prints. People who did this kind of work rarely left that kind of evidence behind.

He keyed the property address in the squad car's on-board computer. The house was registered to Lori and Jack Crawford. *Jack Crawford.* Her husband was the guy they pulled out of the river. He punched the keys of the computer to bring up the case

199

and read the report. Jack Crawford's car had a tire blowout. It sent him through the guardrail into the river three months ago. He was a computer programmer at SpringWare . . .

Abernathy stopped mid-sentence. *Damn!* He sat there for a few seconds, letting the thoughts connect in his head: Karla Phillips, killed in her home by a burglar. George Packwood's death looked like a suicide, but he was really murdered. Jack Crawford died in a one-car accident. The victims were all employees of SpringWare. Now the Crawford's house is ransacked? *What the hell?*

He recalled Nathan saying once that there were no coincidences in life. Abernathy agreed. In his experience, events like these were always connected. *Serial murders?* Maybe that pain in the ass reporter knew what he was talking about after all.

CHAPTER

47

RITA HAD BEEN driving for a few hours when she pulled her car into the parking lot of a seedy motel along the edge of the highway. She got out of her car and strolled into the office.

Jacob had left thirty minutes ahead of her, so he should already be at the rendezvous point they had identified from a Google webcam search. She thought she spotted a quick flash of light, letting her know he was parked at a partially hidden spot across the street from the motel.

They had counted on Rita's phone being tapped, and on Trench Coat Man following her to this place. The red SUV turned off his headlights and pulled in between two cars at the far end of the motel's parking lot.

Rita told the manager she'd be staying for what was left of the night and leaving later than the normal checkout. He eyed her carefully as she paid with her credit card. There weren't many people checking in that wanted to stay more than a few hours or that didn't pay in cash. He figured he'd treat her to one of his nicer rooms in the back.

She emerged a few minutes later with the key to room 183 and spotted the red SUV hiding in the back of the lot. *Perfect!* She casually glanced up toward Jacob's car as she got her empty roller bag out of the trunk to signal him that she would just be a few minutes. Jacob kept his eyes trained on the red SUV while Rita walked around the side of the motel toward the rooms in the back.

The smell of cigarette smoke and stale beer overwhelmed her when she opened the door. In the bathroom, she briefly turned on the shower, wet the towels a bit, and put a couple of pieces of toilet paper in the toilet. Then, she walked over to the bed and rumpled the sheets and pillows. The filthy comforter made her gag. She placed a half empty can of soda on the nightstand.

Rita parted the curtains slightly and scanned for anyone loitering. Seeing no one, she used her burner phone to call Jacob. He confirmed that the man was still in his car.

This was her opportunity. She took the roller bag and trotted quickly across the back embankment of the hotel property and over to the next block where Jacob was waiting for her. She crawled into the car and melted into the front seat, allowing the adrenaline to subside. They headed back to Cooperville, wondering how long Trench Coat Man would watch her car in the morning before he got suspicious.

CHAPTER

48

AT 8 A.M., the phone in Nathan's cubicle started ringing. Nathan didn't have to be psychic to know who would be on the other end.

"Nathan Schilling." He was completely prepared for how this call was going to go. *Stay calm and in control.*

"Who the hell do you think you are? Making the deaths of two of my employees a sensational story worthy of the National Enquirer? Where's your respect? Do you realize that SpringWare is the economic pillar of this community? Run another headline like that, and you'll be talking to my lawyers!" Mason's tirade seemed to go on forever. The longer he went on, the bigger Nathan's smile grew.

Just the reaction I was expecting.

"Mr. Mason? I understand your concern, sir. I think you might be interested in some new information that has come to my attention since I wrote that article. Are you in your office? I'd like to come over and talk to you about it."

"Yes, I am . . . I mean, no," Mason stammered. "Whatever you have to say to me, you can say on the phone."

"All right," said Nathan. "I have confirmation from the ME's office that George Packwood's death was a murder, not a suicide . . . that certainly changes things, don't you think, Mr. Mason?"

Total silence. *Gotcha!*

"Mr. Mason? Are you there?" Nathan thought for a minute that he might have hung up or passed out.

"Uh, yes. I . . . I have no comment." The call abruptly ended.

And there it is. Nathan knew that a reaction like that meant one thing and one thing only: Mason was guilty.

CHAPTER

49

NATHAN FLEW OUT of the office to his car. SpringWare was only a few blocks away, and he wanted to get there before Mason left the parking garage. He parked on the one-way street across from the garage exit and waited, keeping an eye on his rearview mirror.

About twenty minutes later, Mason's red Tesla exited the garage and turned left onto Main Street. A black 4x4 pulled out shortly afterward and fell in several cars behind Mason. Nathan disciplined himself to do the same. After three cars filled the gap between him and the 4x4, a total of six cars between Nathan and Mason, he felt it was a safe distance at which to follow. Mason's red Tesla was easy to spot, even in the distance.

The phone call had provoked the reaction Nathan wanted. He could visualize Mason immediately calling Carl Baxter to give him the news about George Packwood's autopsy.

This was a major slip up in their master plan. They had evidently not thought to pay off the medical examiner. Perhaps they believed that a small-town ME wouldn't pay much attention to the details of what appeared to be an obvious suicide. Nathan was now hoping that Mason was panicked enough from the pressure he had applied to make another mistake. A mistake that would help them garner more solid evidence toward his involvement in these murders.

Mason turned onto the highway. Nathan was relieved, as the traffic was heavier on this road. He kept his distance, trying to blend into the traffic. Several miles later, Mason's car exited on the only exit to Denton, with the same black 4x4 following. The hair went up on the back of his neck. Was the 4x4 following Mason too? Nathan thought about this possibility. *Perhaps Baxter doesn't trust his partner?*

Nathan held back a little further. For once, he was grateful for Christmas shopping traffic. Denton was the site of the only large mall within a reasonable driving range of Cooperville, and it seemed that many people were headed there. The exit had a steady stream of traffic getting off, providing more cover for Nathan's old Miata.

Nathan knew Denton very well, so he took the upcoming fork in the road that ran parallel to the street Mason had taken. The only logical place Mason could be headed was the mall, so Nathan raced ahead to beat him there. At one point, at a cross street, he glimpsed the sight of the Tesla as he sped ahead.

He veered into a parking spot near the mall entrance where he could see either driveway that Mason might enter. Then, two minutes later, Mason's car turned into the first entrance to the mall parking lot. Nathan spotted the 4x4 pass the entrance Mason had taken and turn in at the next driveway.

Nathan got out of his car and sprinted to the entrance while both cars found parking spaces. He studied the situation from behind a pole just inside the door, watching Mason heading his way. It appeared that the person in the black 4x4 was going to wait in the car. *Hmm. That's odd.* Nathan thought he'd want to see what Mason was doing here. *Or does he already know?*

Nathan kept an eye on Mason while loitering near the lockers in the hallway that led to the restrooms. From there, he could see him walking rapidly toward the food court. *He looks really stressed out.* Nathan smiled at the thought and casually followed at a distance. He stopped, pretending to look in the window of the men's clothing store at the edge of the food court.

The tables were already packed with an early Saturday morning crowd having breakfast before starting their marathon holiday shopping. The smell of cinnamon buns filled the space, and a few parents were already trying to corral the kids running around the play area off to the side of the eating area. Mason almost mowed one of them down as the boy ran between the chairs in front of him. Annoyed, he said something to the apologetic parent and continued to weave his way through the tables to where a man was already sitting on the other side of the food court. Mason took the seat next to him. Both men had their backs to Nathan.

Nathan needed to get to the other side of the food court to get a look at the other man. He strolled the perimeter of the food court toward the McDonald's and bought a soft drink. When he turned around, the other man was in full view. *Pay dirt!*

Nathan scanned the immediate area, but there were no available tables near them. *Oh, to be a fly on the wall to hear that conversation.* Nathan casually reached into his pant pocket and pulled out his cell phone. He sipped on his soft drink and inconspicuously snapped several pictures as he casually passed near their table.

Nathan had to stifle a laugh. *Smile pretty for the camera, boys.* Deep in conversation, neither Mason nor Carl Baxter looked very happy.

CHAPTER

50

BAXTER LOOKED CLOSELY at a visibly stressed Mark Mason. "Mark, pull it together. Tell me what happened."

"You saw the paper?" Baxter nodded. Mason continued, "I admit, I saw that insinuating headline and I lost it. I called the paper and gave that reporter a piece of my mind. He said he had other information and wanted to come over and talk. I told him to tell me on the phone." Mason stopped to catch his breath, struggling to keep his voice down. "Then he drops the bomb. He says the ME's report shows Packwood was murdered! Carl, what are we going to do? You know they'll start looking closer at Karla's death too. How am I going to explain this? I've already had a message from my CEO that I've yet to return."

"Mark, calm down. It's unfortunate that we didn't handle the ME's office. But actually, it will bolster the rest of the plan that's already in place. I've had my men place some incriminating evidence on George's home computer and in Karla's apartment. We knew the cops would go back and take a harder look when they put two and two together. When they find everything we've planted, Karla and George will be exposed as drug dealers. We've got a snitch ready to confess to killing them both. He's agreed to do some time, and when things have quieted down, he'll escape to the islands a very rich man. At least that's what he thinks the plan is."

Mason shuddered. Baxter was ruthless. "I don't know, Carl. George and Karla led good lives and worked for Spring-Ware a long time. People who know them won't buy into that story."

"There is always a side of us we never let others see. People thrive on gossip. They love to think that other people's lives weren't so rosy after all. We're making it convincing, Mark. Besides, the only people that have to believe it are the police. Once they arrest our guy, he'll confess, and this is all over. The news cycle will run its course and start to focus elsewhere. Trust me. This isn't our first rodeo." Baxter paused, watching Mason closely.

"We've been following Browning and Johnson and listening to their phone recordings. Nothing showed up on the computers we took from Crawford's house, so she seems to be in the clear. We'll continue to monitor things through the holidays before making any other decisions." Baxter conveniently left out a lot of things he didn't think Mason needed to know yet.

Mason did not look appeased. He looked like a man on the edge.

Baxter continued anyway. "I finally received the security clearances on the two men that will handle the software. Now we can see what's on that last file and understand how much

Jack really knew. They'll be hacking into it this afternoon, and I'll let you know what they find. Hopefully, it won't take long. Stay calm. It's all under control."

He didn't wait for Mason to respond because he didn't really care what Mark thought. Baxter got up and strode away.

Mason sat at the table for a long time. The police would be questioning him and other employees at SpringWare. He would call that reporter, Schilling, back and apologize for being emotional on the phone. He cares about every employee who works for him, and this news has been very upsetting to him. He'll stay calm and just keep professing his own astonishment at these events. If he, or the police, don't buy into it, he'll refer them to the company lawyers.

Baxter was right. After all, the NSA was handling this. They were the ultimate professionals. *What could possibly go wrong?*

CHAPTER

51

NATHAN HAD SUGGESTED that his house could be a temporary place for them to stay. He had plenty of space for them, and he hoped they would be able to get a well-deserved night's rest. They had to stay sharp, so they didn't make mistakes like the ones Baxter and Mason had made with George.

He entered his home office quietly to upload the pictures from his phone onto his computer. It was clear that Baxter was involved in this to some extent. Nathan guessed that he was the only one, or maybe one of just a few, that would even know about this project. He was even more certain that Baxter was the one who had coordinated the murders. After his talk with Mason this morning, he realized that there was no way Mason had orchestrated any of this. *Develop the software, yeah. But not the murders.* Mark Mason did not have the stomach for that kind of work. With all that Baxter had done in his career, it would be nothing for him. They must keep the pressure on Mason if they wanted to get to Baxter.

He also needed more questions answered and solid evidence before he let Delacourt in on what he and Lori knew. He wasn't about to endanger more of his colleagues. Lori was right when she said he'd be in danger.

Nathan's involvement had its obvious advantages. He could hide the group, gather information, and move about more freely in the circles he needed to be in. However, because he had written that article and talked to Mason, it put him directly in their crosshairs. Because Lori worked with him, it could also cause them to be suspicious of both of them. He must stay very alert to anything unusual.

A few minutes later, Rita and Jacob walked into the room. Jacob had been busy in the basement on his laptop, looking through the files on George's disk.

"Did you guys get any sleep?" Nathan asked.

"A few hours. SUV Man should be figuring things out soon," said Rita. "Where's Lori?"

"She insisted on spending the night at her house. I don't know how she could stay there. I mean, the entire house was trashed. She was meeting with Abernathy at the police station early this morning. I expect her any time now." As if on cue, they could hear Lori following their voices back to the den.

"How'd it go, Lori?" Nathan could see by looking at her that she had gotten little sleep. He would insist on it tonight. "Did you park in my garage?"

"Yeah. My car is now officially tucked away with Jacob's. Abernathy asked a lot of questions," she said. "He also asked if I thought this might have anything to do with Jack's position at SpringWare." The room went quiet.

"Hmm. Sounds like he's suspicious," Jacob said.

"That's not a surprise. I mean, three deaths at the same company? They'll investigate, but they'll never be able to find the motive. They won't be able to discover what we have. The NSA will cover their tracks, just like they did with Jack, and this will just become two more unsolved cases for them," said Rita.

"Unless we have them help us," Nathan said. The room went silent again. Nathan looked at each of them. "Look, Abernathy is a good guy. We can trust him. Let's see where he goes with this on his own, but let's keep our options open about telling him more." Slow nods from the rest of the group indicated they were cautious, but amenable to Nathan's idea. They were all wondering if they could really do this on their own. There may come a time when they would need all the help they can get.

Nathan meant what he said about Abernathy. He had written the story about the convenience store robbery. It was a justified shooting, but Abernathy had never gotten over it. Nathan had known many cops in his career, some good and some not so much. His instincts told him that even with all the payoffs and the drinking, somewhere deep inside Abernathy slept the good cop that he had been before the shooting happened.

"I'm going to get back to work on this disk," Jacob said, opening his laptop. "There's a damaged file on it, and I don't think Jack would have put it on there if it wasn't important. Hopefully, I can repair it and get a look at what's in it."

"I hope you can, Jacob." Nathan turned to Lori and Rita. "Let's go over the evidence to see what's missing and how we can tie together what we already have."

Lori nodded and began spreading out the items from the brown envelope on the table as she talked about them. "Okay . . . we've got my cloud account with Jack's files that Jacob is working on. We have the copies of the emails between Mason and Jack. There are these numbers in some sort of series. And Jack's interpretation of the underlying program Mason and Baxter created. We still don't know if there's anything different on George's disk."

"I'll get to that next," interjected Jacob.

"Let me play devil's advocate here." Nathan began to summarize. "Mason's emails only dispute what Jack said was a problem with the program. At the time Jack was writing them, I'm not sure he knew what the scope of the problem was. At best, Mason's responses sound dismissive, not incriminating. Jack's summary of what he finally found is only an idea of what he thought could be possible. We also have no proof that this program really exists. The fact that Jack names Mason and the NSA really gets us nowhere without some proof that links them directly to it. I'm certain the software that Mason would produce would be the original version, the one Jack worked on before they altered it."

Rita looked dismayed, but Lori picked up where Nathan left off. "We also have George's planner. It's not much, but with everything else, it could help show a connection between Jack, Baxter, and SpringWare."

Rita's forehead furrowed as she spoke. "Yes, but it's really not a very strong connection. It was just Baxter's name and the letter 'k.' Outside of the context of what we know, it could mean anything. We need that phone log from Mason's office. That notation is in Mason's handwriting and would be critical physical evidence. But it's impossible now for Jacob or me to get into Mason's office. We're supposed to be out of town. Our security passes for the elevator would register that we were there."

"I can get in," Nathan volunteered. "Look, Mason knows I want to talk to him. I'll give him a good enough reason that he'll have to see me. If I can get into his office for a meeting, I can get the phone log book."

All eyes focused on Nathan. Objections were on everyone's lips, but none were spoken. They needed all the evidence they could gather, even if it meant standing in front of a murderer to get it.

CHAPTER

52

ABERNATHY SAT ON the metal chair in the interrogation room. He read through the post mortem results for Jack Crawford. Clearly a drowning. But that was only the cause of death, not the cause of the accident.

One-car accidents were sometimes puzzling but always interesting to him. Now, with the current events at SpringWare, he felt it prudent to look a little harder at this old case. Hindsight was always helpful. The Cooperville police department had not investigated the crash, so he didn't have firsthand knowledge of the accident. He would have to rely on the reports on file.

Abernathy closely examined the pictures taken at the scene. The report stated that Crawford's tire blew, but he couldn't see anything in the pictures that would have caused that to happen. There was no road debris of any kind. In fact, there were no skid marks that indicated braking until well into the spin of the car. He found this odd too. *Why didn't he brake right away?* Crawford had crossed three lanes of traffic before he had reacted.

He made another notation on his notepad to ask if there had been an inspection done on the tire itself. Was there a defect in the tread? It was standard protocol to thoroughly inspect the car for malfunctions when someone died, especially when only one car was involved. *Pretty big red flags here.* Even a beat cop could see problems in this report.

Abernathy didn't have much cause to interact with the State Highway Patrol, but he thought there was no time like the present to have a conversation with Parker Barnes, the investigating officer on the scene. After several transfers, they located Barnes on duty in his patrol car. Abernathy identified himself and the case he was referencing for the call.

"I have two homicide cases I'm investigating and am curious if this accident might be related. All the vics work at the same company . . . and three deaths in three months is a little unusual." He could hear Barnes tapping on his onboard computer. Abernathy figured he was bringing up the file to jog his memory. He didn't want Barnes to get defensive, so he asked him if he remembered anything unusual about the accident.

"No, the guy's tire blew out. His car spun across three lanes of traffic, hit a pole, and went over the guardrail into the river. ME said he drowned." He sounded vaguely aggravated, and Abernathy found that interesting. "Just like the report says." *Hmm. Sarcasm too.*

"Any idea why the tire blew out?"

"Probably some road debris. Nail or something."

"I didn't notice anything like that in the pictures or noted in your report. Did you have the tires checked for defects?" Silence followed Abernathy's question.

"You accusing me of not doin' my job?" The voice had changed from annoyance to anger. In Abernathy's mind, he had his answer. Standard procedure had been overlooked on purpose. He didn't know why, but he'd bet on it with a round for the house.

"Not sayin' that at all. Just hoping, one cop to another, you'd have information that might help me with my two cases." Abernathy waited for the response. There was typically a courtesy extended across law enforcement lines, at least at this level. Even if it was off the record.

"I got nothin' other than what the report says." The line went dead.

Well, that certainly makes things a lot more interesting.

CHAPTER

53

MARK MASON SWIVELED from side to side in his leather chair, recounting everything that had happened the past week. *Baxter is clearly running the show now.* There was no more strategizing or consulting with him. Mason was just along for the ride.

With each hour that passed, the dread inside of him grew stronger. What was it that Baxter said at the mall? *We'll continue to monitor things through the holidays before making any other decisions.* He glanced down at the calendar on his desk. It wouldn't be long before the holidays were here and gone. Mason couldn't help but wonder if those decisions might include him.

Carl was right about one thing, though. Blowing up at Schilling had been a big mistake. He needed to be calm and stay the course, if for no other reason than self-preservation. And he certainly didn't want to give Baxter any more reasons for making "decisions" about him. He would just have to trust that Baxter had all the bases covered, as far as Karla and George were concerned.

Mason knew that he would eventually have to talk to Nathan Schilling, but he hadn't expected another call from him so quickly. Nathan phoned earlier to tell him that an exposé on SpringWare was going to run in the paper on Tuesday. He offered Mason the opportunity to give his perspective of the events from SpringWare, or he would be happy to print his own point of view of the events involving the SpringWare employees. *What did Schilling think I would say? Sure, print whatever you want?*

Mason agreed to meeting with the reporter. He jotted down a few of the points he wanted to make, and thought about the potential questions Schilling might ask. Being well-prepared for whatever may come up in conversation would keep his emotions in check. Mason leaned back in his chair, rehearsing his typical PR speech on all that is good about SpringWare. He felt confident that he'd send the reporter out with his notepad tucked between his legs, just like a scolded dog does with his tail.

The knock on the door startled him. He chided himself that while he had left word with security to send the reporter up when he arrived, he forgot to tell them to call and let him know he was on his way up.

"Come in and have a seat," Mason said, gesturing to a chair. Schilling held nothing but a notepad and pencil. Security would not let him bring up anything else.

"Thanks for seeing me on such short notice," Nathan said while taking off his coat.

"I'd like to apologize for my outburst when I last talked to you. It's just that Karla and George were excellent employees, and of course, SpringWare is also very important to me. I took those headlines personally and got a little emotional. It's also company policy to not comment to reporters until the facts have been sorted out, so I'd like you to know that this is really just a courtesy visit today."

"I understand. So do you think things are sorted out?" Nathan paused to let that question hang in the air. Of course, the question went unanswered. "It's refreshing to hear that someone in your position, at such a large company, would care so much about two of his employees." Nathan felt stupid making this ridiculous comment, but Mason took him to be sincere. He looked down at his notepad for a minute, then got down to reporter business. "What positions did George and Karla hold at SpringWare?"

"George was a senior software designer, who had worked here for about fifteen years. Karla was George's assistant for the last six months."

"Oh, so she had just started working here?"

"No, she had worked for Ja—uh, she'd worked here for three years." Mason hoped that his slip of the tongue went over Schilling's head. Nathan pretended not to notice. He wasn't about to let Mason know that he suspected anything about Jack's death.

"Is there any information about SpringWare they might have had knowledge of that could have led to their deaths?" Nathan went for the jugular. *Keep him off guard.*

"Of course not!" Mason fumed. He took a breath to calm down. His next words were very measured. "We create gaming software. It's a reasonably innocuous and uneventful job." He shifted the focus. "You told me that George was murdered. If what you say is true, which of course, I have not heard about from any law enforcement agency, well, I would be as astonished at that as anyone."

"I'd like to ask you a few questions about SpringWare," Nathan asked as the phone began to ring. *Ah, Perfect timing.*

At first, Mason ignored it, then he remembered that Rita was not here to get it. "Sorry for the interruption," he said, picking up the handset.

"Hello? Yes, this is Mark Mason. Officer who? Hold on one moment, please." Mason put the caller on hold. "I'm sorry," he said to Nathan. "I need to step out for a minute." He walked into Rita's outer office, shutting the door behind him.

The door opened a minute later. "I need to end this interview. I have important business to take care of, and I didn't realize how late it was. Thank you for coming in." Mason was polite, but obviously rattled.

"Well, uh . . . okay," Nathan responded, looking puzzled as he put his coat on. "I'm sorry we weren't able to talk about SpringWare. I'll just fill in my own blanks."

An ashen Mason showed him to the door and closed it firmly behind him.

The weekend guard on duty was reading a book when Nathan entered the security area of the lobby. He seemed annoyed at being interrupted. Nathan put his keys, pencil, and notepad on the tray. *Rita was right.* He let Nathan walk right through the metal detector with his coat on. He retrieved his belongings from the dish and headed out to the car, where Lori was waiting.

"A convincing performance at the perfect moment, Officer Georgia Karlton! I wonder if he'll recognize the irony in the name you chose. He looked like he'd seen a ghost when he came back in the office." Nathan laughed as he buckled up in the car.

"Did you get the phone log book from Rita's desk?"

"That was the easy part. His door was closed when I got there, so I just helped myself before I even knocked. Ah, but this . . ." He paused while he reached inside his coat. "This is a bonus prize!" Nathan laid the planner on the seat between them. "It was on his desk under some papers. I took it when he left the room to talk to you. I don't know what you said to him, but it sure shook him up."

"Oh, I just told him that someone from the station would be coming by to ask about Packwood's death and the *murder* of Karla Phillips."

CHAPTER

54

MASON HAD BARELY shut the door behind Schilling when his cell phone rang. He looked at the number and was tempted not to answer. *Probably not a good idea.*

Baxter's voice pierced his eardrums. "We decoded that file on the disk. It was Jack's rundown of the details of our program."

He gets right to it, doesn't he? Mason quietly took a breath before he proceeded.

"It doesn't matter. There's no proof that the software even exists. You have the only copy of the program, Carl." Mason responded as calmly as he could. *Which, of course, isn't true.* Just in case he faced unforeseen trouble down the road, Mason had kept his own copy for added protection.

"They also found a damaged file on the CD we recovered from the Crawford house. My men are trying to repair it now to see what it is. Jack had theories about the program, Mark. *Our* program. Theories that sound pretty good." Baxter was quiet, letting that comment sit for a few seconds.

Damn! Mason's mind was racing, trying to find an explanation.

"How the hell do you think he knew that?" Baxter let the silence fill the air once again, this time for what seemed to Mason to be an eternity. "We really don't know if I have the only copy now, do we?"

"What are you going to do?" Mason's voice wavered ever so slightly, but his stomach was doing cartwheels. More silence.

Now Baxter knew that somehow Jack must have had access to the altered program. *I had hoped to take that secret to my grave.* Baxter didn't say so, but Mason knew Carl was thinking he was to blame.

"I'm going to extend the surveillance on Johnson, Browning, and Crawford until I'm totally satisfied that they know nothing. I haven't ruled out taking other actions as well. The security of this project takes precedence over everything else." The line went dead.

The words "other actions" hung heavy in the air. Mason sat with his head in his hands. *Damn it!* He pounded his fist so hard on the desk that it shook.

The trust he had worked so hard to build was suddenly on very shaky ground, if not gone entirely. He just needed to hang in there for a little while longer.

Of course, he couldn't possibly know that Carl was already taking further steps to keep the project secure: at that very moment, two men were searching his house and computer. This time, unlike the Crawford job, there would be no clues left to tip Mason off that they were there.

CHAPTER

55

IN SPITE OF everything, the events of the day lifted their spirits. Nathan's visit with Mason was a little victory, but they'd take it. They ate the pizzas Lori and Nathan had brought with them with renewed enthusiasm.

Officer Georgia Karlton had thoughtfully made another call from the phone booth, this one to the local pizzeria. She was praised repeatedly for her acting and culinary talents. Lori took a bow.

Only Jacob was quiet, still at his computer. Lori took notice. "Jacob, what's wrong?"

"I've been working on this damaged file all morning, and I can't seem to fix it." His voice dripped with disappointment. He was well aware that they needed more tangible proof, and he was hoping he'd find it in those files.

"Hey," Nathan said. "We had a successful day today. Take a break and enjoy it. Besides, I've got a special dessert that you are all going to love!"

"I hope it's something chocolate!" Rita chimed in.

"Nope. Even better," Nathan teased. He dropped his half-eaten slice of pizza on the paper plate and sauntered over to his desk. He opened a drawer and pulled out a large piece of paper. With great drama, he hummed a burlesque refrain in preparation to unveil his surprise.

"How photogenic do you think these two guys are?" He laughed, turning the picture around for all of them to see.

"Oh my God!" they cried out in unison. Jacob ran over and picked Nathan up off the floor in a big bear hug. Lori and Rita followed with hugs and kisses.

"That ties them together!" Rita exclaimed. "Maybe not exactly in an indisputable way for our purposes, but they cannot deny that they know each other."

"Yeah, and they don't look very happy, do they?" Lori added. This was a major coup.

It was Nathan's first opportunity to recount his trip to the mall. "And here's another thing. I think there was a black 4x4 following him. It makes me think that . . ."

"Baxter doesn't trust Mason," Lori said, finishing his sentence. Nathan laughed, nodding his head.

"I bet Baxter doesn't trust anyone. He's got too much at stake," said Jacob. "And that makes him even more dangerous."

"Yeah, I agree. Baxter is the predictable one in this scenario. He's got the resources to do whatever he sees as necessary. I see Mason as a loaded gun with a faulty trigger. They both have a lot to lose, making them both serious adversaries." Nathan moved on to recount his recent interview and how Mason had been really shaken after Lori's call.

"We've certainly got him feeling pressured," Rita noted. "Maybe it'll cause him to make a mistake in our favor."

"I'm going back to George's disk right away," Jacob said with renewed enthusiasm. "I want to see if I can figure out what those pages of numbers are, and I'm not going to give up on that corrupted file."

"Good idea," said Rita. "We need to examine this evidence again and see where the holes are. We also need to protect this stuff. Do you have a safe place to hide these documents, Nathan?"

"Sure. Joe has a safe in his office that only he has access to. I'll tell him I'm working on something that needs to be kept in there. Joe would go to jail before revealing anything having to do with the confidentiality of our sources. I'll also send copies to Alex, my reporter friend in Atlanta and ask him to store it safely." Nathan started making duplicates of all their printed information and gave Jacob a couple of blank CDs so he could make more copies.

"Rita and I will put some fresh eyes on George and Mason's planners to see if we can find anything else," said Lori.

The room went quiet. Everyone was absorbed in their own tasks. But the one question no one wanted to raise hung heavy in the air. *Who are we going to take this to that will believe us?*

CHAPTER

56

JACOB WAS THE first to break the silence. "I knew it! These are definitely bank account and routing numbers. They look different because they are overseas accounts. I'm betting Mason got a nice little bonus on this NSA deal."

"I hadn't thought much about how money was exchanged before," said Lori. "The NSA must have paid for the program. But how did they do that and not let anyone at SpringWare know who the client was?"

"Mason's probably handling all of that himself. The company accountants would ask too many questions," Rita replied. "The only person Mason reports to is the CEO, and he's pretty hands off. Mr. Caplan has had a good ride since he hired Mason, so I doubt he'd question anything Mason did. It wouldn't be hard to get the programs created on company time and then pocket the money for himself."

"Yeah, and I'm sure Baxter paid him through layers of shell companies set up to look like real businesses. That would make it almost impossible to track the original source of the money. Baxter would make sure that the NSA stayed hidden well behind the scenes. Even if they did run the money through SpringWare, it would appear as if they were just doing business with another new client. It keeps the project legitimate, and no one has to ask questions, even the accountants at SpringWare." Nathan rubbed his chin, deep in thought again.

"I think Rita's right. It would mean less risk to Mason to *not* run the money through SpringWare. I mean, the money must be Mason's motivation. If he ran it through the company, it would be harder for him to get it out." Lori bit into another slice of pizza, already deep into another thought.

"True. So . . . unless Mason has the skill of creating complex layers of shell companies, which I'm betting he doesn't, it should make it easier to connect the money to him. We've got to find out more about those routing numbers." Nathan sat back, looking quite satisfied with himself.

"Yeah. No pressure, guys. Working on it," Jacob laughed, turning his attention to his keyboard once more.

"That brings up something else I've been thinking about. Why didn't the NSA create this program themselves? They certainly have the talent that could do it," Lori said.

Jacob paused his work. "Lori, Jack thought this software program has capabilities that have never been used before. If it is capable of what he thinks it can do, it would be a huge privacy issue. I would imagine that even some NSA employees would have a difficult time with the ethics of this and wouldn't stay quiet about it." Lori nodded in agreement. This pertained directly to the information she had been researching for Joe.

"I'm not sure I fully understand what those capabilities are. Can you explain it?" Rita then added, "In a way that I can understand it." She laughed, and the others joined in. Jacob returned her self-deprecating statement with a warm smile.

"Well, let me explain it as simply as I can. When you log into a website, say Amazon, their site leaves what is called a 'cookie' on your computer. It's a way for Amazon to remember your computer, track the items you look at, as well as the items you buy. The next time you log in, their server recognizes your computer and still has all of this data about what you did the last time you were there." He paused to be sure this was making sense. He saw three heads nodding.

"Retail companies track the spending patterns of their customers so they know what products to carry and how much inventory they might need. Tracking demographics and using your search history is valuable information for any company, especially a company like Amazon. In gathering this information about their consumers, they use this data to make suggestions to you to sell even more products, and they sell the information they gather to other advertisers. It's big money from every angle."

"That's why after looking at something on a website, I see ads for it later in other programs or websites that I'm on," Lori added.

"Exactly! But what *this* program can do is much more than that." Jacob went on to explain. "If Jack is correct in his theory, this program has a worm, kind of like a destructive cookie, that not only infiltrates the user's computer hard drive, but that can self-replicate and plant another worm in their email system. Those worms then infiltrate the emails and hard drives of all the computers it communicates with, searching for specific information to send back to the NSA that they have asked it to find."

"I've been researching this for Joe so he can run some educational pieces on it in the paper. The president had authorized the NSA to monitor the communications of people with suspected terrorist ties, even American citizens. People went crazy over the idea of the government monitoring its own citizens," Lori commented.

"That has been primarily aimed at phones and social media. This program takes that to a much higher level because it actually invades a person's physical property and presumes that *anyone* is a potential terrorist. It indiscriminately infiltrates any computer it comes in contact with." Jacob paused to let that percolate before continuing.

"Think about how many different people you might email. Then how many people *they* might email, guilty or innocent of anything. It's just a matter of time before the NSA is able to monitor just about everyone in the world who uses email on any device. And it could search for anything they wanted it to look for." Jacob could almost see the lightbulbs in their heads going off around the room as they absorbed the enormity of what this program could do.

"Wow. This is definitely no ordinary terrorist tracking system. If there were no way to discriminate who actually had potential terrorist ties and who were average citizens, I imagine that even high-level NSA employees would have a problem with this kind of invasion of privacy," Nathan commented. "But I'd also guess that very few people besides Baxter will ever know about this program."

"Baxter has much at stake. It's not a mystery to me why he is killing people he thinks might be in a position to let this information become public." Lori absently tapped her fingers on the table, feeling the weight of her words.

"And even though it was risky to take it out of the agency, it made it easier in some ways. Mason split the work up so that no one knew what they were actually working on," Rita observed.

"Right," Jacob agreed. "I had no idea how my part of the project fit in to the whole. I never would have been the wiser had you not come to me with this. Which still leaves the question about how Jack found out about it."

Nathan shifted in his chair. "You know, the government has used this strategy before. There's this bunker in West Virginia that's not too far from here. It was built in the Cold War days as a government safe haven in case of a nuclear attack. It's an amazing structure built under the Greenbrier Hotel."

"Really, under a hotel open to the public? And they kept it quiet?" Rita sounded flabbergasted.

"Yeah. They split up the companies used for the construction of the bunker into doing many different small sections of it. No one person on the job had knowledge of the overall project they were building, except for a handful of undercover government employees. It was a virtual fortress, capable of housing the president and all of Congress for months if there was a nuclear war. It was kept a secret for many, many years. A reporter is the one who finally made it public." Nathan sounded a little proud of that.

"That's amazing. Yeah, here it is. Wow!" Jacob had already searched for it on the internet as Nathan was talking about it.

"If they could keep this project a secret for thirty years, running a software program like this would only need to be monitored by a couple of people. If they reported only to Baxter, it's possible that no one would ever discover its existence."

"I wonder how George found out? Do you think Jack told him?" Lori said.

"Possibly," Rita said. "If Jack felt strongly that this software was dangerous, maybe he thought he needed help and brought George into it. How else would George have gotten a copy of Jack's file?"

"George was a senior executive in the design department. He would have had the skills and the access Jack needed to help him deal with this. Who knows what they had in mind to stop the NSA from using the program?" Jacob said.

"I'm not sure about that. It's possible that Mason had to bring George in on it. Lori heard Mason tell Baxter that George was the one to contact if there were issues with the software." Lori nodded at Rita's comment.

"Or maybe Mason brought George in, not knowing that Jack had already told him about it. Either way, I suppose it doesn't matter. With both of them gone, we'll probably never know." Lori's voice conveyed the deep sadness she felt.

"Jacob, are you sure those numbers are bank accounts?" Rita asked, suddenly shifting the conversation. A few thoughts had occurred to her during the course of the conversation.

"Yeah. One set is a normal routing number, so I can identify the bank. If I knew who the account belonged to or had an account number, I could hack into it. The other numbers are definitely overseas accounts. I'm not sure I can get into those because of the higher security level."

"I would think they belong to Mason. These numbers are important pieces of evidence for us." Rita's index finger drummed against her temple. "I've been gathering a file of personal and business information on Mason for the last two months. There's information in there that can help us. With everything that went on yesterday, I forgot to bring it with me. I'm going to go home and get it."

"Rita, I don't think that's a good idea," Lori said. Jacob and Nathan strongly agreed, but even after a good twenty minutes of trying to persuade her, Rita wasn't having any of it.

"Don't worry. It's dark out. I know the back alleys to take, so I won't be seen. Besides, everyone thinks I'm on my way to California, remember? I'll be back in an hour." Before any more objections could be made, Rita had her coat on and was out the back door.

CHAPTER

57

HE'D HAD LITTLE sleep over the past thirty-six hours when the phone woke him up. Baxter picked it up and was ready to give whoever was calling a piece of his mind.

"Sir, I'm sorry to disturb you at this hour, but you said to call if we discovered something important. I have the information you requested on the results of the search of Mark Mason's home. We found a disk that contained a copy of the software program. What are your orders, sir?"

"Damn!" Baxter mumbled. He was wide awake now. "Destroy it. Nothing else at this time." He hung up the phone, knowing that he had slept all he would tonight. *I knew I shouldn't have trusted him. Son of a bitch!*

Baxter had to admit that he would have kept a copy of the program if the tables were turned. But he thought he'd made himself abundantly clear about the security issues in this case. *Is Mason a complete moron?* He was getting paid too well to pull this crap.

He got up from the sofa in his home office, where he'd

finally dozed off, and poured a drink. *Might as well.* He poured some more into the glass.

He lowered his body into the chair, glaring at the phone. It had become a source of never-ending frustration. Just a few hours ago, the tail he had put on Rita Johnson called to tell him that he had lost her. Recalling the conversation, he was surprised he hadn't melted the landline with his anger. *Isn't anyone competent anymore? It's a simple damn job. Get in a car and follow someone.*

Baxter knew from the wiretap on Johnson's phone that she was headed to California to see her daughter and was bringing someone with her. It was the holidays, so that wasn't unusual.

Red SUV man had followed her to a cheap hotel, where he watched her go to her room. He went to the office to get a room for the night, rather than stay in the freezing car. He requested a room with a full view of her motel door. He took care to let the air out of one of her tires, so she wouldn't be sneaking off without having to call a tow truck. *One smart thing, at least.*

Later the next morning, he saw a maid enter the room with her pass key, and he knew there was a problem. He flashed his phony badge to the maid and saw that the room was empty. It appeared that she had slept and showered there. He couldn't figure out how she had managed to slip out without him seeing her. Her car was still in the parking lot, so she must have left with someone else.

Red SUV man didn't know if she was trying to give him the slip, or if she had left in the morning with her friend at the very moment when he had been in the bathroom. *Yeah, probably more like you fell asleep.*

He ordered the man to find her and do what was necessary to eliminate any further risk. He was certain that his tone had conveyed what he meant by that—and that the Red SUV man knew he would face the same fate if he failed.

Baxter was furious as he slammed down the last drop of liquor in his glass. He felt it burning the ulcer being formed in his empty stomach. *Can't anyone just do their damn job?*

CHAPTER

58

DAMN, IT'S COLD!

The man pulled up the hood of his parka to provide some warmth between his head and the icy car window. He fidgeted in the car, pushing the front seat back as far as he could to straighten his stiff legs. He laid his head back against the window, knowing he didn't dare fall asleep like he had at the motel.

The identity of the man that hired him was unknown, but there was one thing he did know: the man was someone powerful and very angry. His reputation was on the line. This old woman had given him the slip twice, and he'd *never* lost a target before. It was pure luck that he'd found her the first time when she was shopping, so he didn't have to call it in.

Now his job description had changed—from surveillance to murder. At least that's how he interpreted the man's instructions. It wasn't a new position for him to be in. He was glad for it too. The bitch had made him look incompetent.

She reminded him of his mother. Another bitch he was glad to have taken care of.

She was supposed to be heading to California. There was no way he was going to catch up with her at this point. But he did have to find her if he wanted to survive this job. Having nothing to point him in any particular direction, the man decided the best place to start looking for clues would be at her house. He had been waiting in the frigid car for hours while the snow fell steadily outside. No one had come or gone.

His instincts told him that her trip had been a ruse, simply a distraction. Had she realized she was being followed? He'd been careful. From everything he was told about her, she was just a simple assistant. It wasn't like she was a super spy or something. He didn't know who she was or what she might have done, but he would find her again. He *would* finish this job.

Having watched the house long enough, he was sure it was empty. Bracing himself for the cold, he pulled on his ski mask hat, then started up the snow covered walk. Making his way around the corner of the house to break in a back door, he slipped on a hidden patch of ice. *Damn it!* As he bent down to retrieve his flashlight, he saw fresh footprints ahead in the snow. They were coming from the other side of the yard by the alley, leading to the back door.

Staying low to the ground, he crept silently back to his vehicle. With the car out of gear, he pushed it silently around the corner until he had a clear view of the backyard. He put it in park behind a large hedge of shrubs, where she wouldn't notice him, but he could still see her.

His decision to come back here had been a good one after all. He would wait for as long as he needed to. Patience was the one and only virtue he possessed. There were no footprints leading back in the direction they had come from, so she must still be in the house. *You won't outsmart me again, bitch.*

Ten minutes later, he saw a faint shadow moving quickly across the backyard toward the alley. *There you are.* Starting the car, he drove to the opening of the alley on the next block, where he paused and looked to his right. *Yes!* She was continuing to run down the dark alley. He had to make a quick decision and commit to the direction he thought she would continue on. If he was wrong, he'd lose her again. He bet she'd take advantage of the darkness of the alley for as long as she could. As he didn't know where she was going, he just hoped she didn't turn off before he had his chance.

He sped forward another three blocks on a parallel street to get ahead of her and turned the corner. Lights off, he crept forward, nearly to the alley, using the building on his right as a shield. He rolled down both front windows and waited, hoping his instincts were right.

The hum of the engine purred softly. He was glad to have stolen a foreign car. They idled much quieter than the American models. He could feel his excitement building. Shifting slightly in his seat, he adjusted the tightness of the pants between his legs.

The sound of running footsteps crunching in the snow was only audible if you were listening for it. If you knew they were coming.

He slipped the car out of park and poised his right foot over the accelerator, his left foot still on the brake.

Closer.

Patience.

He anticipated her stride and her speed. The crunching of the snow beneath her feet grew louder, like a climax.

He jammed the gas pedal to the floor, his tires getting enough traction to lurch the car forward into her unsuspecting body, but not too far to hit the building behind her. The body flew through the air before thudding to the ground twenty feet in front of him.

He waited. Low beams on now. No movement.

The white snow turned crimson around her gray hair in the glow from the headlights.

He clicked off his headlamps and turned the corner, accelerating quickly again. *Take that bitch! No one makes a fool out of me and lives to talk about it.* Fully erect, he flipped open his cell phone to call in the news.

CHAPTER

59

IT WAS TOO early in the morning to be out of bed, especially because he had only been in it for two hours. The incessant ringing of the T-Mobile jingle was more than Abernathy's raging headache could bear. He groped in the pocket of his pants, which were still on after he passed out. The chief's deep voice rang in his ears.

The chief knew it was his day off, but he was shorthanded. There'd been a hit and run, and he needed a veteran cop on the scene. Now.

You've got to be joking.

Abernathy groaned as he stood up. The room spun around him. The wave of nausea sent him half running, half stumbling to the bathroom. He fell to his knees as he reached the toilet just in time.

Ten minutes later, with nothing left in his stomach, he splashed some water on his face and put on a clean uniform. He picked up the flask of vodka, took a big swig, then followed it with a Listerine chaser. There was no time to sober up. The cold helped clear the fog in his head as he made for his patrol car.

The corner of Ward and Cleveland wasn't far from his house. Flashing lights from the ambulance and squad car lit up the night sky, making it easy to spot his destination. He popped a few Altoids before approaching the rookie cop already at the scene.

"Hit and run, sir. Residents heard the tires squealing and came out to investigate. They found her lying here." Rodgers was the name on his shiny new badge.

Abernathy replied with something resembling a grunt. He pushed past Rodgers and surveyed the scene. The snow was covered in footprints. The residents had destroyed any chance of potential evidence near the body. He looked around the intersection. Tracks from the ambulance and squad car had obliterated any other tire marks in the snow. Both had arrived from two different directions.

"Tell me exactly what you heard," Abernathy asked a man standing near the building, shivering in his robe and overcoat.

"I . . . I was watching the late show, and I heard this loud noise. It sounded like tires spinning; you know . . . like when you accelerate too fast? Well, it was loud. Then I hear this big thud. I threw the cat off my lap and ran over to the window. By the time I got there, all I saw was the body in the street and the back end of a car going down the alley that way." He pointed toward the way the ambulance had come in. "I've never seen a dead body before." The man looked like he was going to throw up. The thought of it made Abernathy's stomach revolt.

"Can you describe the vehicle? License plate?" Abernathy knew that was a long shot, but he had to ask. Eye witnesses were pretty unreliable, and looking at how shook up this guy was, Abernathy didn't expect much.

"Not really, it was pretty dark. Just lights from the other buildings. There are no street lamps back here, and the car didn't have its lights on. I could only say it was a dark color. Red, maybe. Burgundy. An SUV, though. I'm sure of that."

"Thanks for your time. Officer Rodgers will get your name and take your statement." He questioned several more residents who were milling around. All had similar stories. Abernathy stood back, surveying the scene once more. *Accelerating* tires. Interesting. Not someone slamming on the brakes to *keep* from hitting someone.

He walked over to the body. *Woman. Early sixties. Gray hair.* The ME's staff had recently arrived and were finished taking pictures. They brought the stretcher over to move the body.

"Wait a minute," Abernathy interrupted. He pushed them aside and kneeled down by the body. He opened her coat. Nothing in her pockets. *Damn. No luck but bad luck tonight.* He'd have to wait for fingerprint or dental record identification.

"Officer Abernathy! I found this in the alley." Abernathy turned to see a breathless Rodgers holding a manila envelope in his gloved hand. He scrambled up from his kneeling position, feeling his stomach lurch again.

"Show me where you found it." Abernathy followed the rookie about ten yards away from the body. He pointed a few feet away, against a building.

"It looks like the woman came from this direction," Rodgers recounted. "Footprints in the snow farther down the alley match her shoes and indicate that she was running. Hers are the only tracks, so no one was chasing her."

Abernathy processed what Rodgers was saying. He played out the scene in his aching head. *Focus.* The car had to come from where Rodgers had parked his car. He imagined the position of the car, the woman running toward the intersection where he was waiting. He accelerates, hitting her, then turns left and leaves down the alley the way the ambulance had come in. If she was carrying this envelope when she was struck by the car, it was possible for it to have been flung in this direction.

"Come on. Let's take a look at what's in here." The new rookie followed Abernathy like a young puppy to his squad car. Abernathy turned on the interior lights and took out a plastic bag and latex gloves. He examined the thick envelope, the kind sold in any office supply store. There were no markings to indicate who it might belong to or where it could have come from. It was slightly damp, indicating that it had not been exposed to the elements for very long. That made it even more likely that it belonged to the dead woman.

He opened the clasp and peered inside. Carefully, he pulled out a two-inch stack of papers and a cracked jewel case with a CD inside. Abernathy started flipping through the papers. This was some sort of dossier on a Mark Mason, an executive with SpringWare. This realization sobered him up better than any cup of coffee could.

SpringWare. Could this woman have been another employee? *Another murdered employee? What the hell is going on at SpringWare?*

"Sir? . . . Sir?" Rodger's voice interrupted his thoughts. "Is everything okay, sir?"

"Uh, good work, Rodgers." Abernathy put the papers back in the envelope and sealed it in the plastic bag. "Get this fingerprinted. As soon as it's done, bring me copies of everything, ASAP. Understood?"

"Yes, sir."

"Good. Now get on it. I'll be at the station in an hour, so have it ready when I get there. I've got to see someone first."

CHAPTER

60

ABERNATHY SAT IN the back booth at Macho's, drinking his second cup of the strongest café con leche on the menu. The steam from the cup helped keep his head clear, and the caffeine from the hot brown liquid was working wonders on the rest of his body.

SpringWare. What is going on at that place? Why was this dead woman gathering so much information on Mark Mason? Abernathy wished he'd had more time to go through those papers to see exactly what *kind* of information she had been collecting. Well, there'd be time for that.

Crawford, Phillips, Packwood, dead. Abernathy believed they were all murdered. He was confident that the state trooper was paid off to cover up the truth about Crawford's accident. *But paid by who? And why?*

He was willing to bet another round for the house that this vic tonight was also an employee. He needed to figure out how these four victims were tied together. *What did they know that got them killed?*

The sound of shuffling drew his gaze upward from the cup he had momentarily lost himself in.

"You look like death warmed over," Nathan told Abernathy as he slid into the seat across from him.

"Thanks, Schilling. Not that you look much better. Showering every couple of days works wonders, you know."

"I'm sure that's true, but you're the one who's got me out at this insane hour of the morning. Have you heard something about the Packwood murder that just couldn't wait?"

"Not yet, but I've got something that might be connected. I read your piece in the paper on the two dead SpringWare employees. I need to know what you've dug up on that company, SpringWare. What was the name of that VP you mentioned in the article?"

"Mark Mason. Why?"

"We may have another dead employee, and I don't think this one is an accident either. I just came from the scene. A Jane Doe, so far. Gray hair, early sixties. We're looking at dental records or fingerprints to figure out who she is."

The acidic taste of bile filled Nathan's throat. A smothering blanket of dread seemed to cover him. Trying to act nonchalant, he dug deep from within to summon up all the objective reporter that he could muster.

"Uh . . . really? What makes you think she's related to SpringWare?"

"I found a package, some kind of dossier on Mark Mason at the scene. I think it belonged to her . . . Schilling . . . Schilling . . . you're as white as a sheet. You okay?"

"I, uh . . . yeah. I'm fine."

Abernathy laughed. "Right. And I'm the president." Then,

in a more serious tone, he said, "You'd make a lousy poker player, Schilling. What's up?"

Nathan motioned with one hand for him to wait a minute. He fumbled in his coat pocket, finally disentangling his phone from the lining inside. His mind, suddenly moving at warp speed, seemed disconnected from a body whose movements he couldn't seem to coordinate at all.

He fought to control the panic rising inside of him as he waited to hear Lori's voice answer his house phone. If what he suspected was true, he was not going to tell Lori on the phone.

"Is Rita back yet?" *Please say yes!*

"No, and I'm getting worried. I expected her back a couple of hours ago. It's one in the morning. Nathan, where are you?"

"Look, I think I know where she is. I can't talk now, but I'll be back in a couple of hours." Nathan hung up before Lori could ask more questions.

It could only be Rita. *Oh, God! I should have gone with her.* Their success yesterday had made them careless. *How am I going to tell Lori and Jacob? What am I going to tell Abernathy?*

"Schilling. Schilling! Are you listening? I asked you who was on the phone? Who's Rita? Do you know my vic?"

"Yeah. I think I do." Nathan could barely get the words out of his mouth.

"You better come clean with me, Schilling. Come on. I'll drive you down to the morgue to identify her. You can fill me in on the way."

CHAPTER

61

BRUTALIZED. MANGLED. ASHEN. Decomposing.

In his many years working homicide cases, he had seen a lot of dead bodies in various conditions. As he stood next to the drawer, waiting for it to be opened, Nathan realized that this would be the first time he knew the person lying there. His knees felt rubbery as he shifted his weight from side to side, nervously wiping his brow.

Where's the damn medical examiner? It felt like he'd been in this ice-cold room for hours.

Abernathy had been mercifully quiet on the way over. Nathan kept waiting for the questions to come, but he had remained silent. Nathan was grateful for that. The drama of the past few days had exhausted him more than he had realized. They all needed sleep.

Nathan had covered a lot of difficult cases. He'd spent days delving into the lives of victims and criminals, watching people suffer great hardships. But none of that had prepared him for what was happening now.

Nathan didn't really know Rita well, but he felt an odd sort of blood-brother closeness in a way that was difficult to explain. They had been thrown together by a strange and dangerous situation that was getting more terrifying by the moment. *How could we not feel close at a time like this?*

Now he was getting ready to look at the body of a woman who had stumbled onto the truth about the death of a beloved colleague. She had just wanted to do the right thing, to bring the guilty to justice. Nathan thought she was one of the strongest women he'd ever met.

The shiny silver door reflected a defeated image. Nathan made a silent promise. *Rita, I will not let them win. For you. And for Jack and George and Karla.*

And for Jacob and Lori. Are they next? I can't let that happen.

Movement caught his attention in the reflection of the stainless steel. He watched Abernathy and the ME approach. He stepped aside to let the medical examiner unlatch the handle.

Nathan leaned against the door next to him and let the chill from the metal run through his body. His legs felt weak, and a cold sweat once again covered his brow. He felt a deep sense of detachment.

The metal tray slid out from the opening, imprinting a sound in his mind that he was sure to remember for a long time. "Jane Doe" was written on the tag protruding from below the sheet. Nathan envisioned it tied around her toe. *Just like in the movies. God, I wish this was a movie.* The ME looked at Nathan for a sign that he was ready for the sheet to be pulled back.

Nathan held his breath and nodded.

She looks peaceful.

Rita deserved at least that, after everything she had been

through these past three months. Unexpected tears fell on stainless steel and then on the highly polished floor. He felt Abernathy's burly hand on his shoulder.

It was time to leave Rita in her new state of peace.

CHAPTER

62

LIQUID BREAKFAST. The twelve-year-old golden liquid seared his throat. He waited for the sensation to pass, then slowly drew another sip from the crystal glass. The warmth could be felt as it traveled all the way down into his stomach. *Who knew scotch could feel this good so early in the morning?*

Mason looked around his plush SpringWare office, where he had safely spent the night. The room had beautiful mahogany furniture, an antique bar cart stocked with the best liquor, and a grand marble bathroom with a shower. It was everything a top executive needed and deserved. The CEO would have given him anything he asked for at this point. Mason had done more than put SpringWare on the map. He'd made it a competitive player in the gaming market, and that was no small feat.

He smiled sardonically at his "Wall of Winning." He recalled having Rita frame the magazine and newspaper articles that he had saved over the years. The glowing accolades of his success, in print, proclaimed for the world to read:

"Sultan of Software"
"VP to Envy"
"Mason Manages SpringWare to the Top"
Forbes
Newsweek
The Wall Street Journal

They hung there, surrounded by the various plaques and awards that had been bestowed on him for a myriad of reasons.

He envisioned the next headlines:

"Maniac Manager Kills Three"
"Cut Employee Costs—Literally"

What have I done? He surprised himself with this sentimental thought.

He'd been drinking since Baxter called. Taking a trip down memory lane, BC. Before Carl. He'd come a long way since the hog farm in Iowa. He had erased it completely from his memory, family and all. Mason had enjoyed more success in his ten years at SpringWare than most men have in their entire careers. Just look at The Wall. It was glaring, indisputable proof.

He was just the man Baxter needed. Driven. Successful. Ambitious. Patriotic. Only he could have given Carl exactly what he wanted: software designed to his specifications, to protect this country against terrorists. And he could keep it a secret, or so he thought.

In return, Mason became a very wealthy man. There was 70 million dollars waiting for him in an account in a Cayman Islands bank. There should have been another 30 million dollars added at delivery of the program, but things had already started to go wrong. Mason wouldn't dare to ask Baxter about the rest of the money.

Jack. Karla. George.

He wondered if Rita, Jacob, and Lori were next, but he didn't have the nerve to ask Baxter. *I should've taken the money and left when he killed Jack.* But leaving would have set Baxter off, so he stayed. The NSA would've found him anyway. Now he had to make sure that his name wasn't on the target list.

Mason knew one thing at that moment. He stared blankly at the Johnny Walker in his hand and thanked it for helping things become so crystal clear.

It's almost time.

He plunked the glass down on his desk and unlocked the bottom drawer. Removing the black leather portfolio he kept hidden there, he unwound the string that bound it and took out his three very important lifelines: his passport, his Cayman bank checkbook, and an airline itinerary to Prague for tomorrow night, with a quick detour to Grand Cayman Islands.

He only needed to make it through one more day by convincing Baxter that he'd never disclose his plan.

CHAPTER

63

ABERNATHY STUDIED SCHILLING'S PROFILE as he walked beside him from the morgue into the adjoining police station.

Tears. From Schilling. Life is full of surprises.

He had let him have his private thoughts on the way over to the morgue, but that reprieve had come to an end. There were lots of questions that needed answers, and he had a feeling Schilling could tell him everything he needed to know. But he needed to be careful. He didn't want Schilling to pull any of that "confidential source" crap on him.

"Officer Abernathy! Sir!"

Abernathy didn't have to look back to know that puppy dog voice belonged to Rodgers. The rookie caught up with them and handed Abernathy a fat envelope.

"It's the copies you wanted, sir. Did you get an ID yet?"

"Good job, Rodgers." Abernathy obliged him. "Vic's name is Rita Johnson. I'm following up now and will handle it from here."

"Yes, sir. Let me know if I can do anything else." He turned and walked away. Kevin Rodgers knew that was all he was going to get from Abernathy. His offer was a formality, not a real desire to help. The guy had a rep for being a drunk ass.

Abernathy saw that the mention of Rita's name made Nathan take notice of the thick envelope he was now holding. *The dossier on Mark Mason.* He could almost see Nathan's reporter's instincts awaken. *Does he know what's in here?* He watched his eyes dart back and forth, almost broadcasting that he wanted to get his hands on what was inside of the envelope. *Leverage, maybe.* Abernathy found his reactions valuable in helping him decide how to approach his interview.

Abernathy led him down the hall toward a door near the end. The starkness of the tiny room made Nathan recoil when they passed through the doorway. It was obviously an interrogation room, and for a moment, Nathan felt like a suspect.

"It's just a place to talk," Abernathy said, noticing the look on Nathan's face. "I know you have a lot to tell me." He gave Nathan a look that let him know that not telling him was not a choice. He could tell that Nathan was weighing his options. They both knew he didn't have to answer any questions. Nathan could claim that he hadn't found anything on SpringWare, or he could say he was protecting his sources.

Nathan's mind was busy. Rita's murder, even more than the others, was causing him to question what they could really do about all of this on their own. It was clear that Baxter wasn't going to stop until every potential threat was neutralized. The group *had* agreed to Abernathy's involvement as a potential course of action, and now he had to seriously consider it. In fact, he couldn't see any other way to proceed at that moment.

It was true that they had evidence that was beginning to tie Baxter and Mason to these four deaths. But they needed proof of the program's existence and that Baxter was intending to use it. Nathan didn't know if it was on the disk that Jacob was trying so hard to decipher. If it wasn't the altered program, they were up the creek. And that meant that Jacob and Lori would always be in danger of being . . . *I can't think like that!*

The blatant reality was that they were dealing with the *National Security Agency*. The likelihood of the three of them bringing a man like Carl Baxter to justice for murder was slim to none. *Who's going to believe us?*

Whether he liked it or not, it was the truth. Baxter could make them all go away, just like he had done with Jack, Karla, George, and now Rita. And he would get away with it. Nathan was terrified and felt sick to his stomach. He was in this story, and he wanted to live to write about it.

They needed help and protection. *Could Abernathy, even the entire Cooperville police force, offer that kind of protection?* No doubt, Abernathy was a drunk, biding his time till retirement. But he had been a good cop at one time, and now he was the only one he *could* trust. There was nowhere else for Nathan to turn.

Nathan gripped the back of the metal chair in front of him with both hands. "Are you absolutely sure that no one will hear this conversation?" Abernathy nodded and closed the door. "If I tell you what you want to know, your life may, no, *will* be in danger," Nathan said, stealing a line from Lori.

Abernathy studied him intently. In his career, he'd inter-viewed a lot of people who were hiding things or lying. Schil-ling was scared for his life. He could see it in every part of his body. *Damn! How bad is this?*

"Yeah, no one can hear us. You want a cup of coffee?"

"No." Nathan pulled out the chair and pointed toward the other chair for Abernathy to sit down. Decision made. "You'll want to be sitting when you hear this."

CHAPTER

64

LORI WAS WORRIED about Rita. Nathan hadn't picked up his phone when she had tried several times to call him. Her body and brain were completely exhausted. They desperately needed sleep. Jacob finally convinced her to go to bed, but after five hours of tossing and turning, she finally gave up.

The smell of coffee lured Jacob to the kitchen, where Lori was putting bread in the toaster. He looked at her questioningly, but she shook her head no. No word from either of them. They ate in silence, wondering.

Lori's burner phone rang, but before she could retrieve it from the bedroom, it had stopped. She walked back into the kitchen where Jacob was busy putting the plates in the dishwasher. "Nathan left a message saying he would be back in a few hours. At least that's something. Do you think Rita is with him?"

"Maybe. You know, her phone is on the table in the den. She probably didn't want to use her house phone to call us. Maybe she fell asleep." Jacob was trying to make Lori feel better, but from the look on her face, it wasn't working. "Hey, let's go get our minds on something else."

They headed back to the den. Lori spread out the papers, looking once again for something they might have missed. Jacob took his seat at the computer, and his fingers began relentlessly tapping the keyboard. They immersed themselves in solving the challenges in front of them.

She had no idea how much time had passed, but Jacob's sigh got Lori's attention. She looked up to see him rubbing his eyes. He seemed defeated.

"Why don't you take a break, Jacob?"

"Maybe. Staring at this screen isn't doing anything but making me crazy. I don't feel I'm any farther along than when I started three hours ago." He yawned, twisting his neck in semicircles to work out the kinks.

"I know. I could use a long walk to clear my head." Lori put her head back down as she set a few papers off to the side, organizing them in a pile.

"I'd settle for a video game to escape into. At the moment though, it would seem that neither of these are possibilities." Lori could hear the rising frustration in his voice. He pushed back his chair and stood up, causing the chair to crash behind him.

"Jacob!" Lori jumped. "What's the matter?"

"Sorry, Lori. I didn't mean to scare you. I'm just so damned aggravated!" He picked up the chair and plopped back down on it. "Every time I think I'm finally getting somewhere, I find another roadblock. I've tried everything I can think of to get in without a password. I'm just brain-dead. The file is really big, so I think it must be something significant. I want to get it open!"

"I can sort of relate to your frustration. Rita forgot to give me the password to access Jack's file. I only tried for an hour before I gave up." Lori stretched out in her chair with a loud groan, tired of looking through the papers in front of her for the umpteenth time. "The irony was that the password Jack used turned out to be something very special to me . . . hey, maybe George did the same thing. Let me look at the letter he wrote to Karla and see if there's something in it that might be a clue." She rummaged through the papers till she found it. Nothing seemed to stand out.

"I don't know . . . negotiating tool. No, there doesn't seem to be much here . . . did you try Karla's name?" Lori put the paper down, disappointed the letter didn't yield anything of value.

But Jacob was already pounding away at the keys, using every case sensitive version of Karla's name that he could think of. "I'll be damned! 'K@rLa.' Lori, that's ama—"

The file had magically opened. Jacob stared at the screen, totally speechless. He stood up, and the chair crashed to the floor again.

"Oh my God! Lori, we just hit pay dirt. This is it! This is it! Look!" Jacob was jumping up and down, his tall frame almost touching the ceiling. Smiling from ear to ear, he could hardly contain himself.

"What is it, Jacob?" Lori sprung off the sofa and ran to look at the computer screen.

"It's the *program*! Lori . . . this is the final piece of the puzzle!"

"No! Really? I can't believe it!" Lori and Jacob hugged and danced around the floor like little kids at a party.

"Rita and Nathan aren't going to believe this stroke of luck." Jacob held Lori's shoulders, tears of joy in both of their eyes. A heavy weight lifted from their shoulders. "This is the mother lode! With everything else we have, we can put these guys away. There's no way they can get out of this now!"

It was the ammunition they were looking for. Proof that the program really existed. Proof of what this software could do.

Before Lori could respond, she heard footsteps coming down the hallway. Lori and Jacob grinned at each other and moved in that direction, excited to tell them the fabulous news.

"Right on cue, Nathan. We've got great news! What great timing you . . ." Lori's voice trailed off as she saw Abernathy come through the door behind him. Lori knew as soon as she saw Nathan's face.

"No! Oh my God . . . Rita?" It was the last thing she would remember before crumpling to the floor.

CHAPTER

65

THE TOUCH OF Nathan's fingers gently stroking her hair brought the world back into focus. Her face was nestled in his neck as he held her on his lap. She chose to leave her eyes closed, longing to hang on to the safety she felt in his arms. But that moment of comfort quickly turned to disbelief as the truth of the situation took hold of her once again.

Rita! Four murders. For what, the security of our nation?

This was not the "freedom" we should be willing to settle for. No, this was the delusion of madmen. Baxter and Mason had lost their minds. That was the one thing she was actually sure of.

Everything that had taken place this past week seemed like a continuation of the tragedy of her life. Before she could absorb one horrible incident, another had occurred. Rita's death was the proverbial final straw in her life. Death had knocked too many times on her door.

Cassie

Dad

Jack

Karla

George

Rita

She felt her disbelief and sorrow quickly mutating into anger—actual rage. Were they coming for her? Jacob? Nathan? Now Abernathy was involved. Would they come for him and the whole of the Cooperville police department? When would it stop?

It stops with me. She found her resolve. Too many people she loved had died. Her rage grew, and once again, it became a source of strength inside of her. This wasn't a bad dream. It wasn't a scary movie. This was real. She must accept the inevitability of her own death if she did not stay strong. If it was meant to stop with her, then so be it.

She had help now, and they would find a way to beat Baxter and Mason at their own game. Finally stirring against Nathan's shoulder, she knew she possessed the courage to survive. She was tired of being a person to whom bad things happened. It was time to turn the tables of her life.

For Jack. For all of them. For herself.

We're coming for you now, you bastards!

CHAPTER

66

BAXTER PACED THE floor in his home office, whiskey in hand. Mason was falling apart. He could hear it in his voice. *Damn civilians.*

He collapsed in his chair, too agitated now even for pacing. Baxter retraced the chain of events in his mind:

> **Jack's accident**
>
> **A curious email from Karla to George**
>
> **George had Jack's file**
>
> **George and Karla, dead drug dealers**
>
> **Rita's hit and run**

He hated to admit that the situation had not always been entirely under his control. It was an unusual position to find himself in. He had run countless successful military operations during his Naval career. They were well planned and well executed. And the very few times that things didn't go as planned, he held accountable those responsible for the results.

Enlisted men knew the consequences of not obeying commands or following protocol. Mason and these civilians thought they knew better. *They don't know crap. They get all caught up in their righteousness, but they don't see the bigger picture: there are real threats to their freedoms, and terrorists live among us. If they only knew what I know, they'd be too afraid to come out of their homes. They'd be begging me to keep them safe!*

Pouring another shot in his glass, he assessed the current situation. There were two people left who he was sure had knowledge of the software. Jacob Browning, who was nowhere to be found. And, of course, Mark Mason. He should have known Mason was just in it for money and ego. *He had me convinced he was a patriot.* And there was still uncertainty around Lori Crawford. Even though he had no proof, he felt she had to know something. At that moment, Baxter could see no other alternative than to continue on the path he had already started down.

He had been very careful to prevent any ties between SpringWare and the NSA, using layers of shell corporations, so the money he transferred to Mason couldn't be traced back to him.

If Mason would have kept their final software version under wraps, none of this would have been necessary. But he didn't. Now anyone who had any potential knowledge of the software's existence had to be eliminated. The software was the only connection between the NSA and Mark Mason's SpringWare. Terrorism threatened the entire country he was in charge of protecting. If a handful of people must be sacrificed for the good of this wonderful nation, then so be it.

He assumed Browning was not on his way to Florida, just as Johnson had never intended to go to California. She had returned here, and so he surmised that Browning was also somewhere in Cooperville. Hiding meant Browning knew something. He had sent in a team to find him covertly, but so far there was not a single clue to his whereabouts. The search of his home had turned up nothing, but it had provided the opportunity to plant some damning evidence. Operatives had already been dispatched to do the same at Rita Johnson's home after he received the call about her demise.

He had no doubt there would be speculation about the deaths of all these SpringWare employees. Once the drug connection with George and Karla had been created, he had carefully calculated how to tie all the deaths to the same motive. It would be apparent when the police found the evidence he had planted and had arrested the right people.

Mason was under close watch and would remain that way for a short period of time. He might still be useful. His men had planted records on his home computer and stashed evidence of drug activity in the attic and under his hardwood flooring. Mason would be forever remembered as the SpringWare drug lord. His fate had already been decided.

Only one very challenging loose end remained. He had not yet found a way to work out the details, but Baxter was laying the groundwork for one more suicide. Severe depression over the death of a husband, of three friends, and an IRS fraud investigation, could make anyone slip over the edge.

Even Lori Crawford.

CHAPTER

67

NATHAN GENTLY RELATED everything that had transpired to Lori and Jacob, sparing as much detail of Rita's death as possible. Jacob stayed mostly silent while tears slid down Lori's cheeks from time to time.

Abernathy sat at a table, back from the imperfect circle the three had formed in the middle of the den. He listened to Nathan sifting and sorting through what he deemed necessary for them to know. It must have been an emotional rollercoaster of a week for all of them. Now he was witnessing a very different side of the hardcore reporter he knew, and he was gaining a new respect for him.

Abernathy had believed that reporting was just a job to Nathan. That like himself, he had become numb to the brutal and depressing aspects of his job. Obviously, this wasn't true. These people cared about something they felt was important, and they were all willing to pay the ultimate price. Even though they were afraid, they had stood up to that fear of doing the right thing. *Impressive.*

Nathan had laid out an unbelievable story about SpringWare and the NSA at the station. Not just the NSA, the *director* of the NSA. Under other circumstances, Abernathy would have thought Nathan had switched from news writing to fiction. But he had watched Nathan at the morgue. He listened to Nathan's account of what Rita and Lori, and now Jacob, had gone through over the past week. There was no doubt in his mind as to their story's veracity, even though he had yet to see the evidence. And that kind of trust, the kind that came before the evidence, was not something Abernathy had ever given before. After years of listening to perps' stories, Abernathy could spot a lie a mile away. None of these people were lying. He had a lot of questions to ask them, but he didn't doubt or question that they were telling the truth.

These last few hours had awakened something in Abernathy that he had not felt in a very long time. *These people mattered.* And not just the four who had already died.

Lori, in the prime of her life, had just discovered that her husband had been murdered.

Jacob was caught in a web he hadn't even known existed. He'd probably already be dead if it wasn't for Rita and Lori. Now he was trying desperately to survive by helping them find the missing pieces.

And Nathan. With Schilling, he assumed it was always about a news story, but not this time. Abernathy had noticed his reaction when Lori collapsed. How he held her protectively until she regained her composure. How he spared her from any unnecessary information about Rita's death. He was in love and didn't even realize it. Lori had captivated him, and he had followed her unquestioningly into a situation that might cost them all their lives.

Abernathy had been waiting for the day his boss called him in to fire him. And he truly hadn't cared. In fact, a part of him had wished it would have happened a long time ago, so he could be put out of his misery. Now, here he was in this room, thinking about how could he save these three people from being the next victims.

He had absolutely no answers. For a cop who had been on the job as long as he had, he found that very unnerving. But he did know one thing. He was ready to join these three everyday people in their quest to bring one of the most powerful men in the government to justice.

"What do you think, Abernathy? Abernathy?" Nathan's voice snapped him out of his contemplation. "So what do you think we should do now?"

He felt all eyes on him, and he knew they were trying to find some comfort in his "official" presence. He struggled for the words, wondering himself, if they had a chance.

"I think I need to see the evidence you've got. Bring me up to speed with the details. And we all need to sort through this dossier of Mark Mason. Rita risked going home for this, so there has to be something in here that she thought was important." *That's all I've got for now.*

For a moment, the paralysis they felt was palpable. Then, Lori stood up and came to the table where Abernathy was sitting. She looked at Jacob, then at Nathan. Her eyes spoke what words could never express. They all took chairs around the table, and Lori took the lead in opening the thick manila envelope that held the information which had cost Rita her life. She handed Abernathy the stack of evidence they had already compiled while she divided the papers from Rita's dossier between the three of them.

Though Jacob had found the software program, they must be able to link the program directly to Mason and Baxter. There had to be something somewhere to incriminate the two men, or at least Mason. He was getting more stressed by the moment. Perhaps they would discover something that could be used as leverage to make him crack and turn on Baxter.

Silence hung thick in the air as the four of them worked diligently in honor of all of those who were not in the room.

CHAPTER

68

"I'LL HAVE THE goddamned warrant this afternoon. Get back to that newspaper and search her office. Get someone watching her house. Track her down, dammit, or it'll be your head on the chopping block!"

Baxter slammed down the phone. It seemed that Lori Crawford was nowhere to be found, either. In his mind, this was confirmation that she knew something about the software. Was she with Browning? *Probably.* Where they were was the fifty-million-dollar question.

There had been no cell phone calls. There were no pings on their GPS or cellular service. They had disabled their phones. *Another confirmation.*

Surveillance of Browning's house and of his mother's had confirmed that he had lied about the trip to Florida, but he had not remained home. Baxter's gut told him they were both still in the area. They knew information they shouldn't know, but what that information was troubled Baxter beyond belief.

Damn civilians. Why couldn't they just let the government do its job? Baxter picked up the phone to make his last call for the day.

"Mark. It's Carl. There's been a few developments. I'm in meetings for the rest of the day. I'll see you in the morning at ten. The usual place." He hung up before Mason could ask any questions.

Baxter didn't worry about Mason not showing up for the meeting. He was a puppet on a string. A scared one, but still waiting for the rest of his money. Loyalty to his country would never come first for him.

A man with such potential. What a waste.

———

Their moods were somber, but there was a renewed energy among them. Each of them had their tasks to perform, and they were going about them with great intensity.

Jacob's fingers flew across keys while Nathan stuffed the evidence in his backpack. Lori pored through Mason's dossier once more, looking for any bit of helpful information they may have overlooked. Abernathy unconsciously clicked the snap on his holster off and on while he went over the details of Nathan's last interview with Mason. If Mason had been upset when Nathan left last time, his upcoming interview with Abernathy should send him flying for the Prozac.

CHAPTER

69

JOE STUDIED THE papers in his hand very carefully. He'd seen many warrants in his life, and something about this one didn't sit right. It wasn't so much the piece of paper that he was worried about, but the name that was on it—Lori Crawford.

Delacourt eyed the agent once more. He didn't believe for a moment that he was who he said he was, but he had called the number on the card the agent had given him and talked with three people that verified him to be an official IRS agent. He had no choice but to let him search Lori's office.

"When is Ms. Crawford due in today?"

"I already told you. She's out for the week. I believe she's visiting family for the holidays. I'll make a copy of this warrant, then show you to her cubicle."

It wasn't unusual that Lori wasn't here. She always took the holiday week off, but Joe was concerned because she hadn't returned any of the messages he had left her. This was highly out of the ordinary, and it concerned him greatly.

Even when Lori was out of the office, she always returned his messages.

The agent followed Joe down the first row of cubicles. His warrant was for personal items and CDs that may contain personal information. Delacourt would monitor every item he looked at and what he took. The agent would be very careful not to reveal what he was really looking for.

The IRS agent had just turned the first corner when he was accidentally blindsided by a man coming from the other direction. The agent's papers flew in all directions.

"Oh, sorry!" Nathan scrambled to pick up the papers. He stood up to face the man he had seen inquiring about Lori just the other day. "My fault. I wasn't looking." He apologetically handed the papers back to the angry man.

He glanced toward Delacourt, who ever so slightly shook his head, silently communicating that Nathan should not ask questions.

Nathan watched the men continue around the corner toward Lori's cubicle. *What is going on?* Heading up the aisle that ran parallel to the one they had taken, he ducked into the empty cubicle that backed up to Lori's. He quietly lowered his backpack and body to the floor. These cubicles weren't sound proofed, but the voices were still muffled. Delacourt's tone gave away his agitation.

As Nathan sat on the floor, he noticed that the electrical outlets under the desk were shared by the cubicle he was sitting in and by Lori's. If he could pull them out, he was certain he would hear their conversation more clearly. He cautiously unplugged the cords on his side and felt how loosely the outlets fit in the manufactured wall. He hoped there wouldn't be anything plugged in on the other side. Carefully and silently, he loosened the two-sided outlet from the wall. *Much better.*

". . . only personal items," Delacourt was saying. "I don't think those CDs have personal items on them. They're clearly marked as research."

"I have to look at them myself," the agent responded. "Anything could be hand written with a marker on a disk. It's what shows on the screen that interests me." Nathan heard the sliding of the CD drawer, then the whirring of a disk in the computer.

"Like I told you," Delacourt said smugly as he looked at Lori's research on the screen. "Research."

The agent opened the drawers of Lori's desk, and Nathan could hear the rustling of papers as the agent rifled through them. This continued as he worked his way through Lori's entire desk. A few more minutes passed before he heard the chair move back.

"I didn't think you'd find whatever it was you were looking for," Delacourt sneered. "I'll show you out."

Nathan heard them shuffle down the hall. He crawled out of his hiding space and made for his office, but he was too late. Delacourt was waiting in Nathan's chair when he came in.

"What are you up to, Schilling?" The look on Joe's face told Nathan it was a question that he could not avoid answering. "Why are you so interested in what's going on with this guy?"

Nathan knew he had to satisfy his boss's curiosity, but he knew he couldn't endanger him with the whole truth. He settled for a partial truth, along with what he had come to do in the first place.

"I think we both know that agent may not be who he says he is." Nathan watched Delacourt's reaction. "I'm working on the SpringWare story. Well . . . let's just say it's gotten very complicated. I need to put some things in your safe, Joe. It's really important that it be protected and that no one, *not even you*, looks at it." Delacourt started to object, but Nathan cut him off.

"Joe . . . really. It's for your protection. If something happens that I can't finish this story, then you can see to it that it gets in the right hands. But for now, the story has to finish playing itself out. That's all I can tell you." Nathan watched Joe digest what he had said, then consider his options. "We've worked together a long time, Joe. You know you can trust my judgment on this."

Delacourt knew he could trust Nathan, but he had to ask the one question that was most important to him. "Do you know where Lori is?"

"Yes. She's okay, but I can't tell you where she is. Joe, for her safety, it's important that no one connects her to me."

Delacourt pushed himself up from the chair and hesitantly reached for the backpack Nathan held out to him. Without a word, the two men walked toward the editor's office. Nathan supervised as Joe put the bag in the safe. He jumped slightly as the heavy door closed with a thump. Joe gave the combination lock a long swirl to the right to reset the pins.

"I hope you know what the hell you're doing, Schilling."

"Me too, Joe." Nathan felt the heavy responsibility weighing on his shoulders. He was so absorbed in his thoughts, he didn't feel Joe's eyes fixed on his back as he met the icy sleet storm on the other side of the door. All he could think of was getting back to Lori. He didn't notice the two IRS agents in the black sedan across the street.

CHAPTER

70

JOE ROCKED BACK and forth in his office chair. *What have Nathan and Lori gotten themselves into?* He opened the bottom desk drawer and contemplated the silver flask. He had lived through a lot of interesting new cycles in his three decades at the *Washington Post*, but it had been a very long time since he found himself wanting a drink during work hours. Murders, the IRS agent, Lori, and now the backpack. *Ah, the backpack. It's definitely calling my name.*

Joe rocked a little harder in the chair as he reminisced. He was fresh out of college and not sure what he wanted to do with his life. His father had a connection at the *Post*, so somewhat reluctantly, he gave the news business a try. If he were honest, he only took the position to stop his dad from complaining about him not having a job. He had little interest in newspapers.

He started as an assistant for Bob Woodward, at the time when the Watergate scandal had shifted into full gear. It was a sudden, deep dive into the world of political news reporting.

Joe had cut his teeth on one of the most important and historic news events with Woodward and Bernstein, men whose reputations were undisputed and later became legendary. Those were times filled with pressure and stress, and a lot of fear. Reporting that the president of the United States was involved in a crime was not your run-of-the-mill story. Though it came with great risks, it was also one of the most valuable learning experiences a young reporter could have. It was fast-paced and exciting, two qualities he never thought would be a part of any career he might pursue. He was hooked.

There had been some pretty tense moments during those times, so having a drink or two at the office was pretty common. He remembered times going home at night, afraid that he was being followed. And he was just an assistant. He could only imagine the stress and fear Woodward and Bernstein must have felt. The Pentagon Papers, then Watergate. *I wonder if Ben Bradlee and Katharine Graham worried about their reporters then?*

Flask in hand now, Joe rocked back in his chair, eyes on the safe. *Should I?* He never imagined he would entertain the thought of breaching confidentiality. But he was very worried about Lori and Nathan.

Fifteen years had passed since he jumped at the opportunity to take the reign at the *Herald.* His colleagues thought that going to the small-town newspaper was a step backward, but Joe didn't see it that way. He viewed it as his chance to create a reputable and unbiased paper, with good reporting about the things people cared about. Joe felt he had accomplished his goal, and now he owned the paper. In an era where newspapers were struggling, the *Herald* was at least holding its own.

Sitting there with his stomach in a knot, staring at the safe, Joe knew that the small-town image Cooperville had was just that, an image. He rubbed his hands together as if to warm them from the chill he felt in his body. The events of this past week had clearly demonstrated that Cooperville was not immune to the perils that any big city suffered.

Joe twisted off the cap and took a swig. Having worked for so long in the most political town in the country, he felt like he had experienced it all—the ordinary, the good, and the bad. *And what I sense happening here is neither good nor ordinary.*

CHAPTER

71

LORI STUDIED THE paper she held in her hand. It looked like part of a bank statement. The ink was dark and smudged, as though the photocopy had been made from a badly damaged original. She turned it sideways and held it up to the lamp next to her, putting the darkest part directly in front of the bulb.

"This copy looks like it was made from something that had been wadded up and put in the trash. Abernathy, look at this." Lori squinted more closely at the paper.

The tone in Lori's voice had also attracted Jacob's attention, and he followed Abernathy over to the sofa where she sat.

"I think this is part of a bank statement. This could be an account number. Can you make it out?"

Abernathy took the document from her and held it up to the light. He frowned and handed it to Jacob.

"I can't make it out, either. But let me try something." Jacob took the paper back to the computer. He pulled a portable scanner from his duffel bag and plugged it into his laptop. Lori and Abernathy stood behind Jacob, watching the screen, waiting for the document to appear. It looked as bad on the screen as it had on the paper. Lori sighed.

But Jacob wasn't finished. He flipped through a few applications until he found what he was looking for. His cursor flew from tab to tab, rapidly changing the appearance of the document. Abernathy watched the document lighten and focus, fascinated by the technology that had passed him by. Another tab, and Jacob zoomed in and magnified the portion they thought could be an account number.

"That's it! Jacob, you're a genius," Lori cried. The entire number was legible.

Jacob printed the magnified portion and returned to the document for another look. He whipped the cursor across the page and let it stop in another section of writing in the bottom corner. He zoomed again. They could make out the letters "PLE'S."

"It's People's Bank. I recognize the font from their logo," Lori observed.

"Yeah, I've got an account there. That's definitely it," Abernathy agreed.

"Good. Knowing which bank to hack into will make my job a lot easier," Jacob remarked, much too casually for Abernathy's liking. He noticed the sideways glance from Abernathy.

"Don't worry, man. It'll be my first try. It'll take a few minutes, though, so if you don't mind . . ."

Lori and Abernathy took the hint and went back to the table to see if they could find any other gems in the dossier. Rita had collected a lot of information. They divided up the last two dozen pages that Lori hadn't looked through. Only a few minutes had passed when Jacob let out a yell.

"I'm in!" Abernathy and Lori were at his side in a flash.

Jacob typed in the account number and Mark Mason's online bank account glowed before their eyes. Jacob scrolled down the activity register.

"Stop!" Abernathy shouted. "Back up!"

As the cursor slowly ticked up the items, the recent twenty-thousand-dollar deposit jumped out at them. Jacob double clicked to show the details of the transaction.

"It's transferred in from another account," Lori said. "Wait!"

She ran to the table and started rifling through the papers, looking for the one with the series of numbers on it. *I know it's in here!*

Lori grabbed what she was looking for and sprinted back to the computer. As Abernathy looked over her shoulder at the paper, he saw the number.

"This transfer is from an international account. Looks like Mason moved some money in. Now we know that he *does* have an offshore account, and I bet when we find it, it'll have more than twenty grand in it. Good job, guys." Abernathy looked satisfied with himself too.

"Let me see if I can find some information on offshore accounts. I bet there's some account number pattern for designated countries. We've got to find this money." Jacob didn't wait for a response but went right to the Google search box.

Abernathy and Lori went back to the table to resume their search.

"Damn! Lori, look at this. Looks like Rita *was* digging through Mason's trash. Here's part of an email. It's not in very good shape either, but it looks like it could be from Mason. Jacob, can you work some magic on this too?"

The three of them stared at the screen while Jacob scanned the document and manipulated it to get the best resolution. This copy was much worse than the bank statement. The body of the email was barely intact. The original document must have been nearly shredded and nothing in the message could be deciphered. Jacob focused on the top portion, which would contain the subject line, the sender, and the recipient's address.

"Something dot gov," Abernathy guessed at the barely visible line.

"I agree. Too bad we can't make out the beginning of that line. We'd know who it was sent to," Lori remarked. "I wonder why Rita had this in here? There's nothing else that I've found that seems to be related to it. Why would she save such a badly damaged document?

"Well, it proves that an email was sent to someone in the government. Maybe she felt it was another tiny piece for the puzzle," Abernathy replied.

"It's definitely from Mason. All of SpringWare employees' email addresses are structured the same way. There's enough of the sender's address for me to recognize that this is Mason's work email addre—" Jacob suddenly went silent, staring at the screen.

"What is it, Jacob? What's wrong?" Lori asked.

"If Mason sent this email to Carl Baxter, it's an important connection."

"Yeah, Jacob. But we don't know for sure that he sent it to him, and we can't even make out what it says," Abernathy added.

"I *know* that. But he sent it using his work email." Jacob looked at them like they were idiots.

"So?" asked Lori.

"So we *can* find out what the email said."

Abernathy and Lori stared at Jacob, bewildered. *What is he talking about?*

"The Shield," said Jacob. "It'll give us everything we need!"

"What's going on?" Nathan asked as he entered the room.

"Ask Jacob. We have absolutely no clue," Lori replied.

CHAPTER

72

MASON OPENED THE front door of his house just minutes after the back door closed. The darkly dressed intruders were never seen as they slogged through the slippery, snow-covered woods that lined the back of Mason's property.

He threw his keys on the foyer table and set his cell phone in the charger.

God, I need a drink.

He opened the door to his den and paused. *Did I close this door?* He walked into the room and glanced around. Nothing seemed abnormal.

Time to celebrate. It wouldn't be long before this mess would be behind him, and he'd be starting a new life. He lifted a Baccarat crystal aperitif glass from the shelf above the bar. No Johnny Walker tonight. This would be his last drink here, so why not go for the big gun—the Paradis. At fifty dollars per ounce, he could afford bottles of this now. He poured the cognac into the glass. The smell drifted up to his nose before he even picked it up from the bar. *Ahh. This will be good.*

Mason carried the glass from room to room in his spacious home, taking one last look at the treasures he had amassed: a small Rodin statue, Dali and Picasso art, Baccarat crystal, a thousand-bottle wine collection in his temperature-controlled room, and too many Armani suits and Ferragamo shoes to count. His generous salary and bonus package from SpringWare had allowed him many perks. It all reflected who he wanted to be— who he'd become.

Tomorrow he'd walk out the door and leave it all behind. He took another sip of the Paradis and wondered what would happen to his possessions. Maybe he should leave a note to donate it to some obscure charity, one last finger to his family. No, he didn't care enough to even bother with that. Let them have it all. His hog farmer brother and mother. They'd sell everything, having no appreciation for the cultural value or the desire to live a life off the farm.

Though he never saw his career coming to this, it wasn't the things that he'd acquired that really mattered to him. He could imagine the stories in the paper about how he walked away from it all. Or had he vanished? Was he kidnapped? Did he kill his employees? Even if the press was negative, he'd still miss the publicity, the fame, the attention. He'd miss the hobnobbing with people who thought he was important. The people that wanted to be seen with him, to call him a friend or colleague. The same thing he had felt when he had met Carl Baxter.

He pushed these thoughts aside and took another sip of cognac. Just like getting on that Greyhound bus for New York City, he had no doubts he'd fail—or return. He was confident that money would get him whatever he needed. It always had. *And now I've got plenty of it.*

Prague wasn't Mason's final destination. But his visit there was every bit as important as his money stop in the Cayman Islands. He had met a shady character many years ago at a bar in New York. He told Mason he had the resources for passports and plastic surgery if Mason ever needed a new start or a new identity. Mason chuckled to himself. He remembered thinking he'd never have any need for anything like that. Of course, that was before SpringWare and Carl Baxter entered his life. He didn't know why, but he had kept the man's card. The man was still in business, and he had everything already prepared for Mason's new identity, historically and physically.

A month or so of healing from the surgery at that beautiful villa, and I'll be on my way as George Cameron. A ghostwriter for some famous novelists, now scouting the world for the setting of my own book. After Prague, the world is my playground.

Aside from the islands, he had not had much time to travel in his corporate life. It was time for him to see what the big world looked like, to have a real adventure. He had the rest of his life to decide where to put down new roots, or with his newfound wealth he could stay on the move.

He took the last sip of cognac and set the glass on the kitchen counter. He collected a roller bag from the hall coat closet. He wouldn't have time to come back here after his meeting with Baxter tomorrow. *Better put a few things together for my trip.*

Like his formative years in Iowa, this was one chapter of his life that he was anxious to move past and forget. A one-way ticket was once again burning a hole in his pocket.

CHAPTER

73

"LET ME EXPLAIN." Jacob realized they had no idea what he was talking about. "I can hack into SpringWare's email system. The company stores information on all employee computer login activity, communications, and internet searches for four months. We can read Mason's emails, even backtrack his internet searches."

"But won't SpringWare have a security system that will alert them when you do this?" Nathan asked.

"Yeah, but not if I use the Shield." Jacob looked at blank faces again. "Look, I'm really efficient at my work, so I have a lot of spare time. I like to play video games on my computer, but I didn't want to get caught playing around on company time. SpringWare is a sweet gig, and I didn't want to lose my job. So I created this software program that acts as a shield. They can't see what I'm doing when I activate it on my computer. It can make it look like I'm working if I want them to think I am, or it acts like an invisibility cloak if I don't want them to see something I'm looking at. I can use it on my laptop, and they'll never know that I log in."

"You sure you're not a criminal?" Abernathy joked, but with a touch of suspicion. "I hope you're never lured to the dark side, because *I* could never figure all of this out to catch you." Jacob laughed, but he decided it probably wasn't a good idea to share his previous work experience with Abernathy.

"When you're done looking for this email, check his internet activity to see what he's been surfing for lately. My money's on buying an airline ticket," Nathan suggested.

"Okay, let me get to work." Jacob lowered his head to his screen and tuned everyone out.

"Well, I think it's time that I make that phone call to our friend. I think it's sufficiently late enough that it will really scare the crap out of him." Abernathy laughed and stretched his legs. It had been a long day.

Jacob and Lori stayed in the den at the back of the house, each involved in their tasks. There was no rest for the weary tonight. Abernathy followed Nathan to the kitchen, where he could make the call without disturbing them. Abernathy put his cell phone on speaker so Nathan could listen in on the conversation.

"Mark Mason?"

"Yes." Silence.

"This is Officer Abernathy, with the Cooperville police department."

Silence.

"Are you there, Mr. Mason?"

"Uh, yes. What can I do for you, officer . . . Abernathy?" *Another damn cop calling me?*

Nathan smiled at Abernathy.

"I'd like to meet at your office in the morning to discuss the murder of one of your employees. Ten o'clock."

"I've already spoken to people in your department about Karla and George. Besides, I have an urgent meeting out of the office at ten that I must attend."

"Well, I'm afraid this is not about a Karla or a George. This is about a Ms. Rita Johnson, Mr. Mason. Would nine be better? Just routine questions. I won't take much of your time."

More silence. Nathan smiled at Abernathy once more.

"My office at nine." The line went silent.

"I'm sure he'll be up late trying to find a way to put a spin on yet another dead employee." Nathan laughed. "We've still got a lot to do tonight, but I think we deserve a drink. How about some lemonade?"

Abernathy let out a belly laugh. Normally, Schilling would be paying for rounds at the bar by now. *Funny. I don't even feel like a drink.*

"Lemonade sounds good." And Abernathy meant it.

As Nathan reached up to get glasses from the cupboard next to the kitchen window, he noticed the sleet storm had finally stopped. The sky was nearly dark. The streetlight reflected on the slick sidewalk out front, and the black sedan's windows were steamy from condensation. *What?*

"Oh, God!" Nathan pulled away from the window. The chill in his body made him visibly tremble.

"What is it, Schilling?" Abernathy came toward him.

"No. Stay away from the window! Someone's watching the house. A black sedan with steamed up windows."

Abernathy froze in place where he couldn't be seen. "It's okay. Can they see you in the window?" The blinds were open. Nathan nodded ever so slightly. Abernathy continued with his instructions. "Look, get one glass from the cupboard. Act normal. Stay in front of the window. Pour the lemonade and take a drink."

Nathan did as he was instructed. "Now, don't look out, but close the blinds. Turn off the light and take your glass with you to the living room. Turn on the television. If the blinds are open in the living room, walk over and close them, but don't seem like you are looking out when you do."

Abernathy followed Nathan to the living room, mindful to stay out of the sight line to the front window. Nathan cautiously glanced out the window as he pulled the curtains closed. Two men in the car.

"Damn! How did they tie me into this?" Nathan collapsed into the recliner, rubbing his temples. Then he had a sudden realization. "It has to be the IRS agent. He must have followed me from the office."

"What are you talking about, Schilling?"

Nathan had come home at such an exciting moment that he had forgotten to tell everyone about the IRS agent with the warrant for Lori's office. He quickly relayed the story of running into him and the conversation he overheard to Abernathy.

"I didn't mean to bump into him, but maybe he didn't think it was an accident. I was so worried about getting back here that it never occurred to me to check to see if I was being followed. How could I be so stupid?" Nathan was beside himself, pacing the room.

"Don't be hard on yourself. You're all under a lot of stress. Hell, I'm trained for this stuff, and I'm not sure I'd have gotten through this as well as all of you have. But this does pose a problem." Abernathy sat quietly for a long time, thinking. Finally, he took out his cell phone and went into the hallway for a minute to put his plan in motion. When he returned, Nathan was still in the chair, looking like a kid waiting to go into the principal's office.

"Come on, Schilling. We've got some preparations to make. Let's go fill the others in on our new plan."

CHAPTER

74

"**JUST REPORTING IN,** sir. There's nothing happening. Schilling came straight home and has been here all night. No one has gone in or out. We just saw him get a drink and take it to the living room. Looks like he may be watching television. I think he's in for the night."

The news from the two men didn't make Baxter feel any better. *Nosy reporters are always problems. Especially ones who work with Lori Crawford.*

He was relieved, though, that he finally had someone with a brain working for him. The phony agent had called in after his encounter with Schilling in the hallway at the *Herald*. He reported that Schilling had acted like he had recognized the agent. But he hadn't remembered seeing Schilling on his first visit to the paper's office. Something just didn't sit right with him.

Baxter instructed the agents to surveil him. Schilling might be the way to find Lori Crawford . . . and Jacob Browning. His gut told him they were together.

"Stay there. Do *not* leave for any reason! I want constant surveillance. Is that clear? Report in if anything changes or there is something I need to know."

"Yes, sir. We're on it, sir."

The man clicked off his cell phone and turned to his partner. "You sleep the first shift. I'm wide awake now after that phone call."

Carl Baxter had too many loose ends dangling in the wind to sleep.

CHAPTER

75

THE DARK CIRCLES under Lori's eyes were an obvious sign she had not slept. Jacob's eyes were red from staring at the computer screen for so many hours. Everyone was exhausted, but committed. The fact that Baxter may be closing in on them went unspoken, but Abernathy could feel their nervous energy.

"So does everyone know what to do? We've got two hours." Three heads nodded in Abernathy's direction. He looked at his team of civilians and wondered if they were up to this. *I can only hope.*

"That's enough time for me to finish downloading and printing the last four months of emails from Mason's computer records." Abernathy heard the printer kick into gear as Jacob continued pressing keys.

"Did you find anything in his internet history for travel plans that looked interesting?" Abernathy wanted to get a team to the airport or train stations in advance of Mason skipping town.

"Yeah. Nathan was right. I'm still having trouble getting by Expedia's security, but it shouldn't take much longer. I'll find out when and where he's going." Jacob turned back to his computer.

"I was thinking about that urgent meeting he has in the morning. Do you think he's meeting with Baxter?" Nathan asked.

"I'd be willing to bet on it. And I'm going to be there for sure," Abernathy replied.

"I wonder what's going through his mind now?" Lori said. "Abernathy, do you think he'll try to contact Baxter about your call?"

"Probably. I'm sure the stress of this is getting to him. It's a lot of murders to ask of a VP of a company. I doubt he has the stomach for it. My guess is that Baxter is pulling the strings and Mason is the puppet . . ."

"I'm in! Looks like Mason *is* planning a little trip." Jacob's voice rang out once again. It didn't take long before they were all gathered around his computer screen. Grand Cayman. Prague.

"He leaves tomorrow night. I bet he can't wait to get on that plane," said Lori.

"Good job, Jacob. Now I know when and where to have a team ready to apprehend him." Abernathy started to dial the number on his cell phone when Jacob stood up from the desk.

"I've got an idea!" They were learning to listen when Jacob had a plan. "Why don't we take their little software creation out for a spin. I'd consider them terrorists, wouldn't you?"

Abernathy let out a long, hearty laugh.

CHAPTER

76

THE AGENT IN the black sedan stared at his snoring partner. It was his turn to get some sleep. He'd let him have another five minutes before he woke him so he could get some shut eye. He pushed the seat back and stretched his legs as far as he could while sitting behind the wheel. He turned his gaze back toward the dark house. *What the hell?*

The flash of fiery orange quickly spread up the curtain in the window.

"Hey! Hey!" The agent shook his partner from his slumber. "Fire!" The men scrambled to get out of the car. As they bolted toward the house, sirens blared.

"Damn! Get back in the car!"

The two men ran back to the car and drove forward to the end of the block. They didn't dare be seen outside of the burning house. They watched in the rearview mirror as a fire truck and an ambulance screeched to a halt in front of the house.

Men charged into the house with long hoses. The sound of the powerful water spraying the blaze could be heard in their car even a few houses away. After a few minutes, the firefighters came out, and the agent could see a stretcher being pushed inside. About fifteen minutes later, the stretcher was wheeled back out and put in the ambulance. One of the attendants got in the back and closed the door.

"Did you see someone on the stretcher?" the agent asked his partner.

"Yeah. Fully covered in a sheet. Looks like the guy might have had a tough night."

As the ambulance tore away from the house, the agent looked at his watch. Midnight. He dialed Carl Baxter's number as they followed the ambulance at a distance.

CHAPTER

77

RODGERS WAS PARKED on the next street. He watched the fire truck and ambulance scream past him. He wouldn't lie. He had been very nervous when he received the instructions directly from the chief. "No room for mistakes. Do whatever Abernathy tells you to do," the chief had told him. Rodgers wasn't sure if working with Abernathy was going to be a blessing or a curse.

As the stretcher was being wheeled out the front door, the back door to Nathan's house opened. The alley that led to the next block was dark and empty.

Looking through the shadows from the trees, Rodgers watched dark figures slip and slide on the ice toward his van. *One, two, three, four. The right number of bodies.*

He inched the van as close as he could toward them, then pressed the button to open the side door. Abernathy's body fell in the door first.

"Damn ice!" He pulled Lori in after him while Nathan crawled in the front. Lori grabbed Jacob's computer bags, and Abernathy hauled him in the back with them. The door closed, and Rodgers drove off toward Abernathy's house with his headlights off until he reached the main street.

"Rodgers, did the chief brief you?" Abernathy was all business.

"He just said to do whatever you asked, sir."

"Did you tell anyone where you are?"

"No, sir." If Rodgers hadn't had both hands on the wheel, Nathan thought he would have been saluting Abernathy. He suppressed a grin.

"Good. You are assigned to the inside of my house until further notice. No one comes or goes without my say so. You are to speak to no one but me—and don't use the phone unless I call you. The safety of these three people is your responsibility. Understood?"

"Yes, sir."

Abernathy got out and opened his garage door for the van to pull in. It reminded him that he had left his car at the station. He'd have to have someone bring it over early so he could arrive on time at SpringWare for his appointment with Mason.

The three passengers watched the young rookie as he got out of the van. They were all thinking the same thing: *Our safety is in your rookie hands?*

CHAPTER

78

JOE DELACOURT HUNG up the phone by his bedside and dressed immediately. He didn't have to question the police chief's instructions. He thoroughly understood the importance they carried.

Now he was even more concerned about Lori's and Nathan's safety. He was sure it had something to do with SpringWare and those two murders. Lori's husband had worked there. *Was his death related too?* It was the only reason he could think of that would involve Lori.

Joe sat back down on the bed for a minute, trying to wrap his head around what he knew for certain. Two murders. A phony IRS agent. A serious and scared Nathan Schilling. Lori, obviously in hiding. And now, this bizarre request from the Cooperville police chief.

In all his years in journalism, he had never broken confidentiality with an informant or a reporter. But this time felt different. Nathan told him he wasn't supposed to look in the backpack unless something happened to him. *That alone is reason to look.*

These are my employees. Even though he didn't show it, he cared about both of them. He surmised that lives had been taken over whatever was in that backpack. As he had sat in front of that safe after that agent had left the office yesterday, he had been as tempted to look in it as he had ever been about anything. Still, he trusted Nathan's judgment, so he resisted.

Now, he had gotten this call from the chief in the middle of the night. He didn't know if the police being involved was a good or a bad sign, but he did know that he didn't like what he was being asked to do. Still, for the safety of Lori and Nathan, he would not hesitate to do it.

But Joe had his boundaries about confidentiality, and he was very close to the line of needing to cross them.

CHAPTER

79

THE TELEVISION CREWS were already outside of the hospital when Joe arrived. He spotted a reporter from his own paper. Delacourt showed his credentials to the guard at the front desk and quickly disappeared down the long, empty hall.

The police chief was waiting in an empty hospital room. He reassured Joe that Nathan and Lori, and someone named Jacob Browning, were under police protection, but he would not tell him where or why. The chief insisted that his silence and patience were essential to their survival. He said that Nathan would be in contact with him soon.

Nathan had also asked the chief to deliver a message to Joe that he was not to do any internet searches on anything to do with the three of them, SpringWare, or anyone who worked there. *I guess Schilling knows me better than I thought.* Joe chuckled inside, but it left him feeling very frustrated. In his mind, he inched a little closer to that line.

After waiting for an appropriate amount of time, Delacourt pinched his cheeks a bit and put on his most grim face.

This would require an academy award-winning performance. The chief headed for the back door, so as not to be seen. He wanted to check in with the officer being sent to Nathan's mother's house to explain what was going on. He prayed she'd honor their request to go along with their plan to avoid the press and stay quiet for a few days.

Joe went out front to face the growing throng of reporters near the front door. A podium and microphone had been set up just outside of the hospital doors. A police officer took her place beside Joe. The crowd quieted as they realized he was about to speak.

"Ladies and Gentlemen. Friends across the media. This has been a tragic evening." Joe paused for effect, waiting until he had their full attention. "It is with great sadness that I tell you that Nathan Schilling, homicide investigator for the *Town Herald*, my friend and your colleague, died in a fire at his home around midnight." Delacourt paused, took an obvious deep breath, cleared his throat, and then resumed.

"The investigation is not completed yet, but early reports indicate that the fire was started by a burning candle as Nathan slept in the living room. Our condolences go out to Nathan's family and friends. I will prepare Nathan's biography and make it available online later this morning for your stories."

Delacourt covered his mouth with his hand and somehow managed a tear for the camera lights flashing in front of him. With just the right amount of drama, he turned slowly, and with slumped shoulders, he reentered the hospital doors. Reporters rushed back to their vans to finish their broadcasts. Others headed back to their computers to write their stories about Nathan's tragic demise. All competitiveness gone, they would write a story worthy of a hero who was one of their own.

The two men made their way back to the black sedan to call Baxter with what they hoped was good news.

———

Four completely exhausted people finally managed to sleep as their rookie guard watched over them.

CHAPTER

80

NATHAN AWOKE TO television reports about his death. The story had broken too late to make even his own paper. He laughed at how loved he was by fellow members of the news media and how much they admired him. *Most of them barely know me.* They had no idea they were in for the story of their lives when he would rise from the dead.

"I had no idea that you accomplished so much in your career. What incredible adventures you've had." Nathan looked embarrassed at Lori's comment. "Really, you're incredible!" She had never once heard Nathan bragging about his accomplishments over the years that she had worked with him. *How did I not know this?*

"Well, you know reporters. They make things sound a lot more exciting than perhaps they really are. Especially when you're dead and can't dispute them!"

They all shared a laugh, but inside, Lori was truly impressed. She knew all the complimentary things they were saying about Nathan were actually true. He was risking his life for them when he had no skin in the game. And she didn't once think that it was simply for the sake of a good story.

———

While Lori, Nathan, and Jacob were sequestered in their new hiding place at his house, Abernathy had left early to give the chief a full briefing. He wanted to be sure that everything was in place before he went to his meeting with Mason.

The chief had some news of his own. He filled Abernathy in on some new developments about the deaths of Karla and George. After George's autopsy proved he had been murdered, the police went back to his house to look for other evidence. This time, they found drugs in the attic and computer files that suggested that both George and Karla were involved in drug trafficking. They also received information that pointed to a possible suspect, another drug dealer. They had already put out an APB and were searching for him.

How convenient. Abernathy didn't think the chief bought into this cover-up any more than he did, but he made a mental note to question Lori and Jacob about them selling drugs. Abernathy briefed his boss as thoroughly as possible on all the information that had been found on Mason and Baxter. Abernathy thought he noticed him cringe ever so slightly each time he'd say Carl Baxter's name. He laid out what his needs would be over the next couple of days if all went according to plan. They both knew that rarely happened, and with the NSA involved, it was all a crapshoot.

The stakes were high. Four people had already died, and the players involved were way out of the league of the small

Cooperville police force. The chief agreed that as few people as possible should be involved for the time being. No internet or phone calls that could potentially tip their hand. The hope was that Baxter wouldn't discover that the police department was involved in protecting Lori and Jacob for as long as possible.

Setting the fire had been the only way to get them out of the house, without having anyone know Lori and Jacob were there in the first place. The chief had coordinated Abernathy's plan with his close friend at the Fire Department. For now, only a few firefighters, two cops posing as paramedics, Rodgers, and the chief knew that it was a ruse. Another trusted officer had also been dispatched to tell the real news to Nathan's mother. It was still too many people for Abernathy's liking, but a scheme like this couldn't be executed without involving others.

Abernathy believed the plan for bringing down Mason was getting easier with every passing minute. He was a man who was starting to come apart at the seams. But Baxter was a formidable force with his incredible resources and powerful connections, and he was certain to have covered his tracks well. Abernathy also knew that he didn't carry these murders out himself. He needed to find the henchmen who were helping him besides Mason.

The chief expressed his concern about being able to nail Baxter. But truth be told, Abernathy knew that the chief was more concerned about *his* ability to break this case. His reputation as a slacker had made its way to his boss's office. Abernathy knew he was on thin ice with the chief, but the situation was moving quickly. He was too far in the middle of it to be replaced by someone the chief might think more reliable. In for a penny, in for a pound. It was a big risk for everyone involved, from getting fired to dying.

The chief questioned the logic of using a rookie cop to stand guard for the three civilians. Abernathy assured him that the rationale for choosing Rodgers was *because* of his newness to the force. He hadn't had time to make friends with other cops on the force or with the press. He wanted someone with no reason to make a phone call to a friend or to take a payoff. Someone who wouldn't have the nerve to question instructions. Besides, Abernathy could see no reason why anyone would fathom looking for Lori or Jacob at a cop's house. Rodgers was really just a precaution anyway. Someone on their side with a gun to make the three of them feel a little more secure.

———

Rodgers looked weary from his wakeful night, but he was in good spirits. Abernathy told him he could get some shut eye when he returned from his meeting with Mason. In the meantime, a few cups of strong coffee would keep him going.

———

Mason was showing signs of stress. He had left three voice messages for Baxter by eight o'clock this morning. Carl hadn't returned any of them. Mason was desperate. What was he going to say to this cop about Rita? Pleading ignorance would not be plausible for much longer. All he wanted to think about was the luggage waiting for him in the car.

Ten more hours till I'm on the plane. I can do this.

Mason sat at his computer and opened his email. He typed a short note to Baxter: "Cop coming to talk re: Rita. Advice?"

Maybe he'll respond now.

———

One email was all Jacob needed. The software program that Baxter and Mason had created had just been used against them. As the email left Mason's outbox and landed in Baxter's inbox, the worm penetrated both systems. In finding a solution to avoid *any* security defenses, Baxter had unthinkingly allowed the NSA's to be compromised.

Jacob sat back in the chair and snickered. He wondered what Baxter was going to do when he found out that they were able to discover every communication he had and with whom, the communications of those people, and those communications with others.

What goes around comes around, and sometimes exponentially greater. Jacob's smile grew even broader.

CHAPTER

81

PROMPTLY AT NINE, Abernathy knocked on the door with the beautifully carved mahogany etchings. He was well prepared to put Mason out on the ledge. The question was, what would he do when he got there? Would he jump alone, or would he take Baxter down with him?

Moments later, a very composed and well-dressed Mason opened the door.

"Officer Abernathy? Please come in."

Abernathy smelled the familiar scent of liquor on Mason's breath. He followed him toward the desk and took a seat in one of the brown leather wingback chairs. Mason, of course, assumed a position of power behind the desk, in a chair that slightly dwarfed anyone sitting opposite him.

Not for long, my friend.

Abernathy purposefully placed a thick manila envelope on the desk. Mason did his best to ignore it.

"What can I help you with? You do remember that I have another meeting this morning," he said in a matter-of-fact tone, which made it clear it was a statement, not a question.

Still trying to stay in charge. "Yes. I'll get right to the point. Why do you think three of your employees have been murdered in the last two weeks?"

"I can assure you, I am as shocked and appalled by this as everyone else. I cannot even begin to guess what is happening. Rita worked as my personal assistant for two years. We were very close. I haven't seen her since I gave her a few extra days off before the holidays."

Mason didn't look very shocked or appalled. He had obviously rehearsed this.

Well, let's see how you improvise. "Maybe you'd like to comment on this?"

Abernathy's stout fingers pulled the thick dossier from the envelope and dropped it closer to Mason. It landed with a thud that caused Mason to sit back ever so slightly in his chair.

Mason picked up the papers and fanned through them, seemingly unaffected. He didn't need to look too closely to know that all these papers pertained to him.

"I've . . . uh . . . I've never seen these before." He tried to hide it, but he was clearly perplexed. And petrified. Abernathy could smell it on him, and he went for his jugular.

"What would you say if I told you that Rita Johnson was carrying this file when she was killed?"

Silence. Abernathy could see Mason's mind racing as his eyes shifted back and forth. He was struggling to stay calm, to find a way to control the direction of the conversation.

"Why would she have accumulated so much information about you, Mr. Mason? Why was she killed for it?" Abernathy was taunting him now.

Mason sprang up from his chair, his composure completely shattered. Abernathy suppressed a smile. *Gotcha!*

"I have absolutely no idea why Rita would have compiled information about me outside of the office. I often have her collect articles that have been written about me. Look at that wall over there. She had all of those framed." Mason's eyes were dilated and bulging as he pointed at the wall. His neck was a bright shade of crimson.

"But these are more than flattering articles, Mr. Mason. This is *personal* information, including bank accounts, emails, partially shredded documents. Why do you think Rita Johnson was so interested in your personal affairs?" Abernathy pressed a bit harder, but his voice remained cool and calm. That unsettled Mason even more.

"I have no idea what you are implying, but until you have something specific to say to me, I think you should leave. I'm late for my meeting."

That was it. Abernathy was dismissed. It had gone perfectly. He picked up the file and stuffed it in the envelope, being careful to leave a few sheets behind accidentally.

Take a good look at those after I leave.

"Thanks for your time, Mr. Mason. I'm sure I'll be seeing you again *real* soon."

Abernathy didn't bother to look back as he closed the door behind him. He already knew that Mason was staring at a number for an offshore account, a deposit slip that showed twenty thousand dollars was deposited in his account, and an illegible email from Mason to a .gov address.

He imagined the crimson from Mason's neck creeping up his entire face. He'd be reaching for the bottle on the bar behind him before Abernathy made it down the elevator to the first floor. *That'll give you a whole lot to talk to Carl Baxter about.*

CHAPTER

82

ABERNATHY HADN'T PULLED surveillance duty in a long time. Now he remembered why he had always hated it. He was freezing, but he didn't dare turn on the car to warm it up. The day was too cold, and he didn't want the billowing exhaust from the tailpipe to attract attention.

He had located Mason's Tesla before he went up to his office and taken care to park where he could see him pull out of the parking garage. It was 9:35, and he figured Mason would be leaving soon to go to his meeting. The miserably cold weather assured Abernathy that Mason certainly wouldn't be walking to wherever he was headed.

There you are.

Red and white taillights signaled that Mason was ready to pull out. Abernathy reached down to put his key in the ignition of the old model sedan from the precinct's lot. He grumbled as they dropped to the floorboard. *Good job, Abernathy.*

Mason steered the Tesla silently out of the exit. *Don't lose him already, dammit!*

Abernathy fumbled with the key and finally got the car started. He yielded to a black 4x4, then turned left at the stop sign. He caught a glimpse of Mason's Tesla up ahead and breathed a sigh of relief.

A black 4x4.

Why did that stick? His instincts kicking in, Abernathy backed off and let a few cars fall in between him and the 4x4. He could still keep his eye on Mason. He remembered that Nathan had mentioned seeing a black 4x4 following Mason to the mall when he met with Baxter. Abernathy assumed it was the same car.

I bet Baxter is even more nervous now about his protégé.

They joined the heavy traffic on the highway and headed south. It was anyone's guess where they were going, but if he *was* meeting Baxter, it would have to be somewhere discreet. Several miles later, he saw the Tesla take the Carronville exit. The 4x4 continued on. Either they knew where he was going, or Abernathy had been mistaken about the tail.

His mind raced to think of anything of note in Carronville. He clicked off possible rendezvous points as he pulled off at the only exit for this town.

The auto salvage yard.

He had lost sight of Mason. Abernathy knew of a small road from another neighboring town off of the exit that provided a back way to the salvage yard. It was mostly only known by the locals and hardly used because it had fallen into such disrepair. Abernathy guessed that Mason was on that old road. He drove in through the entrance of the salvage yard and aimed for the back. The salvage yard backed right up to that road. There'd be plenty of scrap cars to use for cover once he got back there.

He took the car as far as he safely could, then scrambled out. He moved toward the barbed wire fence that ran along the back. *Damn. It's cold!* Rounding a pile of crushed cars, he saw Mason getting out of his car. He walked toward a limo that was waiting about twenty yards down the road.

Abernathy carefully positioned himself parallel and slightly behind Mason. Hidden from sight by the row of junk cars, he compared his position to that of the limo and felt confident that he couldn't be seen by whoever was inside. The fence separated him from Mason, but he was only about thirty feet away. The stack of cars directly opposite the limo would provide a good vantage point. He turned on his body cam and the camera on his phone.

Perfect.

As Mason walked up to the car, the driver got out. Abernathy started recording with his phone and aimed his body camera in the direction of the two men. Faces and license plates. He hoped he was close enough for the audio to be heard on the recordings. He could vaguely hear them, and he hoped his devices could do better.

"Mr. Mason. Good morning. Mr. Baxter got tied up in a meeting, so he asked me to come pick you up." The driver opened the back door, and Mason crawled in.

Damn! He was supposed to be meeting Baxter.

There was no way for Abernathy to follow them now, though he supposed he could crash through the fence with his car. He cursed himself for not having better foresight. The limo moved slowly down the bumpy dirt road as he watched from behind the mass of iron and steel.

I can't believe I was so—

The thoughts in his head went unheard as the limo exploded into a massive fireball. Abernathy dropped to the ground and covered his head as debris pelted down around him.

CHAPTER

83

COPS SWARMED THE salvage yard and the road next to it. The explosion had blown apart the fence, so getting through now was no longer a problem. Abernathy's legs dangled out of the back of the ambulance while the paramedic tended to the big gash on his forehead and removed a large piece of shrapnel from his forearm.

"You need to go to the hospital for some stitches."

"Right. Look, bandage it up for now. I'll go later." Abernathy waved to a passing Cooperville cop to come over.

"Hey, Abernathy. You don't look so good."

"People tell me that all the time. Look, I need to know everything about that limo, the driver, the explosives. Everything. And I need to know yesterday." Abernathy took off his body camera and gave it to the cop. He'd go over the pictures and video on his personal phone as soon as he could. Maybe Jacob could work some magic on the audio.

"Okay, but you know how backed up the lab is now—"

"Don't give me excuses! Take this directly to the chief. Tell him it's from me. He'll take care of it. Now get moving!" Abernathy grabbed his arm and pulled his face within inches of his. "Talk about this to anyone, and the chief will have your badge. Nobody!" Confused, but warned of serious consequences in no uncertain terms, the cop took the camera and headed for his car. *The chief? What the hell was this about?*

Abernathy already knew *why* that limo blew up. What he was interested in was the evidence. Something that would tie Baxter to it. He needed a thread that tied it all together.

God, my head hurts.

Abernathy lifted his body off the back end of the ambulance. A familiar feeling of drunkenness came over him, though he'd had no drink. The paramedic steadied him at the elbow and encouraged him to sit back down. He suggested that he should go to the hospital to get screened for a concussion. "I'm fine," he retorted as he pulled his elbow away and headed to a group of cops nearby.

He made one last round with the investigating unit, still being vague as to why he was there in the first place. He used his head injury as an excuse to "write it all up in his report later." The fewer people that knew anything, the better. Even his fellow officers needed to be kept in the dark. He doubted that even the entire Cooperville police force could protect Lori and Jacob from Carl Baxter. They were on their own until they found a way to bring him down. Staying under the radar was their only advantage.

Abernathy sought out the lead officer.

"I don't want any leaks of this incident. No one, and I mean *no* one, is to talk to the press, their wives, even their four-year-old, for God's sake. That order comes directly from the chief.

Am I clear? Run everything through him." The cop shook his head fiercely.

"Yeah."

"Good. Now I'm going to watch you go tell this to every person on this site. Right now. And don't forget the paramedics and the firemen."

Abernathy watched to make sure his orders were carried out. He was grateful this location was so isolated, that it was Christmas Eve, and that there were no onlookers to start spreading rumors or posting on social media. If this had to happen, the location and timing were definitely to their advantage. But they had also lost Mason. He had hoped to break him and use him as leverage to nail Baxter. Now there was only the man himself. He gingerly lowered himself into his unmarked car, unsure if this incident would help or hurt their case.

Abernathy was almost home when his cell phone rang. The chief said they brought in the drug dealer they had been looking for. He thought he might want to be there when they questioned him.

Uh, yeah. The perfect remedy to clear his foggy, aching head.

He turned on the lights and siren and made a U-turn. He'd be at the station in five minutes.

CHAPTER

84

MASON HAD SCREWED everything up. Baxter didn't know how, but he was the only one who could have allowed Jack to discover their secret. Once Jack was eliminated, he was relatively confident that things were under control. But just in case, Baxter had Mason monitor all communications of the SpringWare employees that had touched the project in any way. At least Mason had the balls to own up to finding that damn email from Karla to George: *George, I had nightmares after what you told me last night. Can we talk at dinner?*

Baxter paced the floor. He threw out idea after idea as to what George could have told her that would have made her have nightmares. He couldn't come up with anything other than what Jack had discovered. *I made the right decision to get rid of them. All of them.* There would be no more opportunity for anything, or anyone else to interfere with his plan to save this nation.

Baxter was working from his home office, an unusual occurrence. The glass of scotch in his hand was also highly unusual, especially for this time of morning. He glanced over at the grandfather clock and took a long sip. He enjoyed the searing sensation of the alcohol as it made its way across his tongue and down his throat.

He was waiting for the call to tell him that the mission had been completed. Then he'd have a reason to celebrate. He'd just saved the agency 70 million dollars, reclaiming the money he had wired to Mason at the Cayman bank that he had recommended. Good banking relationships were invaluable.

He'd also just tidied up one more obstacle. Two more to go.

CHAPTER

85

NATHAN PEERED IN through the partially closed door. Lori was sitting in a worn, overstuffed chair, staring out the back window at nothing in particular. He could only imagine what was going through her mind. *She's been through so much.* She was vulnerable, but far from broken. Over and over since the story broke about Karla, actually since Jack died, he had seen her stand strong.

They had worked together at the *Herald* for fifteen years, as close colleagues in a professional environment. But after Jack died, he felt something change when he was around her. Nathan had never felt awkward around women, but there was something about Lori Crawford that made him feel off balance. Whenever he had the opportunity to interact with her, it was as if all of his tactful reporter skills and instincts deserted him, and he became very proficient at putting his foot in his mouth.

Looking at her now, he could hardly believe this was the same woman he had dinner with at Mel's Diner. He admired the determination and strength she demonstrated, even in the midst of her fear and grief. Nathan had never met another woman like her. He was just now realizing that he wanted to know more about the complex woman sitting in that chair. *When this is all over.*

The thought snapped Nathan from his musing. He had lost track of how much time he stood there watching her. He rapped softly on the door. "Can I come in?" Moist cheeks and red eyes undermined the smile she attempted when she looked toward the door.

Nathan plopped down on the bed across from her. Lori watched that familiar curve in his lip as he smiled out of the corner of his mouth. "You look like you could use a hug." He patted the bed beside him. She eased herself out of the chair and perched herself beside him. Lori breathed in deeply, enjoying the comfort and security of Nathan's arm around her shoulders. She laid her head on his chest and began to softly cry again. He felt her tears on his fingers as he stroked her face and hair.

"I feel like I'm in the middle of some bad dream. I thought that Jack's death was the worst thing that could ever happen to me. But the nightmares became even more horrible since I met Rita that day in the park. I keep wondering if all of this is my fault. If I would've ignored that note she left me, maybe she would have dropped all of this, and everyone would still be alive."

"Lori, don't think like that. Rita told you because you had the right to know. She knew the risks when she started looking into those files. Like you, she was a strong, determined woman. There's no doubt in my mind that she would have pursued this with or without your help. Besides, I don't think they were the least bit suspicious of Rita in the beginning. It was Karla and

George's emails that made them start to worry. They killed Rita because things were getting so out of hand. I think Baxter would get rid of anyone he *suspects* knows anything."

Nathan felt Lori's body tense, and he grimaced at those last words that had come out of his mouth. *You idiot!* He wished he could grab them back. She was scared enough.

"I know, Nathan. It's just that everything has happened so fast. I can't seem to get my head around it. Just last week my biggest worry was how to get through the first Christmas without Jack. Then, all of this . . ." Lori's voice trailed off.

They sat together on the bed, soaking in the comfort they felt in the moment. They were in this together, and they'd see it through. When Lori finally turned to face Nathan, the tears had dried, and she spoke with resolve. "We've got to get them, Nathan. We *can't* let them get away with this!" A sense of purpose had once again overridden her sadness.

Nathan gripped her shoulders and met her gaze. He was pulled into the depths of her watery hazel eyes, and he could feel her raw fear, anger, and strength. It stirred feelings deep within him. Unexpectedly, he felt his own will strengthen. He wouldn't let them take her from him. It had snuck up on him while he was most unaware. He wasn't sure how, or when, or even why.

Now the words stumbled from his lips. "Lori . . . I . . . I'll never let them hurt you." He drew her to his chest and his arms enclosed her, as if to protect her from the world. He hoped that she could feel what he was feeling. His hand lifted her face to his, and he kissed her softly on her forehead.

"Nathan . . ." She didn't finish her sentence; instead, she raised her lips to meet his.

CHAPTER

86

RYDER COPELAND SPAT his words through his thick red mustache, his long beard pumping with every word. His disdain for the cop questioning him was apparent as Abernathy watched through the two-way mirror.

The officer paced in front of the suspect, watching him carefully. He slammed his fist on the table. "I know you killed them, Ryder. I've got your redneck hillbilly prints at George's house. Tell me the truth!"

"I'm tellin' y'all like it is, man. My job be takin' the crank to the boys out on the street, man. Dat's *it!* I don' no nuthin' 'bout those two bein' whacked. I ain't no killah. George or Kahla call me up, I go get it. Dat's *it*, man!" Ryder jumped out of his chair, anger raging through every pore. His southern hillbilly accent was getting thicker with every word. "I ain't chewin' my cabbage twice. You'ns oughta be askin' thems book-red boss hisself 'bout all dis!"

The detective grabbed the big man's shoulders and drove him back into the chair. His fury was growing too.

Abernathy opened the door to the interrogation room. He took the detective aside and whispered, "Why don't you put him back in the cell and let him think about this for a while? Let's sift through the rest of the evidence and see what we've got before he remembers to call a lawyer."

It wasn't really a question that Abernathy posed, more like an order. He had made it clear that the arresting officer could run the interview, but it was Abernathy's case, and it would go his way. "I want a full report as soon as you know something else."

The detective started to object. Abernathy was just a street cop. And he was a lousy one. Everyone on the force knew that. But the detective knew better than to let even a frown cross his face. The orders had come from the chief himself that Abernathy was in charge of this case. He grumbled something under his breath and left to escort Copeland back to his cell.

Did I just hear him implicate Mason? In his wildest dreams, Abernathy could not imagine Mason dealing with the likes of Copeland.

CHAPTER

87

JACOB SCROLLED THROUGH the list of Baxter's communications since the worm had infiltrated his email. *Jack was right.* The software was performing exactly as Baxter had planned.

Jacob was relatively confident that he had not implemented the program yet. Baxter would want to deal with all loose ends before he risked executing his plan. Unfortunately, he was one of those loose ends. That thought sent a chill through his body. *We've got to nail this bastard.*

The people Baxter communicated with were quite impressive—the president, the secretary of defense, Homeland Security, the secretary of state. While this list was imposing, even a bit frightening, there were a few other names that really interested Jacob.

Mason's email to Baxter would tie the two of them to Rita: *Cop coming to talk re: Rita. Advice?* He was grateful for the dates and time stamps on the emails too.

But there was another one, addressed to c.reyes, that really attracted Jacob's attention. He had no idea what it meant, but the content was too peculiar to be disregarded. "Pick up Mason. Ten a.m. Usual place."

What the hell is that about?

Jacob took another look through Mason and Baxter's files. He couldn't see anything else that seemed important but clicked the save function, just in case. He'd come back to the c.reyes email.

It was time to keep searching for an overseas account. Because Mason had purchased a ticket to the Grand Caymans on his way to Prague, Jacob had been searching through several banks there. The first four had turned up nothing, but there were plenty more to go. The Caymans are a hot spot for offshore accounts because of the privacy the banks provide and the protection from US taxes.

First Caribbean International Bank was next on the list. He quickly initiated the "Shield" so he could take his time and not worry about being detected by the security software. It took Jacob fifteen minutes to hack his way in. After locating the accounts file, he typed in the number he now knew from memory. The data started to appear.

Yes! Finally.

Jacob hit a few more keys. He stood up to stretch and did a little dance while the information downloaded onto his screen. Another piece of the puzzle. Things were coming together now. *I'm on a roll now, baby! I can feel it!*

Lori and Nathan came into the room to see Jacob singing out loud and dancing to a Britney Spears tune.

". . . Oops, I did it again!" He twirled around and stopped dead in his tracks when he saw them in the room.

"Oops!" Jacob burst into uncontrollable laughter, with Nathan and Lori joining in. It was the stress relief they all needed.

Lori was the first to compose herself. "Do you mind telling me why we are laughing so hard?" She looked at Jacob.

"Oh, that felt good," Jacob acknowledged, when he finally caught his breath. "I just found Mason's offshore account! First Caribbean International Bank. Come on . . . let's take a look."

Three sets of eyes scanned that the computer screen was full of data. But there was no more laughter as they saw Mason's account balance—$69,980,000—it was just shy of the $20,000 they already knew was taken out.

"Oh, my God," whispered Lori. "So that's how much these lost lives have cost?"

It was a question that needed no answer. No one could've spoken anyway. Obviously, Mason thought seventy million was enough to take four lives. But to the three people in this room, it was incomprehensible.

CHAPTER

88

"OH, MY GOD! Are you okay, Abernathy?" Lori jumped out of her chair and ran to the disheveled cop standing in the doorway. She took his unbandaged arm and led him toward the sofa.

"You guys look like you've had a day as bad as mine. What's up?" Abernathy said, referring to the three glum faces he had seen when he walked in. He looked around. "Where the hell is Rodgers?"

"I told him to go up to bed," said Nathan. "He was so tired he would've probably shot one of us if we moved too fast."

Abernathy glanced at his watch. *Five o'clock! Where did the day go? The kid had to be exhausted.*

"It's getting close to flight time. Is someone watching the airport for Mason?" Jacob asked.

"What happened to your head?" Nathan asked.

"And your arm?" Lori chimed in.

"Whoa! Hold up a minute. Too many questions. Sit down. My head is throbbing." Abernathy sat down on the sofa, and everyone took seats around him. "It's been quite the day."

Abernathy related the events of the past ten hours. He saw the same foreboding in the three of them that he had seen when Nathan had told them about Rita's death. He could feel their fear. Baxter had killed Mason. They knew he wouldn't stop until Lori and Jacob were dead too.

Abernathy moved on to tell them about Ryder Copeland. "Lori, Jacob, do you think George and Karla were running drugs?" The question sent a shock wave through the room.

"What? George was the straightest guy I've ever known," cried Jacob.

"Never. George even hated the drugs they gave his wife when she had cancer. Not even a possibility," Lori said flatly.

"I didn't think so either, but this may be Baxter's way of connecting the dots with these murders. Drugs were hidden in their homes and there's evidence on their computers of trafficking. We weren't looking for it when we first found the bodies, but after learning they were murdered, a second team discovered the evidence. And we just arrested a drug dealer that says he worked for Karla and George. It sounded like he was trying to implicate Mason as well.

"I've sent a team to have a look around Mason's house for evidence of drugs. If they find it, and I'm sure they will, I'm going to bet this guy Ryder takes the rap for the murders."

"Why would he do that?" asked Lori.

"Baxter probably put money in an account somewhere for when he's released," said Nathan.

"Yeah, but before he gets out, there'll be a prison fight and Ryder will be no more. It won't be the first time it's hap-pened." Abernathy sounded truly disgusted. "I got a phone call on the way here. The investigators found some evidence that indicated the limo driver was a key drug figure in DC, a Carlos—"

"Reyes," Jacob interrupted.

"How did you know?" Abernathy was stunned.

"Well, I've got a bit of information to share too."

Jacob and Nathan took turns telling Abernathy about finding the offshore account and about the emails exchanged between Mason and Baxter.

"I had a hunch that the email Mason sent to Baxter was going to be important. But I had no idea that it would tie him directly to two murders!" Jacob let his own words sink into his head. The room was stone silent. *They had done it.* Baxter would not get out of this one.

"Jacob, can you send Baxter an email from Mason's computer?" Abernathy asked.

"Yeah. But he's . . . dead?"

"Baxter may not know that for sure. If the 4x4 I saw was indeed tailing Mason, they didn't get off at the exit because Mason would have seen them following him on the road he took. They didn't actually witness the explosion."

Nathan had never seen Abernathy smile so broadly before.

CHAPTER

89

THE GREEN LETTERS of the email glowed as hot as the temper flaring inside Carl Baxter. Mason demanded Baxter come to his house tomorrow at noon.

What kind of crap is this? He stared at the sender address of the email. It belonged to Mason. How could it be?

He's supposed to be blown to bits!

He picked up his phone and dialed the number to the team assigned to Mason. "Dammit! You better pick up!" He paced the floor as the phone kept ringing.

"Yes, sir?" answered an anxious voice. A call from this number was never a good thing.

"What the hell happened? Did it blow up or not?"

"Yes, sir. We heard the explosion, sir."

Silence.

"You *heard* the explosion?" Baxter's rage was building. "You didn't *see* it?"

"No, sir, there was no place to follow him where we wouldn't be seen. We pulled over on the highway, where we knew we would hear it. Saw the smoke and everything."

The phone shattered against the brick of the fireplace. "DAMN IT!" he screamed at the top of his lungs. Baxter stared at the glass of whiskey on his desk. It followed the same trajectory as the phone.

Mason was still alive!

He collapsed into his chair, letting out a howl that even a wolf would envy.

"Damn incompetent civilians!" He punched the keyboard so hard it hurt his fingers. He hit the send button, confirming the meeting. Now Mason knew that Baxter had intended to kill him. This changed everything.

Baxter opened his desk drawer and withdrew the gun. The pearl handle felt smooth in his hand as he stroked it with his long fingers. He wiped the shiny silver with his sweater. There was plenty of time to formulate his plan. Christmas Day was the only day he ever took off work. It looked like this year would be an exception.

"I'm ready for you, Mason. When I'm finished, you'll wish you had blown up in that limo."

CHAPTER

90

THEY WERE BUSY making calls from Abernathy's landline and cell phone. No one dared use their own. They were too close now to risk being detected.

Abernathy called the chief. The others wished they could hear the conversation on the other end, but of course, Abernathy's house phone was dated and had no speaker function.

"I know it's Christmas Eve . . . I know tomorrow is Christmas . . . I know it sounds impossible . . . Chief, we've got Baxter nailed! Use your connections with the Bureau . . . Yes, I *know* it's Christmas . . . just get him there." Abernathy shocked himself as he hung up on his boss.

———

Lori reached Delacourt on his cell phone, careful not to identify herself or use Nathan's name. Joe was overcome with relief in hearing her voice. He was especially overwhelmed when she told him who was coming to the *Herald*'s office.

"He needs the backpack out at seven in the morning."

"No problem. I'll meet him there." Once again, Joe asked no questions.

———

They all needed a good night's sleep. The morning was going to come early, and tomorrow would be a very big day.

CHAPTER

91

JACOB HURRIED TO gather all of the new evidence he had found. As he watched the last sheet emerge from the printer, he felt a sense of pride, quickly followed by remorse. He had used his skills in finding the pieces they needed to put a really bad man away forever. *If only I could have figured this out before he got to Rita.*

———

Nathan grabbed the papers from Jacob and hurried out to meet Rodgers in the van that was still hidden in the garage. For some reason that Nathan couldn't fathom, Rodgers looked as nervous as Nathan felt. But then again, Abernathy was acting as his boss. Nathan speculated that if he was in Rodger's shoes, he would probably feel the same reporting to someone like Abernathy.

His thoughts turned to the task at hand today. Nathan wondered how Delacourt was managing. Joe was worried about

Lori. He had to give a press conference announcing Nathan's fake death. He was surely was more than curious about what was in the backpack. *I wonder if he looked?* Nathan tried to imagine the situation if the roles were reversed. *Would I look?* He couldn't be sure, but he wouldn't think less of Joe if he had. Joe sounded tough, but Nathan was seeing the teddy bear side that he had always suspected was there. It was evident in the way he worried about Lori, and Nathan was pretty sure he was concerned about him too. He could also imagine Delacourt loving all of the intrigue. So *All the President's Men.*

It was Christmas Day, so no one would be at the office. Lori and Jacob waited with Abernathy, while Rodgers escorted a "dead" Nathan to meet Joe at the back entrance of the paper's building. But he didn't let him out until the rookie had driven around the block twice to be sure no one was watching the place.

Once the meeting time was confirmed with their special visitor, Abernathy would bring Lori and Jacob to meet with all of them. He wanted them under wraps till the very last minute.

Not long after the sun rose, Delacourt pushed in the final chair around the conference table. His hand massaged his chin as he surveyed all the details. Paper, pens, water glasses, and coffee mugs. He sniffed the air and confirmed the coffee was brewing in the next room. He lifted the backpack onto the vacant end of the table. The urge to open it was irresistible. *No. It'll happen soon enough. Might as well be as surprised as our guest.* He said a silent prayer for all of them to arrive safely.

Those who believed that he was making a mistake going to a small-town paper would be eating those words in the morning. He didn't know exactly what the story was, but he was betting that his little paper was about to become famous for breaking one of the biggest government scandals in history. *Eat your heart out,* Washington Post.

CHAPTER

92

NATHAN TRANSFERRED SEVERAL small stacks of paper and multiple jewel cases from the backpack to the conference table. He and Jacob exchanged a few whispers as everyone took their seats.

Joe conducted the introductions, then turned the meeting over to Lori. You could have literally heard a pin drop for the next hour as she, Nathan, Jacob, and Abernathy took turns, confidently and methodically, laying out the timeline of their discoveries. Periodically, Jacob would pass the irrefutable physical documentation that supported their case against Carl Baxter across the table to the three men.

Delacourt was astounded. He studied the men for reactions as they listened to the incredible story unfold. Their faces were expressionless, giving absolutely no clues as to what they were thinking. *They'd make great poker players.*

Abernathy concluded by describing the plan they had put in motion to meet Baxter in Mason's home office.

Joe hadn't realized that he had been sitting on the edge of

his seat. He sat back with a sigh, immediately conscious of the sound he had made. *Screw 'em. I don't care.* In his opinion, these four very ordinary people were about to bring down the head of the National Security Agency. *The damn NSA, for Christ's sake.* From what he had heard, there was absolutely no doubt that they had the evidence they needed to bring Carl Baxter to justice for murder and a slew of other charges. The nervousness that he had felt earlier had morphed into something he could only identify as pride.

The proof of Baxter's deeds and his plan was overwhelming, yet their guest seemed to be having a hard time accepting it. He picked up several pieces of evidence from the table. He carefully studied the papers, then passed them to the other two men who had accompanied him. Still, he did not speak.

The air was thick with agonizing silence.

Delacourt saw Lori shift in her chair. He caught the slight shoulder shrug as she exchanged looks with her counterparts, as if to say, "What's so hard about this? Can't he see how dangerous Baxter is?" It was obvious to Joe that they were exercising all the self-control they could muster to remain quiet. He was doing the same. *What's the problem here?*

After what seemed to be an eternity, their guest finally spoke. "Officer Abernathy, it's only a couple of hours until noon. I don't have sufficient time to debrief a team from Washington and set things in motion. I only have two agents with me. I need you to provide the remaining staff we need to make this meeting happen."

"No problem, sir. I've already got my men ready to go."

Delacourt sensed a collective sigh of relief from one side of the table, and a profound sense of disappointment from the other. *Or is it disgust?* It was hard to determine exactly. He gathered the papers from the table and put them back in Nathan's bag. "I'm going to keep this in my safe until all of this is sorted out." There was no way Joe was taking the risk of anything happening to this evidence. And he was not letting them take anything yet, even though Nathan had assured him they had copies of everything at Abernathy's house.

Their guest looked deliberately at each of them before he spoke, shaking his head in disbelief at everything he had heard. "I need Baxter to confess, and I want him to tell us why."

Delacourt studied the man intently. He imagined it was hard for him to believe that Carl Baxter, a man who had dedicated his life to this country, could have killed five people and had created software that went against the very democracy that he maintained he wanted to protect.

"Now, let's decide how this should go down."

CHAPTER

93

THERE WERE TOO MANY opportunities for things to go sideways. Gathered in Mason's home office, they had developed a plan. Abernathy wasn't happy with it. He had tried to hold firm for how he envisioned the meeting should go, but the big guns from Washington wanted full command. He suggested that he and Rodgers be inside the house, closer to the confrontation.

"What if he brings others and they search the house?" *The sidekick finally speaks.* Abernathy kept a lid on his sarcasm and admitted that was a possibility. He agreed that everyone had to keep their distance until they saw who showed up and Baxter was in the house.

"Maybe we should have Nathan pointing a gun on him when he enters." *A not so brilliant idea from sidekick number two.*

"Nathan, do you know how to use a gun?" Abernathy smiled as Nathan nodded in the negative. "So that's not an option." *But, hey, I'm just a small-town cop. What do I know?* What he knew was that if things went badly, it'd be his fault.

They also wanted Baxter to confess to what he'd done. Abernathy agreed wholeheartedly, but that meant that no one from the Washington group or law enforcement could confront Baxter directly. He'd clam up and demand his lawyers, giving him time to call on his powerful friends. This would end up in the courts forever, despite the evidence. A confession would prevent all of that.

To get Baxter to own up to what he had done, the meeting would have to be confrontational. Baxter had to be provoked, and that could get very dangerous. He would be coming to that house angry that his mission to kill Mason had failed, planning to kill Mason himself.

Since they obviously couldn't produce Mason to do this dirty work, the only players in the room that were capable of doing this were Lori, Jacob, and Nathan. Obviously, this was the part that worried Abernathy the most.

Exhausted, inexperienced civilians. Not a good choice, but I can see no other option.

He worried about their ability to handle such a dangerous situation. He eyed them carefully while Delacourt and the others looked on. This was no time to beat around the bush. There was no time for gentle preparation. "Look, Baxter will be an enraged man with a gun, ready to do the job no one else has been able to do. Instead, he'll be face to face with the other two people he's been looking for. That's you, Lori and Jacob. It's the perfect opportunity for him to tie up all the loose ends at once." Abernathy watched the three faces tense with anxiety. "We will be watching every move through that camera above the door from the command post. As soon as you get the confession, we'll move in immediately."

"Glad you're not sugarcoating anything, Abernathy." Lori tried to laugh and lighten the mood. They were all stressed to the max, but there was no turning back now.

If the three of them couldn't get a confession out of Baxter, no one could. As Nathan had years of experience as a reporter getting people to tell him things, he volunteered to take the lead. The three of them strategized how to make that happen in the quickest way possible.

Abernathy went over every detail of the far from perfect plan. They rehearsed it, again and again, until he was confident that they had it right. He talked about other possibilities, like what to do if he pulled a gun. He assured them that his team was already watching the house and the neighborhood to minimize any other potential surprises.

He double, then triple checked that everyone was where they were supposed to be. "All right, it's almost time. Everybody, let's move out and get to the command post across the street so we can test the equipment." Abernathy gave Lori a hug and shook hands with Nathan and Jacob. "You've come this far, guys. I know you've got this." He tried to sound convincing. *I sure hope so.*

Lori, Nathan, and Jacob came together in a group hug in the middle of the den. Now, there was nothing more to do but wait—wait until both hands were on the twelve.

CHAPTER

94

BAXTER'S BROWS FURROWED as he purposefully planted one foot in front of the other on the way to the idling car. His anger over Mason still being alive had turned into rage. He was done with incompetence. One team had let Mason escape. The others hadn't located Browning and Crawford. *Damn freelancing civilians.*

His eyes burned holes into the back of the heads of the two men in the front seat of the Escalade. *You'd better be reliable, or I'll kill you too.*

They were there for backup, just in case. This time, he would deal with Mason himself. He was done relying on others. This loose end was way too important to leave hanging. He knew that Mason had kept copies of the software, and he suspected he kept copies of other things too. Mason was too smart not to cover himself if he were to get caught. He'd want evidence to use against him if he needed it.

You won't escape this time, Mason. I don't fail. Ever. This mission will damn well be successful.

CHAPTER

95

THE POLICE RADIO crackled softly at his waist. Fingers tense, he pushed the button. "Yeah."

"Sir. Security guard just let Baxter in the gate. Two men with him."

"Copy. Stay alert." Abernathy figured he wouldn't come alone. He pressed the button down again. "Team two. Suspect is through the gate. Two accomplices. Eyes on them at all times. Take them out if you have to, but let's try to let Baxter meet his judge in court, not at the pearly gates."

He checked the camera monitor. Lori, Jacob, and Nathan were in their places in Mason's den. They didn't have sound as part of their communication, but the visual was comforting. He made a mental note to present this example to the chief as a reason to find the money to update their equipment. If all went well, he was confident there'd be no more budgetary excuses.

He pressed the button twice. The red light on the camera alerted them that Baxter was on his way. Nathan gave him a wave.

Abernathy said a silent prayer to a god he wasn't sure existed. They had reached the point of no return.

———

Nathan would be the focal point when Baxter entered the room. "There goes the light," Nathan whispered to the others from his place behind Mason's desk. "Are you ready?" Lori and Jacob nodded and managed nervous smiles. "We can do this." Nathan chuckled anxiously to himself. *Why am I whispering? He's not even here yet.* But he knew it had nothing to do with that. He was afraid that his fear might have disabled his speaking voice.

Jacob dialed the number Abernathy had given him and set the handset of Mason's landline on the desk. "All set here." Everything was now in place so Abernathy could hear and record the conversations taking place in the room. Jacob watched the light blink, letting them know they could be heard.

Nathan reached into the slightly open desk drawer. He pressed the start button on his cell phone to record the confrontation that was about to take place—just in case they needed a backup. He watched the dial start to spin and pushed the volume up to the max. Baxter's confession was the final piece they needed, and he wanted a fail-safe just in case something happened on Abernathy's end.

An ashen Jacob gave Lori a quick hug; then he took his place next to a tall plant that would conceal him when Baxter entered. He felt like wallpaper glued to the wall, but he trusted that his legs would move when it was time. Once more, he rehearsed the lines in his head, then he prayed. He had never prayed before, having never felt it of value. Where the words in his mind came from was a mystery, but he felt slightly better for having found them. He asked for this nightmare to end peacefully so they could all get back to their lives.

Lori stood behind the partially closed door to the den. Flashing a brief smile at Nathan, she held her hands out in front of her. It surprised her to find they were still. She thought she would be afraid, but once again, she channeled her fear into focus. Baxter needed to be punished for the hurt he had caused so many, for the lives he had forever changed. Feeling the adrenaline kick in, she placed her hand over her heart, as if to keep it from beating out of her chest. *Keep it under control, Lori.*

They heard the knock on the door.

Once again, the feeling she had looking at the state trooper on her doorstep washed over her. Lori heard Nathan's voice. "In the den." She felt paralyzed. It was as if time had stopped, and it seemed an eternity before the door of the den slowly opened. But instead of the officer standing in front of her, she saw the back of Carl Baxter, the man that had killed four people she cared about.

CHAPTER

96

"NOT THE DEAD man you expected to see, Baxter?" Nathan's courage miraculously seemed to double with each word that left his lips. He was enjoying Baxter's confusion, not being able to put a name to his face. After all, Baxter had never met him in person. But Nathan knew he'd seen his picture. He probably had an entire dossier on his life.

"Schilling. Nathan Schilling." Nathan helped him out. He saw it register in Baxter's eyes. "Yes, I'm supposed to be dead too. Right along with your sidekick, Mark Mason."

"What the hell is this about?" Baxter demanded, trying to clear the astonishment from his head. His eyes darted rapidly from left to right as he struggled to make sense of the situation. "Where's Mason?"

"Oh, I don't think he'll be joining us today. But some other folks will."

On cue, Lori stepped out from behind the door to confront the man that had killed her husband. He turned as the movement to his right caught his attention. Her eyes bored into his.

"Yes, we're here for all the people you killed. Jack, Karla, George, and Rita."

Again, Nathan could see that he couldn't put the name to her face. Baxter unconsciously took a step backward, like a person too close to a hot fire. As he did, he stepped right into Jacob, who had crept up behind him from the left. He whipped around and looked up into a dark, angry face. Jacob had found his courage.

"Where's Mason? What are you people doing here?" There was a slight bit of panic in his voice, and Nathan didn't want to give him the opportunity to recover. With his reporter instinct in full gear, he stepped out from behind the desk and came toward him.

"Don't play games with us, Baxter. You know damn well you blew Mason up in that limo." They had successfully surrounded him on three sides and had maneuvered his back slightly toward the wall.

"Mason isn't dead. He sent me an email . . . He asked me to meet him here. I have no idea who you people are or what you want." He was still in reaction mode, but Baxter wasn't giving anything up. They needed to press harder. He gave Jacob a slight nod.

"Oh, we know about Mason's email, Baxter. In fact, we have the software program Mason created for you. We know what you're planning on doing with it." Jacob remembered his lines. "We also know about the email you sent to Carlos Reyes telling him to pick up Mason at the usual spot so you could blow them up in the limo."

Baxter realized he was in trouble. Nathan could see that he was deciding what to do. After all, three against one weren't good odds. He fingered a button on his jacket, appearing to be nervous, trying to buy time. The button signaled the two men outside to come in.

Nathan saw the light blink on the camera over the door. He knew that was Abernathy's signal that someone was coming. *We need that confession, now!*

"Look, Baxter. Let's cut the crap. Everyone in this room knows what you and Mason have done. We know about the software; we know about the murders. We have all kinds of documents that link you to this. We just want to know why you killed four innocent people . . . then we'll tell you how we can all get out of here with our lives and reputations intact." Nathan paused and let him digest that thought.

But instead, Nathan saw a smug look come over his face. There was no way Baxter was going to work any deal; he'd just let them think so until whoever was coming to help him arrived.

"Civilians," he said with disgust. "Don't you know there are no innocent people, just people who are used to serve the greater good?"

"You bastard!" Lori lunged at him, but Nathan stopped her before her hand could strike Baxter's face. Her eyes seethed with rage as Nathan held her arm. Lori stepped back, forcing herself to regain control. They had to get his confession, or all of this would have been for nothing.

"This is exactly what I'm talking about," Baxter went on, mocking her, unfazed. "You think everything is about right and wrong.

"You let your emotions rule you to the detriment of our national security. There are terrorists out there *right now* just waiting for the opportunity to strike out at the citizens of this country. They have to be stopped *at all costs*! Why is it so hard for you to see that?"

"You killed my husband. You killed people I care about!" Lori spat at him.

"Your husband," Baxter shouted sarcastically at her. "Your husband was interfering with my plan to expose terrorists. So did the others. So are the three of you. I won't let that happen on my watch. You are all sacrifices that have to be made for the greater good of this country. I have sworn to serve and protect. It's my duty, and nothing is going to keep me from winning this battle. It's really not that damn complicated, lady."

"Who gave you the right to say who lives and who dies? I think *you're* the terrorist!" Lori was inching forward again.

"No. They appointed me director of the National Security Agency, and I'm just doing my job."

Nathan could tell from the tremor in her voice that Lori was on the verge of losing it again. He glanced her way and saw he was right. That's when he caught a movement outside the door.

"Lori! Get down!"

Two men burst through the door, guns drawn. Lori threw her body into Baxter, propelling him into Nathan. Baxter and Nathan went crashing into the bar cart next to Mason's desk.

Jacob attempted to dive to the ground as one of the men aimed his gun at him, but he was too late. Jacob's arms flew to his head as the man fired a round into his chest. He fell to the ground and went still.

The other man focused his weapon on Lori, who was on her knees, struggling to get up. The bullet hit her square in the middle of her back. She fell back to the floor with a scream.

Nathan and Baxter scrambled to get up from the broken bottles and toppled furniture. Nathan saw movement again in the direction of the door. He threw his body behind the desk, somehow managing to catch his foot behind Baxter's ankle. Baxter fell back into the glass and alcohol.

Blasts of gunfire ripped through the air as Abernathy took out the first gunman and Rodgers killed the second.

"Get up, Baxter!" thundered Abernathy's commanding voice. "Now! Hands up!" Baxter moaned as Abernathy and Rodgers both steadied their guns on him.

A visibly shaken Nathan slowly crawled out from behind the desk. He watched Carl Baxter rise slowly above him from the broken shards of glass. Baxter grabbed his back, groaning as he tried to straighten up.

"Hands up!" Abernathy boomed again.

Nathan caught a glimpse of silver. In one quick motion, Baxter yanked the gun from under the back of his jacket and aimed straight at Abernathy. Nathan sprang forward from his crouched position, hearing the cracking of bones as he rammed his shoulder into the side of Baxter's knee. The gun fired into the air as Baxter's body fell to the floor and Nathan crashed into the toppled bar cart once again.

It took a minute for Nathan to focus, the smell of alcohol helping to clear his head. His eyes finally landed on Lori's perfectly still body on the floor.

"Lori! No!" Nathan stumbled over to her while Abernathy put cuffs on Baxter. Rodgers leaned down and helped Jacob to his feet.

Nathan saw the bullet hole in her blouse. *No! You can't be dead!* He knelt down and gathered her into his lap. Nathan put his face to hers, kissing her forehead and stroking her hair.

"Lori! It's me, Nathan! Open your eyes, Lori. I know you can. Lori, open your eyes!" Tears landed on her cheek. "I can't lose you, Lori. I just *found* you."

A quiet murmur came from her barely moving lips. "Nathan." And in that moment, he knew everything was going to be fine.

CHAPTER

97

TWO AGENTS STRODE on either side of Cooperville's guest, Gabriel Dotson, the director of the Department of Homeland Security. They stopped the paramedics, who were wheeling Baxter's stretcher to the waiting ambulance.

"Baxter, what the hell were you thinking?" Dotson looked down at the man he thought he knew.

"Gabe . . . it's not what it looks like . . . these people are part of a terrorist cell—"

"Save it, Carl! I've seen everything they have on you, and we've got that whole scene in there on tape. Do you have anything else to say for yourself?"

Baxter glared at Dotson. His voice rang out like thunder. "You have no idea how you're putting this country at risk. Homeland Security? This nation isn't even close to being secure." Baxter spat in Dotson's direction. "You don't have the balls to do what it takes to win. I did. We can find anyone we want with this software. I found a way to win this war we're fighting, and now you've screwed it all up! It's *you* that should be explaining yourself."

Gabriel Dotson looked at Baxter with a mix of sadness and disgust. Before him was a man on the ledge. *No, he's already jumped.* Dotson had seen enlisted men melt down before. It was commonly seen in those who had experienced the kind of atrocities that Baxter had witnessed over his long career. But this was especially frightening. Thankfully, it was very rare to see it happen to someone in the position of power that Baxter held.

"Carl Baxter, by order of the president of the United States, you are hereby relieved of your duty as director of the National Security Agency. You are also under arrest for the murders of Jack Crawford, Karla Phillips, George Packwood, Rita Johnson, Mark Mason, and Carlos Reyes; for conspiracy to commit the murders of Nathan Schilling, Lori Crawford, and Jacob Browning; for conspiracy and treason against the United States of America, and for any number of other things I may decide to add to that list." Each agent cuffed a wrist to the bars of the stretcher. If Baxter's look could kill, Dotson would have been able to add his own name to the list.

"Alvarez, read him his rights."

Gabriel Dotson watched the agents climb into the ambulance with Carl Baxter. Never in his lengthy career had he witnessed this kind of insanity at this level of power. He wondered how long Baxter could have kept his plan a secret, even at the NSA. The truth of the matter was that the lack of oversight might have made it longer than most would think. He felt especially unsettled, wondering if there were other Carl Baxters in his midst. *The enemy within.*

Dotson shifted his gaze to the other ambulance parked to his left. No doubt, he was experiencing a myriad of unnerving negative emotions around this discovery about Carl Baxter. But watching the paramedics attend to Lori, Jacob, and Nathan, he felt tremendous respect for these courageous individuals. Even with all that he had found out about Baxter, they had helped restore his faith in the goodness and resilience of people. He was grateful and truly in awe of these three very ordinary, very brave people who had done much for the greater good today. Dotson would see to it that their courage didn't go unnoticed. He would also make sure that those whose lives were lost would be recognized.

CHAPTER

98

THEY WERE QUITE the trio sitting in the open back door of the ambulance. They were unaware of Joe's camera snapping pictures of America's heroes. He'd capture the moment in pictures, but would leave the storytelling to Nathan. He couldn't have put his admiration for them into words anyway.

"Thank God for bulletproof vests," said Jacob, his arms hugging his aching chest.

"Hmm, yeah. It managed to keep out most of the broken scotch bottles too." Nathan laughed. He groaned as he lifted his arm to put around Lori, his bandaged hand dangling off her shoulder.

"My back is killing me," Lori said. The mere weight of Nathan's arm made her flinch, but there was absolutely no way she would ask him to move it and the security it gave her. "But I'm glad to be alive to feel it."

The three exhaled simultaneously, the relief palpable between them. The weight of the fear they felt had been lifted. The reality of what they had been through, of what they had accomplished, was sure to set in over the next few days. For now, it just felt good to breathe freely, even if they had to do it carefully until they healed.

They watched Abernathy saunter over to them, chuckling at the sight of them. His belly heaved as he said, "You look like the Three Stooges after one of the fight scenes!" He howled at his own joke. Unfortunately for their bruised bodies, his laughter was contagious.

"Thanks a bunch, Abernathy." Lori rolled her eyes. Clutching herself, she tried to avoid moving her body while she laughed at Nathan and Jacob. "You two look like synchronized swimmers, groaning and grabbing your sore bodies in perfect unison!"

Abernathy's face grew serious. "Damn civilians. You got enough out of him. Along with all the evidence you've gathered, Baxter won't be seeing the light of day for a long time. I'm proud of you. I'd take you on as partners any day of the week."

"You could've come in a little sooner, Abernathy. You know, kept us from taking those bullets. It was a bit of a close call, don't you think? I won't be able to play video games for a week! "

"Well, those goons locked the front door behind them. Rodgers had to put two bullets in the lock before we could get in. But look at the bright side. Now you've got an even more exciting story to tell your coworkers."

"Yeah, and the bruises to prove it," Lori replied. Smiles spread across their faces, the only place that didn't hurt.

Abernathy told them they'd take official statements at the station tomorrow, after a well-deserved night's rest. He gave them each a hand, easing them off the back of the ambulance with a surprising gentleness.

"Come on," Abernathy said. "We could all use a drink. Nathan, you may have saved my life today, so I'm buying. Lemonades all around!"

Join your favorite characters from **A Knock on the Door** *in their next adventure:*

AND THE TWO SHALL MEET

ONE MURDERED TEEN. His friend and mother in witness protection. Can the trio of heroes find the killer before they meet the same fate? And who proves to be the darker force, the Mob or the Triad? Lori Crawford gets an up close and very personal answer to that question.

TURN THE PAGE **FOR A SNEAK PEEK!**

PROLOGUE

THE BOY DANGLED his legs over the side of the dock. His toes barely registered the icy water as his mind swirled with the images he had seen an hour ago. The sound of gunshots still rang in his ears.

He should tell his mom, but he wasn't sure if she would believe him after all the trouble he'd had. He could report it to the police, but he had little faith these small-town cops would believe anything he said. Being Black in Virginia wasn't much different than in Mississippi. He was in a place he shouldn't have been, hanging with a kid that violated the terms of his probation. It was a clear violation of the agreement that had kept him out of the juvenile detention center.

His teeth chewed on the remainder of a jagged fingernail. *What if they find me?*

The sudden blow to his head erased any potential for further thought as his body collapsed against the old, splintered wood beneath him. Concrete made the splash much bigger as his body disappeared into the dark water, settling into the thick grasses deep at the bottom.

The man uttered a sarcastic, "Sleep with the fishes, kid."

Dante's question had been definitively answered.

CHAPTER

1

LORI STARED AT the stacks of books on the table in front of her. Her fingers absently slid over the embossed letters of the book's title: *A Knock on the Door*. She leaned back in her chair, a long sigh escaping her lips.

The symbolism of the title sometimes overwhelmed her. It triggered visceral emotions that transported her back in time to the memory of the sheriff delivering the news of her husband's death. Then to the sound of Carl Baxter knocking on the office door, where things could have gone very badly. The former director of the NSA was Jack's murderer. A year later, knocking still evoked the horrific moments that profoundly changed her life. Her fingers trembled slightly as her peripheral vision caught the movement of a young woman approaching from her left. Lori hoped she didn't notice that she startled her.

"Ms. Crawford." She smiled eagerly. "I wanted to bring you some water before I open the doors. You've got a big crowd out there!" Kelly handed Lori a bottle of water, suddenly looking nervous as a thought occurred to her. "I hope we ordered enough books." Inkspot Books was one of the few independently-owned bookstores left in Washington, DC. It had been a big win for Kelly to get Lori Crawford here for the book's first signing event. She wanted everything to go smoothly.

"Thanks." Lori understood Kelly's nervousness, though for very different reasons. "I'm nervous too. And don't worry, I've got a trunk full of books that the publisher insists I carry around. Everything will be fine." Lori's graciousness seemed to put Kelly at ease, and remarkably, it had the same effect on herself.

Today was the first signing event since the book was released a week ago. It already landed on the bestseller list. Nathan was supposed to be here, but Joe Delacourt, the newspaper's owner and editor, had called him in at the last minute for what she assumed was an important story. Lori looked at the cover again. Lori Crawford and Nathan Schilling. Coworkers who became coauthors under the most unusual of circumstances.

"Well, if you're ready, I'm going to open the doors!" Kelly turned to make her way to the front of the store. Lori opened the inside of the book. Published in 2016. Hot off the presses. Maybe this would be a better year. For no logical reason, the tightness she felt in her stomach told her life was about to change once again.

CHAPTER

2

"STUGOTS, MARIO! FIND that kid now, or you'll be at the bottom of the lake too!" The Boss's raging voice was unsettling but not unusual. Vittorio Romano was quick to fly off the handle, using every Italian curse word in the book.

Mario let the phone fall into his lap. He'd had to make a choice: the kid on foot or the kid on the bike. Unable to outrun the bicycle, he snapped a few pictures of the biker with his cell phone. He would find him later.

I'm getting too old for this crap. Using the sleeve of his shirt, Mario wiped the sweat from his forehead. The pressure was coming from too many directions. He wanted to run from all of it, but that was no longer an option. *Twenty-five years. What else could I do?* Hunting and killing had been his life. Questioning orders the Boss gave him had never entered his mind. Offing the kids was no exception.

Mario closed his eyes and let his head fall back against the seat's headrest. He was tired after everything that had already happened today, and he was tired of his entire life. After both parents died in a car accident, Mario lived with his grand-mother. The only thing he gave that woman credit for was teaching him how to curse in Italian. Now those were the only Italian words that he allowed himself to speak. He made a conscious effort to speak only English for the next nine years, and finally, he silenced the sound of his mother's gentle voice in his head.

By the time he was nineteen, he was desperate to get out from under his grandmother's suffocating thumb. The sales pitch from the Boss was irresistible. It was time to be his own man, not the servant boy his grandmother had made him. "This is your chance to be part of a real family," Romano had promised.

The violence he witnessed nearly every day bothered him in the beginning. He'd vomit after seeing limbs chopped off or heads blown to pieces, and he experienced a lot of sleepless nights in those early years. But soon, he became numb to it. The job became like any other job. You go to work. You're told what to do. You do it or get fired. Though, in his case, he'd be popped.

No one in the organization ever used the word kill. Elimi-nate. Put down. Off. Whack. Clip. Pop. Burn. Smoke. It made the job easier if killing sounded like something else.

Mario got "made" when he was only twenty-five, and he was proud of that. It took most wise guys much longer to gain that status. Now, as the Boss's right hand, he didn't whack low-lifes anymore. That job was for those of lesser rank. So when Romano called on him, he knew it was big. Big meant more responsibility and more severe consequences if he screwed up. *And I screwed this up big time.*

The kid had been easy to follow into the woods behind the salvage yard. He was frantic, running like hell until he was out of breath. Mario wasn't sure if the kid even knew he was following him, but he let him get far enough ahead to think he was safe. It had rained all night, and the wet ground made it easy to track him.

Sitting low, hidden in the bushes at the edge of the lake, he watched the kid pace back and forth, trying to decide what to do. Mario scanned the surrounding area. There was nowhere else for the kid to go. Swimming a mile to the shore on the other side wasn't feasible. The area around the lake was barren, leaving him nowhere to hide. *No, when the kid left, he'd most likely go back the way he came.* Mario was confident that he would wait a while to ensure that everyone would be gone from the salvage yard.

Convinced that he had plenty of time, Mario headed back to the car to get what he needed out of the trunk. Rope and concrete blocks were as much a part of his tool kit as a doctor with his stethoscope and thermometer.

BOOK CLUB
QUESTIONS

1. What do you see the title of the book, *A Knock on the Door*, as a metaphor for?

2. Who is your favorite character, and why? What more do you want to know about them?

3. Multiple characters have different roles and perspectives in this story. Typically, the chapters are each told from a different character's point of view. If you had to choose to tell the story from only one character's point of view, who would you choose, and why?

4. What did you like and dislike about the book?

5. Does one chapter or scene in particular stand out to you as particularly thought-provoking or interesting, and if so, why?

6. Do you feel the author's telling of the story from chapter to chapter compels you to keep reading? If not, why?

7. Does the story evoke any emotions, such as sadness, fear, or anger? If so, what are they, and why?

8. The author describes Lori and Jack's relationship as a Cinderella story. Do you believe such relationships exist? If so, why?

9. Discuss the fairness of Rita's decision to tell Lori about what she discovers about Jack's death. If you were in Lori's shoes in those first few chapters, how would you feel? Would your feelings shift like Lori's do?

10. Rita, Lori, Nathan, Jacob, Abernathy, Mason, and Baxter all had life experiences or careers that helped shape their personalities and perspectives. Choose one or all to discuss why this statement is true for them. Do you feel that experiences, events, and careers shape most people, and why?

11. Is there ever a time when national security should outweigh the rights of individual privacy? If so, when and why?

12. Defend this statement from Baxter's perspective: The ends justify the means.

13. In the story, the use of the software program is prevented. Discuss the potential ramifications of keeping Baxter's scheme from becoming public knowledge or of exposing it to the public.

14. Are you satisfied with the story ending on a lighter note? If not, what would you like to happen?

15. If you could talk to the author, what burning question would you want to ask?

Submit highlights from your book club discussions to Roberta@RobertaFernandez. com and receive a free gift!

ABOUT THE AUTHOR

IN HER SIXTY-THREE years of life, Roberta Fernandez, a board-certified hypnotist, didn't know that she had a story waiting to be told.

In 2006, she attended a weeklong memoir-writing class conducted by a bestselling author, Joyce Maynard. Joyce worked hard to bring out Roberta's best work, in spite of her self-perceived lack of talent. While it was an awesome experience to be instructed by a well-known author, Roberta determined that writing about herself was not a talent she possessed.

As a first-time author, Roberta now understands she was simply destined to write in a different genre. She enjoys cre-

ating relatable characters and watching the story unfold as she types. Like her readers, she wonders what's going to happen next. A sequel is already being written as this book is published. Who knows what words will flow across the page in the next fifteen years!